Sand and Blood

D. Moonfire

Copyright © 2014, D. Moonfire

All Rights Reserved

Cover art by Dan Howard (http://www.danhowardart.com/)

All characters, events, and locations are fictitious. Any resemblance to persons, past, present, and future is coincidental and highly unlikely.

Broken Typewriter Press
5001 1st Ave SE
Ste 105 #243
Cedar Rapids, IA 52402

http://brokentypewriterpress.com/

To the English teachers of Prospect High School, Mount Prospect, Illinois.

It took me twenty years to finally thank you properly.

(Class of '93)

Acknowledgements

Despite the popular image of writers working in dark-lit rooms hunched over a typewriter, it took more than a few people to get this book in your hands.

Firstly, I have to thank Susan. Without her patience and tolerance, I would never had gotten the courage to return to writing. Or to keep writing for over a decade.

To the Nobel Pen writers group, thank you for pushing me, suffering through endless revisions, and for listening to my grand schemes. And to the folks on Reddit who were just as helpful with the final steps. And to Shannon, Mike, Jo, and Chandrakumar who graciously read the entire piece and gave me feedback.

To Shannon, Allison, Dylan, and Melanie: If it wasn't for your kind words and encouragement, I wouldn't have kept chasing after you.

And finally to JoSelle Vanderhooft for editing, Dan Howard for the cover illustration, and Matt Davis for putting together the cover.

Contents

1	Rutejìmo	1
2	Confession	7
3	Morning	15
4	Rivals	25
5	Decisions	31
6	Heading Out	41
7	Middle of the Trip	47
8	The Morning Sun	53
9	Blood and Bone	65
10	Separation Anxiety	77
11	Standing Alone	83
12	Investigating the Night	91
13	Breaking Up	101
14	Coming Back	111
15	A Quiet Conversation	119

16	Pushing Forward	125
17	An Evening Run	133
18	Quiet-Voiced Threat	141
19	Humiliated	149
20	Shimusogo Karawàbi	159
21	From the Shadows	165
22	Shadows from Sunlight	179
23	One Mistake	187
24	Alone in the Dark	197
25	Lessons Taught	205
26	Preparing for Battle	215
27	Pabinkue Tsubàyo	221
28	The Offer	231
29	Rescue	239
30	A Year Later	265
	About D. Moonfire	271

Chapter 1

Rutejìmo

> When a child is waiting to become an adult, they are subtly encouraged to prove themselves ready for the rites of passage. In public, however, they are to remain patient and respectful.
>
> — Funikogo Ganósho, *The Wait in the Valleys*

Rutejìmo's heart slammed against his ribs as he held himself still. The cool desert wind blew across his face, teasing his short, dark hair. In the night, his brown skin was lost to the shadows, but if anyone shone a lantern toward the top of the small building, he would be exposed. Fortunately, the shrine house was at the southern end of the Shimusogo Valley, the clan's ancestral home, and very few of the clan went there except for meetings and prayers.

He held his breath as he tested the brick tile on the shrine-house roof. It shifted underneath his bare toe and he stepped back. Braced on both hands and one foot, he tested the second brick. It held and he eased his weight onto it before lifting his other foot. He was light and thin, slightly over five stones, and thankful of that as he shifted his balance. He glanced up to his destination, an opening in the roof to let out smoke and incense. It was only a few links beyond his fingers, but he didn't dare jump for it.

Shifting his weight to his forward foot, he walked his hands along the tiles until he found two more stable footholds. Inching forward, he stretched his foot and tested the next tile. It was solid and he leaned to put more weight on it.

A loud crack shot out and he almost lost his balance when his footing sank an inch. He let out a cry but then clapped his hands over his mouth to avoid alerting the guard inside. If it was Gemènyo, he would just be sent back to his home. But, if Hyonèku was on duty, then he would be suffering for days. His stomach knotted in fear, and he listened for the telltale blast of air that always followed when anyone in the clan used magic.

A sand fly landed on his neck, its little legs pricking his skin. He tensed as he fought back a whimper. Sand flies bit when disturbed. He tried to lean forward, avoiding the tile, to encourage it to fly off, but it just crawled up to his earlobe.

Another fly landed on his shoulder. He caught sight of it in the corner of his eye, its black eyes were illuminated by the dim light spearing up from the opening. It fluttered its wings as it crawled along, looking for some delicate spot to bite.

He forgot about the first fly until it bit down. The sharp pain broke his concentration, and he let out a yelp. He clapped his ear but missed the insect.

The cracked tile shifted again, spreading apart. His foot, resting along the crack, twisted as the tile shattered and he lost his balance.

"Sands!" he screamed as he slipped down the sloped roof. His back crushed another tile before he rolled off. He tumbled in the air and saw the earth rushing up to him. Closing his eyes, he threw his hands in front of his face to protect himself.

A blast of wind slammed into him a heartbeat before he fell into a pair of muscular arms. The wind howled around him, quickly dying before Rutejìmo could finish slumping into the man who caught him. From the flowery perfume that remained, it was Hyonèku who had caught him. His wife had a distinctive perfume.

"Damn the sands," muttered Rutejìmo as he looked up into the face of his rescuer.

Hyonèku was almost six feet tall, with the wiry build all Shimusògo clan warriors shared. He had a short-cropped beard, but the hairs were still as black as the night. In the light from the shrine, his green eyes glittered.

"What were you doing, boy?"

Rutejìmo cleared his throat and wished he was anywhere else. He tried to reach for the ground but Hyonèku refused to set him down.

"I asked a question," said the older man.

"I was just looking." It sounded pathetic when he said it, and he could feel the arms holding him tighten.

"You were trying to steal a vase, weren't you? You're seventeen years old, not twelve."

Rutejìmo turned away. It was exactly what he wanted to do. Inside the shrine house were hundreds of vases, each filled with the ashes of a fallen warrior. The plan was to steal his great-grandfather's vase and bring it to the entrance of the valley. It was an impromptu test of skill, speed, and stealth. From what he heard, Chimípu had done it twice, once to steal her great-aunt and once for her twice-grand mother. Both times, she left the vase on the threshold for the guards to pick up in the morning. She didn't have to say anything, but everyone knew she did it.

Her accomplishments rankled Rutejìmo; he hated that Chimípu did everything better than him. It wasn't fair. She was only a year older. Just because her father was the greatest warrior in the clan, she was given freedoms he could never enjoy.

Hyonèku set him down. "You're an idiot."

"Yes, Great Shimusogo Hyonèku."

In the language of the desert, being polite not only required a deferential tone but also using someone's full name, with the clan coming before the given name. Only the last part of the name was accented. He knew there was nothing he could say to prevent his punishment, but he hoped a proper tone would help defer the worst of it.

"Come on," Hyonèku said as he gestured toward the path back to the rest of the valley, "I have to tell Yutsupazéso."

Yutsupazéso was the oldest of the clan members in the valley. She was also a dour and angry woman who delighted in making Rutejìmo's life difficult.

Rutejìmo's eyes widened. "Please, don't tell her, Great Shimusogo Hyonèku. Anything but her. I promise I won't try it again. She made me clean out the fire pit last week! It took me four days!"

Hyonèku chuckled. "You did dump a pot of soup while roughhousing."

"It was an accident."

Hyonèku shifted the bandoleer of throwing knives to his other shoulder. "And was climbing on the shrine roof an accident too? Maybe you fell on the tiles?"

"No." Rutejìmo sighed and stared at the ground. "It wasn't an accident."

"Then you'll be doing chores until your hair turns gray and your legs wither."

Rutejìmo whimpered. He stepped back from Hyonèku, but froze when the warrior glared at him.

Hyonèku turned his head to follow Rutejìmo, his green eyes shining in dim light. "And what do you think I should do, boy?"

"Um, let me go?"

Hyonèku laughed, a loud, booming noise. Rutejìmo winced at the sound, worried it would carry down the valley. "Let you go? You just tried to break into the sacred shrine. I should have cut you down the second I heard you climbing on the roof." He turned toward Rutejìmo. "Or let you hit the ground."

Rutejìmo bowed his head again. "I'm sorry, Great Shimusogo Hyonèku."

"You should be." There was a pause. "Besides, you should have climbed up from the other side."

Rutejìmo gasped. He looked up to see Hyonèku smiling at him.

"The tiles here are fancy, but fragile. The back of the shrine is built with solid brick. Nothing to crumble or crack. Of course, if you had figured that out," his voice grew tense, "you'd make some other stupid mistake, and I would have my knife at your throat while you pissed your trousers."

Trembling, Rutejìmo forced his gaze back to the ground. He couldn't tell if Hyonèku was being generous or threatening.

The older man grunted and toyed with his knives. "All right, the elder doesn't have to know."

Rutejìmo look up thankfully. He started to say something, but Hyonèku held out his finger.

"But you must tell your grandmother."

Stepping back, Rutejìmo held up his hands. "No, anything but her."

"Yutsupazéso then?"

"I-I can't tell any of them."

"Funny, you say that as though you have a choice," Hyonèku said without a smile. "If you don't tell either, I'll make sure to tell both."

Rutejìmo thought furiously, trying to figure out the lesser of two evils. As much as he feared his grandmother, he dreaded the clan elder more. "I will tell my grandmother, Great Shimusogo Hyonèku."

Hyonèku nodded and gestured down the path. "Then I will ask her in the morning how she dealt with you. Until then be safe, boy."

Rutejìmo sighed. He had to tell her now. Keeping his hands clasped together, he sullenly headed down the trail.

"Don't walk, boy, run. Run like you belong to Shimusògo."

He ran.

Chapter 2

Confession

> It takes a strong man to confess with the knowledge of the punishment that will follow.
>
> — Rador Malastin

Like most of the other clan homes in the northern part of the Mifúno Desert, the Shimusogo Valley ran east-west along the rocky mountains. The valley itself was two miles long with caves cut out of the living rock and paths leading from opening to opening. No one lived along the bottom of the valley among the crops, livestock, and common areas.

Rutejìmo's home was near the top at the middle of the valley. Sun-charged crystal lights lit up pools of orange and blue along the trail. He jogged as he headed home, running but not hurrying. He wasn't ready to face his grandmother. She had ordered Rutejìmo to bed hours before, and beatings were her favorite form of punishment.

He slowed as he headed up the steep trail leading to his grandmother's home, he slept in one of the side caves until he was old enough to live on his own. Light poured through the curtains that covered the entrance of the cave. Rutejìmo stopped, took a deep breath, pushed aside the curtain, and peeked inside.

His grandfather, Somiryòki, rarely moved from his favorite chair and spent his days huddling underneath a blanket and drinking tea. He sat only a few feet from the fire that heated the cave, but the years had left their mark on him and he shivered constantly. His back was to Rutejìmo, and Rutejìmo knew he could easily sneak past the former clan warrior.

It was his grandmother Rutejìmo worried about. Tejíko spent her nights sorting through the maps she had created during a lifetime of running for the clan. Her map room had been carved out just inside the entrance to her home, and he could hear the scuff of paper as she moved. Fear shivered down his spine. Where his grandfather was deaf to the world, his grandmother managed to remain alert late in her twilight years.

Taking a deep breath, he inched past the curtain and crept along the far stone wall. He hoped she wouldn't catch him and he could retreat to his room. He would tell her in the morning before Hyonèku spoke with her.

"Boy," called out his grandmother, "why are you up?"

For a moment, Rutejìmo debated whether or not to respond. He glanced over his shoulder at the opening in the cave that led into his grandmother's den. Not a single inch of stone was visible beyond the papers that covered every wall of the square-cut room.

His grandmother sat in the middle of the floor. Bound into a thick tail, her long, white hair snaked down to the ground where she had tied the tip to a carved wooden ring. She wore her sleeping outfit, a heavily embroidered cotton top and bottom. The fabric was white except for the orange trim highlighting her bare feet and hands. She didn't look at him, nor did she stop going through papers, but Rutejìmo knew she was waiting for an answer.

"I..."

She placed a page on a pile. "Speak up, boy, I can't hear through the mumbling."

"I"—he took a deep breath—"I went out."

His grandmother stopped sorting her maps and held herself in mid-motion. Her grip tightened and she crumpled the page in her hand.

Rutejìmo's skin crawled as his stomach twisted. The sudden stillness worried him.

"Did you meet anyone?" Her rough voice was threatening and quiet. A calm before the sand storm.

He straightened and clasped his hands. He took a long, deep breath and squirmed from the tightness in his chest. "Yes, Great Shimusogo Tejíko."

"Who?"

"Great Shimusogo Hyonèku."

"Hyonèku was on shrine duty this evening. He would not be wandering the valley."

Rutejìmo's insides clenched violently. He wanted to throw up or run away. He gulped and forced the words out. "Yes, Great Shimusogo Tejíko."

She peered over her shoulder at him. She had pale-green eyes, the color of the rare leaf that sprouted in the desert. Everyone Rutejìmo knew had green eyes. It was a mark of the desert, but his grandmother's were brighter than most.

For a long moment, she said nothing.

Rutejìmo squirmed as he waited for her response.

His grandmother finished setting down the page. She made a soft, grunting noise as she staggered to her feet. She leaned one hand against a wooden frame as she swayed, then she turned the rest of her body to face him. "Boy," she sighed, "why were you at the shrine?"

"I—" He hoped that honesty would lessen the beating she would give him. "I was trying to take great-grandfather's ashes."

His grandmother's eyes darkened. "You were trying to steal papa's ashes?" Her voice was a growl, rough with age but brimming with the threat of violence. She stepped forward. Rutejìmo stared down at her hands, which were balling into fists.

"Y-Yes, Great Shimusogo Tejíko," he said as respectfully as he could.

She hit him across the face with her palm. The second and third blow caught him on the shoulder and throat. "You inconsiderate, moon-choked bastard of a sand snake!" She yelled as she continued to smack him rapidly.

He staggered back toward the entrance of the cave.

"You don't deserve your clan! Get out! Get out of my home!"

His grandfather looked up, blinked once, and returned to his cup. Any hope for rescue wouldn't help from him.

Rutejìmo's grandmother continued to smack him as she shoved him out the entrance.

"Of all the sun-dazed, childish, self-serving things—" she continued to rail.

Rutejìmo backed away, shielding his head with his arms. His back foot slipped off the ledge of the trail. He grabbed the wooden railing, but almost let go when his grandmother continued to beat him.

"Excuse me," a man interrupted her ranting, "Great Shimusogo Tejíko?"

His grandmother stopped, panting lightly. She spun around to face the newcomer.

Gemènyo's dark-skinned form welled out of the darkness. In the lantern light, the clan courier was a blot of shadows except for bright teeth and the whites around his eyes. Smoke rose from a pipe he held with three fingers. In his other hand, he carried a half-full bottle of what appeared to be fermented milk, the strongest alcoholic drink in the valley. He was slightly taller than Rutejìmo with curly black hair. Unlike many of the other adult men in the valley, he kept no beard along his brown chin. He wore a pair of trousers but no shirt, his usual outfit for wandering along the valley. The trousers were a deep red, one of the two colors of Shimusògo.

Rutejìmo's grandmother let out an exasperated sigh. "This is none of your business, Gemènyo."

"I just wanted to make sure the screams of a little child were for a good reason."

"He tried to steal Byodenóre's ashes."

"Oh, did he succeed or fail?"

"Failed, of course."

Gemènyo waved his pipe in the air. "Then I agree, a beating is appropriate here. Please, go right ahead, Great Shimusogo Tejíko."

Tejíko turned back to Rutejìmo, who cowered against the railing. The furrows in her brow and the tension in her body faded, leaving only an old woman. She waved her hand. "Bah, he's just a pathetic little worm."

Taking a draw from his pipe, Gemènyo nodded. "Yes. He is." As he spoke, smoke curled from the corner of his mouth.

Rutejìmo blushed at the insult, but said nothing.

Gemènyo turned slightly to Rutejìmo and gave him a wink, stunning the young boy. Then he returned his attention to Tejíko before gesturing to Rutejìmo. "May I?"

Rutejìmo's grandmother narrowed her eyes, but consented with a nod.

Gemènyo strolled over to Rutejìmo. Rutejìmo tensed up, waiting for a blow, but Gemènyo just sat down on the ground next to him and leaned against the railing. "Sit, boy."

Rutejìmo sank to the ground, panting from his efforts. He watched as his grandmother disappeared into the cave. "Sorry."

"For what?"

"Trying to steal great-grandfather's ashes."

Gemènyo chuckled. "Not really. You're sorry you got caught."

Rutejìmo blushed. "Maybe."

"What happened?"

Focusing on the cave entrance in case his grandmother came out, Rutejìmo described his attempt to crawl into the shrine. He stalled when he got to the point where Hyonèku caught him.

Gemènyo nodded as Rutejìmo finished. He tapped his pipe upside down to knock out the remains. Once it was clean, he handed the bottle to Rutejìmo. "Should have gone up the back of the roof."

"I know that now." Rutejìmo paused as he toyed with it. Even from a foot away, he could smell the strong fumes wafting from the bottle. "Wait, does everyone know that?"

Gemènyo grinned and said, "Only those who got caught."

Rutejìmo stared in shock. "You got caught?"

"Yeah, all three times. I only made it out of the shrine once, but they caught me before I was a chain's distance."

Surprised, Rutejìmo said nothing for a long moment. "I... I just want to show them I'm ready to be a man. That I'm not just..."

"Useless?"

Rutejìmo flushed again and he nodded. He brought up the bottle and sniffed at it. His eyes watered from the smell. He took a tentative taste, pulling a face as it burned down his throat. The second gulp wasn't as bad. He let out a soft gasp as he finished. "I heard that Chimípu has done it twice."

"Three times, actually. That girl is quite good at sneaking. Last time, she also stole Hyonèku's knife when she ran by."

CHAPTER 2. CONFESSION

Rutejìmo rolled his eyes and took another gulp. The drink burned in his stomach and he gouth the urge to cough. "Why can't I be as good as her? Why did she get all the talent?"

Gemènyo raised one eyebrow as he stared at Rutejìmo. He was beginning to go gray along his eyebrows and the sides of his head. "Because you suck rocks."

Rutejìmo froze as he stared in shock at Gemènyo. He was expecting something other than a harsh response.

Gemènyo shrugged and held up his hand. "It's true. You aren't as good as Chimípu. You're a fast enough runner, but you just don't have her strength and determination. I had the same problem. Can you imagine what it was like to grow up with your brother around? To hear the elders going on about how he would be the greatest warrior since your grandfather ran the sands? Like having your face ground into the sand time after time. It never stopped even after we became adults."

"I can be just as good."

"No, you can't."

Rutejìmo folded his arms over his chest. "Yes, I can."

"Then do it. You aren't a man yet." Gemènyo chuckled.

"I will, once I finish the rites."

"Becoming a man doesn't magically change you. What you are today is what you'll be tomorrow. You might make a few changes here and there, but ultimately, you are still going to be the same Rutejìmo you were yesterday. The only difference is that you'll hear Shimusògo and you'll be able to use the clan gifts. But, it won't make you a better man. It won't make you stronger or faster. It will just—"

Rutejìmo scrambled to his feet. "I don't have to listen to this."

"No," said Gemènyo as he looked up at Rutejìmo, "but if you want to be more than just a courier in this clan, you should listen. If you want to be greater than Chimípu, you have to change."

"But you're nothing but a courier, Gemènyo. You aren't the best or even the second best here. You aren't a warrior."

Gemènyo stood up and tucked his pipe in his pocket. He reached out for Rutejìmo. Rutejìmo flinched, but Gemènyo just patted him on the shoulder.

"Maybe that means I know what I'm talking about, Jìmo. Just think about it. I'm heading up to the shrine to take over for Hyonèku. I'll tell him that your grandmother beat you."

Rutejìmo turned to watch Gemènyo head down the trail toward the shrine house. He balled his fists as he struggled with his emotions, then looked up at the cloudless sky and the lace of stars above him.

He always knew he could be better than Chimípu. Right now, she beat him every time when they raced. And she won every wrestling match. Even when they sparred with knives, she won. The only thing he almost beat her was with hunting bolas.

"Tomorrow, I'll wake up early and train."

Even as he said it, he knew he wouldn't. He made the same promise every time Chimípu bested him. But no matter how passionately he promised, every morning he rolled over and went back to sleep.

With a sigh, he headed back inside to go to bed.

———————— Chapter 3 ————————

Morning

> In a culture that prides itself on survival and relationships, punishments frequently involve isolation.
>
> — Laminar Gold, *Growing Up in the Desert*

Yawning, Rutejimo pushed aside the heavy curtain covering the entrance to his family's cave and stepped out into the brilliant desert sunlight. Automatically, he whispered a quick prayer to Tachira, the sun spirit. He still did the pointless ritual because if someone caught him skipping the well-remembered words, he would spend a week doing the more noxious chores around the clan's valley. He was already in a great deal of trouble and had no reason to add more.

He looked down into the valley. Only a few dozen people were making their way toward the cooking fires. As with most clans, only the elderly and the youth remained in the valley during the peaceful times. The able adults spread out across the desert for water, food, and trade. For the Shimusògo, trade meant running courier jobs. The entire clan was in the valley only two times a year, and neither day would be for at least seven months. Every other day, the valley was quiet except for the occasional sound of children playing.

Rutejìmo couldn't wait until the rite of passage would let him join his brother Desòchu on the sands. There was no set time when the clan elders would allow him to take the rite. He wasn't even sure he would know when it started. He heard of children being plucked from their beds in the middle of the night and tossed into the desert. Rutejìmo's mother said her rite started when she was caught drinking too much fermented mare's milk, but Chimípu's father started his with pomp and ceremony.

He sighed and tore his thoughts back to the present. It would happen when he least expected it, and there was nothing he could do to speed it up.

To his right, he heard rhythmic thumping and the hiss of steam. He watched as Opōgyo, the oldest of the clan's mechanical dogs, came tromping up the beaten path. Made of iron and brass and powered by an arcane fire device, it stood shoulder-to-shoulder with Rutejìmo and easily weighed ten times his own weight. It was mostly legs and pistons with a pitted metal barrel for a chest. Despite water being precious in the desert, Opōgyo remained valuable for its tireless strength and ability to haul tons from one end of the valley to the other.

The dog struggled with the steep trail as it dragged a large sled covered in boxes and bundles. Steam escaped from the joints on its shoulders and back right leg as it steadily chugged forward.

"Come on, walk faster!" cried a young girl, Mapábyo. She bounced on Opōgyo's back as she encouraged it to walk faster by smacking its metal ears. Her movement caused the mechanical dog to stagger and jerk.

Rutejìmo shook his head. "Pábyo! Get off Opōgyo and let it do its job!"

Mapábyo, Hyonèku's adopted daughter, slid off. Like all desert folk, she had dark skin and green eyes. But where she was as dark as obsidian rock, Rutejìmo was the softer brown of sun-bright soil. She wore a simple dress of white, which was startling against her dark skin. A bright-yellow ribbon cinched it around her waist, and she had a matching one in her long, black hair.

In contrast, Rutejìmo wore a pair of white cotton trousers and remained bare-chested. A few sparse black hairs dusted his pectorals. The only representative traits of the Shimusògo were hard, muscular legs and lean bodies adapted to running across the desert for hours.

Mapábyo bowed her head as she said, "Sorry, Jìmo. Mípu said I could ride."

Rutejìmo tensed at Chimípu's nickname. He forced himself to be polite. "How is Chimípu's mother? Has she beaten the poison?"

He and everyone else in the clan knew Chimípu's mother wouldn't survive, which was why Chimípu asked to hold off on her own rites of passage for her mother's final days. Unlike Rutejìmo, she was important enough to dictate the terms of her rites.

"No," sighed the girl.

Rutejìmo saw the sadness darkening her eyes. He changed topics before Mapábyo started to cry. "Well, still, don't jump on Opōgyo."

"J-Jìmo?" She ran over and grabbed his leg. "Would you come with me? Up to Papa?"

He looked down at the girl clinging to his leg. He was told by his grandmother to get breakfast for his family, but he had no desire to return to his furious grandmother. He made a point of sighing dramatically. "All right, but only if you grab something off the sled."

With a brilliant smile, Mapábyo ran over and hauled a large bucket off. It hit the ground with a thud. Grunting, she dragged it behind her. Rutejìmo reached picked up another two buckets. He staggered under the weight, but the mechanical dog picked up the pace as it continued to plod up the path. Behind it, the sled scraped along the stone.

By the time they reached the end of the valley, Rutejìmo's stomach was rumbling and his mood had darkened. His back hurt from carrying the two buckets. Mapábyo had swapped out her own bucket for a much lighter box, but she was also trudging. They came around the switchback that lead to the outcropping over the entrance of the valley. There were always guards there, warriors and couriers of the Shimusògo clan who were healing from injuries or just resting between jobs.

Even though he knew that Hyonèku would be there, his stomach lurched when Rutejìmo saw him standing at the end of the path. Gemènyo sat next to Hyonèku and the two were chatting while they kept an eye out on the desert stretching out beyond them.

Mapábyo saw Hyonèku and dropped her box. "Papa!" She raced forward to grab his leg.

Hyonèku knelt down and swept her into a tight hug. "Hello, my little desert flower. Did you come up to help me guard?"

"No... but I brought food! And supplies and Mama gave you a letter."

Rutejìmo set down his buckets, thankful for a small break. He ducked his head to avoid attracting attention.

"A letter? Why would she write a letter?" Hyonèku looked curious as Mapábyo dug into her simple shift and pulled out her travel pouch. It was small and filled with momentos of her previous life before her parents died and she was adopted by Hyonèku and his wife. It took a second for her to find what she was looking for.

CHAPTER 3. MORNING

As she handed him a balled-up piece of paper, Hyonèku gave her a reproaching look. He smoothed it over his thigh and flipped it over. His cactus-green eyes moved back and forth as he read the neat script.

"What does it say?" asked the little girl.

Hyonèku's cheeks grew darker. "It's, um, a story."

"About what?"

"About Ojinkomàsu, one of the four horses of Tachìra."

"Really!?" Mapábyo's voice grew excited as she hopped up and down. "Can you read it to me?"

Her father didn't start reading aloud. Instead, he shifted his feet and his face darkened with embarrassment. Rutejìmo turned so his smile couldn't be easily seen.

Gemènyo peeked over Hyonèku's shoulder for a moment. Then, he smiled broadly. "I'm not really sure one should—"

Hyonèku yanked the letter away and balled it up.

"—ride a horse that way. Of course, I didn't know you named a horse after your wife."

Hyonèku spun around, his face flushed with embarrassment. "Gemènyo!"

Gemènyo glanced over at Rutejìmo and gave him a wink. He turned back to Hyonèku. "No, I want to hear about this story. It sounds... fascinating." His voice dripped with amusement.

Hyonèku shoved the letter into his belt. "Later. Never."

"Papa?" asked Mapábyo, obviously not seeing the significance of Gemènyo's comments.

"Later, flower." Hyonèku looked embarrassed as he turned and seemed to notice Rutejìmo for the first time. "Rutejìmo? I would have thought after last night your grandmother wouldn't have let you out of the cave."

It was Rutejìmo's turn to look uncomfortable. "I was told to get breakfast." He sighed. "And not to delay."

"You can't get much farther from the cooking fires than out here." Hyonèku gestured to the wide expanses of desert behind them. From the height of the perch, Rutejìmo could see miles of sand and rock.. To his right, smoke rose from the Ryayusúki clan's valley. A pair of horseback riders raced from the valley as they followed a trail toward Wamifuko City.

"Mapábyo was having trouble with Opōgyo. I decided to help."

"You did, did you?" Hyonèku looked surprised and happy.

"You mean," said Gemènyo as he came over to clap Rutejìmo on the shoulder, "you were actually being responsible for once? Nèku, I think I'm dying. Mapábyo, run down to the village and get the old witch. I must be poisoned, for I'm hallucinating. If Rutejìmo is behaving, the world is about—"

Rutejìmo glared at Gemènyo. "Drown in sands, old man."

Gemènyo chuckled. "Sure you want to try that? I can run circles around you."

Rutejìmo realized he was dangerously close to disrespecting one of the clan's warriors. He bowed his head. "Sorry."

"Don't be," said Gemènyo, "I remember what it was like before my rites. I wanted to go out there"—he pointed to the desert—"so badly I was causing trouble up and down. Just ask Hyonèku when he's drunk. He was right next to me, getting bitched out by Yutsupazéso. You would think the old woman would be nice to her youngest grandson, but Hyonèku always got the worse of the punishments. Of course, he was also the one—"

"Gemènyo," said Hyonèku in a tense voice, "help Jìmo unload the sled so they can get breakfast."

Mapábyo tugged on Hyonèku's shirt. "Papa, do I have to go back? I want to eat with you."

Hyonèku swept up his daughter and kissed her on the nose. "Can I eat you?"

She giggled. "No."

"I bet you'd be delicious."

"No, I'm not!" she said, still giggling.

Rutejìmo smiled and turned back to the sled. He ran his hands along the mechanical dog and found the lever that would switch it to standby mode. He flipped it and the dog shuddered once before dropping to its knees. It curled up to arch its back. Two panels opened along its spine, and coils of metal rose out of the device's chest. A loud hum rang out as the air shimmered with heat. Steam hissed from its joints.

"That thing needs repairs again, huh?" muttered Gemènyo as the warrior came around to grab a stack of boxes from the sled.

"I guess," said Rutejìmo as he picked up his buckets, "I don't really understand things like that. I know it isn't supposed to be leaking steam like that."

Gemènyo took him to a small hut built into the side of the valley. He set down his poxes and pointed to an empty spot.

Rutejìmo set down the buckets in the indicated spot.

The older man stopped Rutejìmo before they left. "I'm serious, Jìmo, just give it a little time. You'll be a man soon enough."

"I know, I'm just...." He didn't have the words.

"You'll be able to impress Mípu."

Rutejìmo glared at the older man. "I'm not interested in Mípu."

"Oh, looking to bind with Hána? Zúchi?"

Rutejìmo grew more embarrassed as Gemènyo listed all the girls around his age. He was old enough that he was uncomfortable with the differences between male and female. He didn't like to be reminded about his awkwardness.

"You know, if you are waiting for Mapábyo, you're going to wait a long time. She's at least nine years younger than—"

"Gemènyo!" The blushed burned hotly on his cheeks.

Gemènyo winked again. "Come on, I'm just giving you a hard time. Let's get this sled cleared off as fast as we can. I'm hungry."

Three more trips to finish unloading. As Gemènyo took the last load, Rutejìmo untwisted the bolts that held the sled together and broke it down. The individual slats of wood folded neatly together, and a rope bound the entire thing.

"Anything else?"

Hyonèku looked up from where he and Mapábyo were wrestling. "Thank you, Jìmo."

Rutejìmo bowed. As he stood, he caught movement across the desert. Four lines of dust rose as runners sprinted toward the valley. He felt his heart beat stronger as he saw two of the plumes pull ahead of the others.

"You know, Hyonèku," said Gemènyo as he watched the runners with a grin, "if you weren't wasting time with your flower, you'd know the village was being attacked."

Hyonèku was on his feet in a flash. "What the... sands! Gemènyo, those aren't attackers! That's clan!"

Gemènyo grinned but said nothing.

Rutejìmo stepped forward, peering over the bright desert. He could just make out people running across the sands in front of the plumes. "Is it Sòchu?"

There was a flash of light over one of the runners. A translucent shape of a shimusogo dépa, the flightless bird named after the clan, appeared and shrank into the body of the runner. As it faded away, the runner accelerated and left the others in a cloud of dust.

Gemènyo laughed. "Yeah, it's your brother."

Rutejìmo's heart lurched in his chest. "Desòchu!" He ran back the trail, then stopped as he looked back at the resting mechanical dog. He knew he shouldn't leave the device behind, but he wanted to meet his brother.

Hyonèku waved him away. "Go on, I'll take care of Opōgyo."

Rutejìmo bowed. "Thank you, Great Shimusogo Hyonèku." He waited until Hyonèku waved again, then spun on his heels to race down the path. He found a safe spot and jumped off the trail to the lower path. His bare feet caught the rocks, and he slid down until he hit the valley's main trail with an impact that rattled his bones. He ran past the threshold of the valley and into the rock-covered sand beyond.

Racing toward him was Desòchu, his arms and legs pumping as he sped across the sands. The cloud beneath him flashed with lights and power as the ghostly images of the dépa appeared and faded over the other runners.

"Sòchu!" Rutejìmo waved for his brother.

Desòchu turned toward him, and there was another flash of light. Translucent feathers appeared in the dust cloud as his form blurred, then he disappeared. A line of footsteps shot across the desert, and the sand rose up in a dark cloud.

Rutejìmo braced himself and shielded his face as the cloud slammed into him. Grains of sand peppered his arms and body. The air was hot and tight in his lungs, making it hard to breathe. Then a wave of force knocked him off his feet. He saw a flash of dark limbs, hands, and feet, as the wind spun around him.

Desòchu reappeared only a few feet away. His arms spread wide as he swept Jìmo into a powerful hug and picked him up. The impact of his movement carried them almost a chain into the valley before Rutejìmo could get his feet underneath him and brace them.

"Jìmo!" laughed Desòchu, "it's been weeks!"

"Big brother." Rutejìmo looked up at his older brother and smiled.

Desòchu was muscular but slender. His hair was long and black, but pulled into a tail wrapped in leather. He was bare-chested and glistening with sweat. "You are taller, aren't you?"

"No." Rutejìmo blushed.

"No, I'm sure you're taller. Your legs are in good shape too. Soon, you'll be running with me. Though"—he pressed two fingers to one of Rutejìmo's bruises—"I see that Great Shimusogo Tejíko was beating you again."

As he spoke, Desòchu's companions came running up. They were all female, small-breasted, and dark-skinned. All of them were armed like his brother, with throwing knives and hunting bolas. Sweat darkened their clothes: cloth wrapped around their chests and matching red pants. Sweat ran in rivulets along their skin as they jogged in place to cool down.

Rutejìmo returned his attention to Desòchu. "Big brother, I thought you were in Wamifuko City?"

"Ah, we were. But Nédo wanted to get home to her husband." One of the warriors bowed as her name was mentioned. "So we ran through the night. Shimusògo kept us company the entire time."

Shimusògo's magic was running and speed. It flowed through older warriors' veins like blood, and very little could outrace the runners of Shimusògo.

"What about the clans of night?" asked Rutejìmo. "What if they attacked you?"

His brother laughed and clapped Rutejìmo on the shoulder. "They could never catch us. Come on, I'm hungry and I want to hear what trouble you got into."

Rutejìmo blushed even though he was excited for his brother to be home. He tugged on Desòchu's arm and dragged him toward the cooking fires.

Chapter 4

Rivals

> The desert clans aren't interested in the third or even the second best. All they care about is who is better and for how long.
> — Palasaid Markon, *Rearing Children in the Mifúno Desert*

Rutejìmo balanced three heavy stone bowls on a plank as he navigated the twisted path leading up to the family cave. The morning sun seared his skin and it was already heating up the stone beneath his feet. In a few hours, it would be too hot to do anything besides rest in the cave.

He took a deep breath. When he inhaled the smells of roasted meat, eggs, and fresh-baked bread, his stomach twisted into a knot. His grandmother insisted he wait to eat with her instead of with the rest of the clan. He peered back over his shoulder to the eating area where Desòchu wolfed down food and joked with the others. He wanted to go back and listen to his brother's tales, but it would mean more punishments if he disobeyed his grandmother.

When he turned back, someone stood right in front of him. He lurched to a stop to avoid running into the broad-chested teenager. The bowls threatened to tilt over, and Rutejìmo swore as he struggled to keep them balanced on the wooden plank.

"Almost got you, Jìmo," said Karawàbi with a chuckle. Even though he was only two months younger than Rutejìmo, he stood a few links taller. He was also considerably stronger and faster. His dark skin glittered with flecks of sand that covered him from head to toe.

Rutejìmo fought the urge to step back. "What do you want, Wàbi?"

Karawàbi shrugged but didn't move out of the way. "I'm bored."

Rutejìmo heard someone crunching on the rock as they walked up behind him. He sighed and didn't look back. "Good morning, Bàyo."

"That's Great Shimusogo Tsubàyo to you." Tsubàyo had a rough, gravelly voice. When he was a young child, he had fallen face-first into an oil-filled pan and the burns never healed. Where Karawàbi was tall and looming, Tsubàyo was short and slender. Ripples of hardened flesh covered his chin, throat, and a wedge down his chest.

Rutejìmo stepped to the side, not wanting to be pinned between the two along the crumbling stone path. "You aren't great yet."

Tsubàyo stepped forward, a glower on his face. "I'm your better, boy, and don't you forget it."

Rutejìmo tried to move away, but the clinking of the bowls on the plank halted his movement. He looked down at the steaming food with a sinking feeling. He couldn't fight Tsubàyo while carrying breakfast.

"I thought so," said Tsubàyo in a satisfied voice.

Looking up, Rutejìmo realized the other boy interpreted his silence for agreement. His hands tightened on the plank. "You aren't my better, braggart, and you never will be."

A glare darkened Tsubàyo's face. He stepped forward and swept his hand up.

Rutejìmo dodged Tsubàyo's attempt to knock over the bowls, but he stumbled into Karawàbi and tripped over the larger boy's outstretched foot. Rutejìmo dropped to his knee to avoid falling over the edge of the path, but the bowls slipped from the board and plummeted down the side of the valley.

"Sands!" Rutejìmo screamed as he flailed helplessly.

"Oops," said Tsubàyo in a sardonic tone.

The ground shook as a blast of wind blew and a flash of a bird raced past them. Rocks tore at Rutejìmo's side and face. Coughing, he managed to focus just as Desòchu caught the third bowl. The other two rested in his other hand. Wind eddied around Rutejìmo's older brother as he gracefully spun around to prevent the food from slipping.

Desòchu glanced up and then stepped forward. He disappeared in a cloud of dust, and a plume of wind streaked to the end of the trail and up toward them.

Rutejìmo yanked his head around, hoping to see Desòchu racing, but his brother had already come to a halt in front of the three teenagers. A heartbeat later, wind blasted around them from the wake of his speed.

"And what are you three boys doing?" There was an easy smile on his face, but a hardness in his voice.

Rutejìmo looked up from the ground, still clutching the plank.

Tsubàyo cleared his throat. "Um, nothing, Great Shimusogo Desòchu."

"Yes," added Karawàbi, "we are doing nothing."

"Funny," Desòchu chuckled, "because I was pretty sure I saw you tripping the brat over there."

Tsubàyo tried to step away from Desòchu, but Rutejìmo's older brother followed him.

Desòchu casually reached out with one of the bowls.

Rutejìmo saw that he was handing it over and he held up his hand to take it.

As soon as the bowl left his grip, Desòchu reached over and dropped his hand on Tsubàyo's shoulder. Tsubàyo winced as he tightened his grip on the joint between the neck and shoulder. "Now, the boy is in trouble right now with my grandmother. Are you sure you really want to annoy Great Shimusogo Tejíko when you spill her breakfast?"

As he spoke, Karawàbi stepped back and held up his hands.

Tsubàyo tried to also walk away, but Desòchu yanked him closer and spoke directly to his face. "Well, Bàyo?"

"No, Great Shimusogo Desòchu."

"Good. Now, run along and stay out of trouble."

As soon as Desòchu released Tsubàyo, the teenage boy broke away. He ran down the path toward the bottom of the valley with Karawàbi following. Rutejìmo followed him with his eyes, watching as they headed toward the eastern end of the valley where there were a few caves that the children used as hiding spots. Rutejìmo knew which one Tsubàyo favored. As soon as his grandmother allowed it, Rutejìmo planned on finishing their discussion in private.

"Jìmo."

Rutejìmo set aside his thoughts and glanced over to his brother.

Desòchu clasped his hands together and regarded Rutejìmo. He wasn't smiling anymore, but Rutejìmo didn't recognize his expression. Desòchu looked torn, as if he were struggling with something.

"Are you planning on... finishing that with Bàyo?"

"Of course."

"Don't."

"Why not?" Rutejìmo snapped. "He keeps insisting he is better than me. And I know he isn't. He just thinks if he can trick me into saying it, somehow he will—"

"Jìmo!"

Rutejìmo clamped his mouth shut.

"Tonight"—Desòchu patted him on the shoulder—"just for tonight, you need to behave. Just be better than you normally are. You know... try?"

Rutejìmo shook his head. "But he—"

"Little brother." Desòchu pulled his hand back. "You need to behave. Please? No fighting and no sneaking around. And don't get revenge on Bàyo."

Rutejìmo opened his mouth to respond, but at the look in his brother's eyes, he closed it. "Yes, Great Shimusogo Desòchu."

"Promise me. Promise on Shimusògo."

Rutejìmo's skin prickled at the intensity of his brother's words. He gulped, then nodded. "I promise on the blood of Shimusògo that flows through my veins."

Desòchu nodded with approval. "Go on, Grandmother is waiting."

Chapter 5

Decisions

> The weight of opinions is measured in years, not from the freedom of a womb but those earned as a true member of the clan.
> — Basamiku Goryápe, *The Snake Killer's Betrayal* (Scene 19)

Rutejìmo didn't plan on obeying to his brother. During dinner, he listened to Desòchu's tale about his trip to Wamifuko City with only half an ear. He was occupied with how to sneak out of the family cave, find Tsubàyo without Karawàbi protecting him, and then beat the boy until he cried.

"Jìmo!"

Rutejìmo jumped at his grandmother's sharp voice. Blinking, he stared across the low table and dredged his mind back into the present. "Y-yes?"

"Were you paying attention to me?"

Desòchu snorted at the obvious answer, and Tejíko glared at him. Desòchu made a show of bowing respectfully, but as soon as she looked away, he pulled a face.

Rutejìmo gulped and shook his head. "No, Great Shimusogo Tejíko."

She leaned over and brandished a knife at him. "Are you paying attention now?"

"Yes, Great Shimusogo Tejíko."

"Good. There is a clan meeting tonight, and I don't want to see or hear a single step from you outside of the cave. Do you understand?" She waved the knife under his nose.

Rutejìmo remained respectful and bowed his head. "Yes, Great Shimusogo Tejíko."

"Good." She turned to his grandfather. "Get up, old man! We have to go to the shrine!"

"Eh?"

She smoothly stood up and smacked her husband playfully on the head. "Hurry up."

"Eh," his grandfather muttered as he shoved himself out of his seat. He reached out for balance.

The scowl faded from her face and she slipped her arm around his chest. She kissed her husband on the ear as she took his weight. Together, they walked to their sleeping quarters to dress in their formal outfits.

Rutejìmo turned to talk to his brother, but Desòchu was already gone. A faint eddy of wind was the only thing to mark his passing. Rutejìmo sighed and stood to clean the table. If he didn't, his grandmother would no doubt punish him again. She said it was being respectful, but it felt as if he were her slave.

By the time he finished scrubbing the last of the plates, his grandparents were gone. Rutejìmo packed the plates and knives into the wooden chest in the corner of the cooking area and closed it.

The cave was quiet except for the crack and pop of the fire. He headed straight for the entrance. He had to hunt down Tsubàyo

CHAPTER 5. DECISIONS

and finish their fight.

Outside, the valley was dark with night. Only a few caves were lit from the inside. Mapábyo's was on the opposite side of the valley, but both Tsubàyo and Karawàbi lived closer to the entrance of the valley. Rutejìmo focused on Tsubàyo's home, but no light escaped the opening. Farther along, he spotted a flicker of movement in the caves by the entrance, and a fierce anticipation rose.

"You wouldn't"—Rutejìmo jumped at Gemènyo whispering into his ear—"be thinking about getting in trouble, are you?"

Blushing hotly, Rutejìmo spun around as Gemènyo stepped out of the shadows. He was wearing only dark trousers and shoes. A cloud of smoke clung to his shoulders. "N-no."

Gemènyo chuckled. "Don't lie, boy."

Rutejìmo nodded sheepishly.

"Don't."

"Why not!?"

"Because important things are being decided tonight. And it would be foolish if you were to..." Gemènyo waved his pipe in the air. "Ruin anything good coming your way."

Rutejìmo hesitated at the serious tone in Gemènyo's voice. "What happened?"

"Great Shimusogo Mifuníko died a few hours ago."

A sick feeling slammed into Rutejìmo. He had heard Chimípu's mother had collapsed after arriving home a few days ago. The elders believed she poisoned during her last courier run, delivering a peace treaty to a warring clan. By the end of the day, her ashes would be in the shrine.

"I-I didn't know."

"Of course not," said Gemènyo with a sad smile, "you aren't a man yet."

"That means that"—Rutejìmo had to swallow past the tightness in his throat—"Chimípu is going on her rite?"

But Gemènyo was gone. The smoke from his pipe pointed down the path, sucked by the speed of his running.

He focused through the dissipating haze to the shrine house, now bright with torches and flames. Clouds of dust rose up around it as clan members appeared nearby, slowing down into visibility to politely walk across the threshold.

Gemènyo stopped at the entrance and looked back across the valley. It was too far to see his eyes, but Rutejìmo felt a shiver as he imagined Gemènyo looking straight at him. The courier tapped his pipe clean on the threshold, slipped it into his trousers, and stepped inside and out of sight.

For a moment, Rutejìmo stood in the entrance of the cave, torn between his sudden choices. Returning to the cave was no longer an option, but his revenge on Tsubàyo paled under the realization that something significant was about to happen.

He took a deep breath to calm himself and started toward the shrine. His bare feet slapped against the stone as he followed the shadows to circle around and come up to the back side of the building. As he drew closer to the rough stone wall, he could hear the older clan members talking among themselves. It was louder than he expected.

Rutejìmo stopped by the wall and rested his hand against the cool stone. Above him, the night sky was pitch-black except for the motes of light that stretched out in a line from horizon to horizon. In the endless depths of night, he felt very small.

Turning his thoughts back to his goal, he peered down the length of the back wall to find the spot Gemènyo mentioned. Just as he was wondering if the courier was tugging his leg, he realized it was right in front of him. The space between the shrine and the stone wall was small enough he could pry himself into it and climb. At the bottom, a barrel of blessed water was just at the right edge to give him a step up.

A minute later, he was creeping along the solid stone toward the vent and feeling ashamed that he had never noticed how easy it was to get on top before. He focused on the opening where a thin tendril of smoke rose up. He could hear the voices better and prayed the din would cover any sounds he made. Heart slamming against his ribs, he crouched and peered inside.

The shrine was a single large room carved from the living rock. A statue of Shimusògo dominated the back wall, and Rutejìmo felt humbled in the raw presence that radiated from the stone bird. He didn't know if the clan could see or feel him, but everyone knew when Shimusògo was paying attention.

Around the statue were stone shelves from floor to ceiling. Tiny vases and other charms of the clan dead were piled on them. Those who earned honor in their lives and deaths were represented by more ornate vases for their ashes. Most of them were smaller clay pots for those who had lived unremarkable lives in duty to the clan.

Rutejìmo was right above the elder, Yutsupazéso. She was a decrepit old woman who could barely walk. But where the weight of opinion was based on age, she had the strongest voice as the oldest living clan member. She sat bundled in a pile of blankets with two large bowls and a pile of polished black stones in front of her. Each one had a white eye carved into it and there were sixty-one of them, one for every year since she went through her rites of passage.

When a vote was brought up before the clan, she would throw her stones into either the red bowl if she disagreed or the black one to agree. The others would throw in their own votes and then the results would be tallied.

The shrine grew quiet, and Rutejìmo leaned forward to pay attention. An older man, Chimípu's father, walked into the shrine carrying a large, ornate vase. Rutejìmo held his breath respectfully as it was presented to Yutsupazéso.

Yutsupazéso reached up with shaking hands and took the

vase. She brought it down to her lap and whispered a prayer to it. She leaned over to kiss the top of it, and Rutejìmo was surprised to see tears sliding down the side of the vase when she handed it back to Chimípu's father.

Rutejìmo watched as the widower carried it over to the statue of Shimusògo and bowed deeply. He set it on the foot of the statue and backed away.

The quiet was almost painful as the entire clan bowed to the statue and the fallen courier.

Rutejìmo tried to show the same respect, but his bowed head was an empty, useless gesture when no one was watching. He looked away to avoid the tears burning in his eyes, then jerked when he realized he wasn't alone.

Chimípu was kneeling next to him, looking down into the shrine in silence. There were no tears in her dark-green eyes, but Rutejìmo could see tension in her wiry frame. Her light-brown skin was pale in the shrine's light, and she made no noise as she stared down.

Rutejìmo stared at her hatchet nose and the line of her throat as he struggled with his emotions. On one hand, he despised her with a passion because she had everything. On the other, she had just lost her mother and somehow managed not to cry.

He opened his mouth to say something but Yutsupazéso's cracked voice rose up. "Is it time for Chimípu to become a woman?"

Rutejìmo glanced over to Chimípu, but only a single tic along her lithe arm tightened indicated she heard the question. She stared down into the shrine with a hard look on her face and a determined set to her jaw.

Chimípu's father walked up and emptied a handful of beads into the black bowl. There were tears still on his face.

After a long count, Yutsupazéso raised her hand. "Any other?"

No one moved.

CHAPTER 5. DECISIONS

"Then tomorrow she will go to Wamifuko City for her rite of passage. Great Shimusogo Desòchu will be guardian for her trial. Agreed?"

Desòchu stepped forward and bowed to the gathered members. He had a grim look on his face, and Rutejìmo wondered what kind of trial his brother would give Chimípu, knowing the conflict between Rutejìmo and her.

No one disagreed, and Yutsupazéso dropped one of her own beads into the black bowl. A moment later, she swept it out.

"I think," Yutsupazéso continued, "that some of the other children should have a chance to visit outside the valley. Karawàbi?"

Karawàbi's mother and grandfather dropped their beads into the black bowl. Another clan member dropped theirs into the red, but it wasn't enough to overcome the opinions already in the black bowl.

Yutsupazéso waited until everyone gathered up their beads. "Tsubàyo?"

A few stepped forward to pour their beads into the bowls. When the last person stepped back, they were almost equal in measure.

She counted them out before announcing he would go.

"Pidòhu?" Pidòhu was a slender, frail boy who lived with his mother on the far side of the valley. He had a talent with repairing the mechanical dogs and other devices, but failed at almost every race and challenge.

No one agreed or disagreed with his inclusion. Rutejìmo frowned, wondering what would happen, but then Yutsupazéso dropped one of her beads into the black bowl.

"He goes. Rutejìmo?"

Rutejìmo tensed as he heard his name. He clutched the side of the opening and peered down, wondering who would answer for him.

His grandmother walked out, holding all the beads in her hand. Fifty-seven bright-red rocks, each one polished perfectly smooth. She reached out and poured all of them into the red bowl. "He's a fool and an idiot. Let him wait another year. Maybe by then, he'll learn his place."

Rutejìmo let out a quiet groan, then clapped a hand over his mouth. He peeked over to Chimípu. When he saw her smirk, the anger rose up and he pulled back his hand, but the sound of beads falling into a bowl stopped him. Snapping his head around, he looked down to see Desòchu's hand over the black bowl. "He's young, Great Shimusogo Tejíko, but we all were at one point."

His grandmother snorted but said nothing.

Gemènyo added his own to the black bowl, but then reached in and tossed one of the beads into the red.

More stepped forward to pour their beads into the bowls. Rutejìmo felt a twisting in his stomach as time slowed down. Most of the clan members poured their stones into the red bowl against him. He didn't realize so many didn't trust or like him.

But, even as the red bowl filled up, stones were added to the black. He tried to identify those speaking for him, but it was difficult. Unlike the others, everyone in the clan had an opinion about him going on the trip, and the press of people made it hard to see who voted for or against him.

Too soon, no one else stepped up to the bowls. Rutejìmo clutched the side of the opening tightly as he peered down. Even without counting, it was obvious that most of the clan didn't want him to go with the others. It was a blow to his stomach, and the bile rose up in his throat. He sniffed and wiped the tears burning in his eyes.

Yutsupazéso lifted her hand. "Any other?"

A gasp rippled through the shrine. He could see people looking at something near the entrance, but he couldn't see what or whom caused the surprise. Desperate to find out, he shifted to the side but bumped into Chimípu.

She made no effort to move aside.

He looked up pleadingly at her, but she was staring inside. And she was smirking.

Rutejìmo grabbed the edge and shoved his head into the opening, trying to get a look at what had caught everyone's attention. As he looked around, he match gazes with Desòchu.

Desòchu's eyes narrowed and he shook his head. His older brother made a point of looking back into the shrine.

Embarrassed, Rutejìmo pulled back shaking and wondered how fast he could run away. He peeked up to Chimípu, but she didn't even twitch from her location.

Then, as if feeling his gaze, she turned her eyes to him and gestured to the opening.

Trembling, he inched forward and peered inside again.

His grandfather stood in front of the black bowl. His hands shook violently as he tried to empty out his stones into it. The white stones bounced on the edge and rolled across the dirt ground but they kept pouring out. Sixty-one stones for someone who became a man the same day as Yutsupazéso.

"Why?" snapped Rutejìmo's grandmother. "He isn't ready."

Rutejìmo's grandfather stopped trying to gather up his stones. Desòchu knelt on the ground and picked them up for him, carefully holding each one out before setting it into the black bowl.

"Why?" repeated Tejíko.

"He's ready," came the only reply.

Chapter 6

Heading Out

> Tateshyúso is the name for large birds that fly high above the desert, content to ride the winds and play in the clouds.
>
> — Gregor Fansil, *Ornithological Studies of the Kimīsu Region of the Mifúno Desert*

When Rutejìmo woke up, his grandfather was back in his customary place by the fire, mute and staring out into the void. Rutejìmo wanted to walk over and thank him, but then his grandmother would know he had been out of the cave. He didn't want to risk his chance to leave the valley, even if it was just to watch Chimípu going through her rites of passage. Instead, he had to wait until one of them told him he was going on a trip.

"Rutejìmo," announced his grandmother.

He tightened with anticipation, knowing what she would say but not how she would tell him.

"I know you were at the shrine last night."

Rutejìmo's stomach did a slow turn to the side. He took a step back, his bare feet scuffing against the stone ground.

"When you get back"—she focused her bright-green eyes on him—"I will beat you until you scream."

Sweat prickled his brow, and he began to tremble. Rutejìmo glanced toward the entrance of the cave, knowing he could never outrun her. He gulped at his suddenly dry throat.

Tejíko turned her back on him and headed into her map room, moving slower than he had ever seen. "Get packed and leave us."

He watched as she sat down heavily in her customary spot and grabbed a fistful of maps. The paper crinkled loudly as he stared at her. "T-thank you, Great Shimusogo Tejíko."

When she said nothing, he ran to his room and pulled out his travel pack. As he grew up, the clan impressed on Rutejìmo what he needed as a courier. Part of the daily lessons was always being prepared to leave with fresh supplies. It had been only a few days since he last inspected it, but he still pulled out the contents and verified that the rations were fresh, the water clear, and the clothes in good shape. He also rewrapped a long length of thin rope around an utility knife.

Hoisting the bag over his shoulder, he headed out of the cave and toward the entrance. His heart soared as he ran down to the floor of the valley. It was a familiar path, but somehow it was different. He was leaving to go somewhere other than the nearby valleys for the first time since he was a toddler.

As he jogged through the common cooking area, he saw Pidòhu ahead of him.

Even though they lived in the same valley, Rutejìmo didn't like being near Pidòhu. There was something different about the younger teenager. He was thinner than anyone else, with long, skinny arms and legs. He looked like a leaf about ready to be torn from a branch. As far as Rutejìmo knew, Pidòhu had never won a race, never beaten anyone at wrestling. He was useless in a clan of couriers.

More than once, Rutejìmo wondered why Pidòhu was still in the valley but kept his thoughts to himself. His grandmother beat him the last time he asked, and the lesson still stung along his shoulders and back. Until the rite of passage, Pidòhu was in the clan just like himself.

Rutejìmo accelerated and passed him.

He smiled to himself, enjoying the chance to beat someone. The smile faded as he saw Chimípu racing along a higher path. She jumped off the trail and landed on the one below him. It was the same thing he did before, but she had leaped further and landed more gracefully than he could ever hope to achieve. Her feet flashed as she sprinted along the next one before she leaped onto the top of one of the storage buildings, over to a second one, and then hit the ground without losing a beat.

Jealousy gnawed at Rutejìmo's heart and he tried to run faster. He would never beat her, but he refused to admit it.

By the time he reached the valley, his heart was pounding and the exertion wrapped around his lungs with a clawed fist. He slowed to a halt as he saw the gathered clan members.

Desòchu was in a knot of a dozen clan couriers and warriors. He was smiling and they were laughing. Hyonèku stood next to him, his hand on Desòchu's shoulder and holding Mapábyo upside down by her waist. His daughter was squealing and thrashing, but laughing just as loud.

Karawàbi and Tsubàyo stood a bit closer to the valley as Gemènyo told a story. Gemènyo's arms waved expansively as he described the scene, and the two watched with rapt fascination.

Rutejìmo scanned the crowds until he spotted Chimípu. She stood right at the threshold of the valley with Jyotekábi and seemed perfectly at ease next to the older woman. Jyotekábi was a tiny and wizened woman with intense green eyes. Unlike everyone else gathered, she didn't wear an outfit for running. Instead, she had a thin silk robe of yellow and green over her shoulders. Underneath, she wore a loin cloth and nothing else. She was also at least two feet shorter than Chimípu but made up the distance in height by standing on a rock to talk to the younger woman.

The yellow and green were the colors of the Tateshyúso clan, unlike the orange and reds of the Shimusògo. There were only three members of the Tateshyúso in the valley and they kept to themselves along the upper ridges. Rutejìmo had never heard of one of them joining in a mission or a trip, but his grandmother claimed they were guardians of the valley. He didn't believe that since they never showed any clan magic besides occasionally bringing a cool breeze down through the valley on the hottest of days.

"Good morning," panted Pidòhu as he jogged up, "Rutejìmo."

Rutejìmo gave him a distracted nod and stepped aside to let him pass, but Pidòhu stopped next to him. Rutejìmo glanced over at the sweating boy and wondered once again if Shimusògo would ever accept such a weakling into the clan.

"Rutejìmo, I saw you on top of the shrine last night," said Pidòhu.

Rutejìmo jumped and looked over guiltily. "Does everyone know?"

Pidòhu ran a thumb along the ridge of his index finger. He shook his head and took a deep breath. "Gossip is faster than the wind."

Rutejìmo prickled at the comment. "None of us were supposed to be out that late. What were you doing out that late?"

"Fixing Opōgyo. Mapábyo managed to tilt it over one of the paths and crushed the outer casing. My father fixed it, but I had to repair some of the guide wires inside, and that took most of the night."

CHAPTER 6. HEADING OUT

Rutejìmo didn't understand Pidòhu's obsession with the mechanical dog, but it kept him away from the others. "At least you'll get a break from all that with this trip."

Pidòhu rubbed his hands together, working at the grease stains on his fingertips. "No, I've been dreading this trip for months." He knelt down to dig into his pack.

"Why? Because of Chimípu?" Rutejìmo jerked as he realized what Pidòhu had said. "For months? I thought this was planned last night."

Pidòhu looked up with murky green eyes. "Do you really think that?"

"Yeah," Rutejìmo said with a frown, "how could it be anything else?"

Pidòhu stood up again with a rag in his hand. He gestured with a finger toward the gathered clan members. "Have you ever seen so many for just a simple trip? And did you know that Jyotekábi is coming with us?"

Rutejìmo shook his head.

"This is more than just Chimípu's rite of passage, Rutejìmo."

"Maybe they just want to see her succeed beyond all expectations," Rutejìmo surprised himself with the spite in his voice.

"No," Pidòhu said with a sigh, "if that were the case, there wouldn't be so many. It only takes Shimusògo to make her a true member of the clan. Look at them." He gestured to the ones around Desòchu. "Can't you see the tension? Something has made the clan frightened."

Rutejìmo snorted and turned away. "You're jumping at the shadows, boy." But, as the words sunk in, he peered at the gathered clan and saw what Pidòhu was talking about. Desòchu was the easiest to see the difference in since Rutejìmo had grown up with him. While Desòchu spoke cheerfully, he tugged on his ears and adjusted his knives far more than Rutejìmo had ever seen.

Other clan members were toying with their own weapons, and the smiles faded during the lulls in conversation.

"This is more than just Chimípu, Rutejìmo." Pidòhu sighed and turned back to the valley. "You know, sometimes I wonder if I'll ever miss this place."

Startled by the sudden change in conversation, Rutejìmo turned to look back. He didn't see anything, but something in Pidòhu's voice brought a shiver of dread. "You'll be back by the end of the week."

"Do you really think that?"

Rutejìmo squirmed at Pidòhu's sullen words. He lifted his gaze to his own home. An uncomfortable tremble coursed along his spine, and the world felt icy for a moment. He started to doubt himself, but it never occurred to him that the trip was more than just a trip. He gulped to wet his throat. When he turned back, Pidòhu was already jogging toward Desòchu's group.

Grunting with annoyance, Rutejìmo drew his mind back to his journey and raced after Pidòhu.

Chapter 7

Middle of the Trip

> The desert has no time for the weak and sickly. The savages slaughter children with minor deformities and constantly push their youth to their limits.
>
> — Paladin Ruse, War Council of Kormar

Rutejìmo's chest ached, and sweat poured down his neck and shoulders. Sunlight bore down on him, stealing his breath as he struggled to jog along the ridge of the dune. For all the lessons, wrestling, and racing in the valley, nothing could prepare him for the difficulty of simply keeping up with the rest of the clan. He ran strongly in the beginning but despite the years of racing and competitions, he was soon straggling behind everyone but Pidòhu. By the third day, humiliation burned brightly and he prayed for death.

He looked for Pidòhu. The other boy struggled to keep moving with every step as he reached the top of a dune a few chains away.

He stumbled and sent sheets of sand pouring down in front of him. As much as Rutejìmo strained to keep up, it was nothing compared to Pidòhu's efforts.

Desòchu paced next to Pidòhu, jogging without any effort. He smiled and held his hand out, but wouldn't grab Pidòhu unless the weaker teenager reached out for him.

Jealousy rose up inside Rutejìmo. Desòchu had never gave him the same attention as he had Pidòhu. His brother always pushed for him to run faster, even in the baking sun, but then sent him to run on his own. Rutejìmo turned away to avoid the anger that surged up inside him. Focusing on his destination, he strained to find some burst of energy to get him through the last chains until he reached the camp.

The clan had stopped in the space between three narrow columns of rock that rose into the sky. They were called Wind's Teeth, and legends claimed they were the bones of some ancient creature that used to wander the deserts. Now, they were just used for landmarks and shelter for the clans who traveled the sands.

As he jogged down the final dune, he peered through the rocks to the camp. Most of the familiar tents were already set up, the bright reds and yellows of the Shimusògo clan comforting. All the tents were small and easily carried by one person. The material was thin but strong; it was also expensive and required a trip to Wamifuko City to obtain. Since he would spend most of his adult life in one, it was an easily justified cost.

Karawàbi and Tsubàyo were gasping for breath with their backs to one of the Teeth. Karawàbi was on the ground, head between his large hands while Tsubàyo bent over and braced himself on his thighs. They were soaked in sweat and shaking violently.

Gemènyo stood next to them, waving his hands wildly as he went on about a dangerous adventure that would, like most of his stories, end with him drunk off his ass. Like most of the adults of the clan, Gemènyo wasn't covered in sweat or even winded. Instead, he hopped back and forth as he tried to cajole Tsubàyo and Karawàbi into standing up.

Beyond the rocks, Chimípu stood calmly as she spoke to Hyonèku with only a triangle of sweat down her shirt and a glistening on her brow. If he didn't know better, Rutejìmo could have sworn she had just started on the trip.

Rutejìmo glared at Chimípu as he came up to the outer edges of the camp. While he struggled to run the last chain without throwing up, she was calm and collected. He slowed down as he fought his jealous thoughts, knowing that being blatant with his opinions would just ask for trouble and mockery from the adults.

"Come on, little brother," called Desòchu from behind, "the last person in camp has to make dinner tonight."

Groaning, Rutejìmo forced himself to speed up again. He had to make dinner the night before and the quips and unceasing demands still wore on his thoughts. His foot caught a thick ridge, and he lost his balance. He barely had a chance to throw his hands in front of him as he slammed face-first into the searing-hot sand.

"You know," said Gemènyo, "if Karawàbi and Tsubàyo weren't gasping for breath, they would be laughing at you."

Rutejìmo glared up at the courier, but took Gemènyo's offered hand to stand up. He sputtered to clear his mouth and wiped the grains from his sweat-soaked face. He looked at Gemènyo, who didn't even have a droplet of sweat on his body. "How do you do it?"

Gemènyo shrugged and held his palms up. "We are the clans of the sun. Just as Tachìra"—he pressed his hands together in prayer and looked up at the sun—"grants Shimusògo the power of speed, so we must honor the great sun that gives us life."

"Besides," Desòchu cheerfully added as he jogged up, "would you really want to run in the dark? You seem to have enough trouble remaining upright when you can see the sand."

Rutejìmo blushed hotly. He watched as Pidòhu staggered into the camp as the last member. It wouldn't be Rutejìmo making dinner. He would have felt a thrill of triumph, except he was too exhausted to care. He gasped for air, then leaned against his brother. "Does it get any easier, great brother?"

"When Shimusògo is before you, the sun stops hurting and the heat doesn't burn quite as much. But, if you don't struggle now, you won't respect the gifts you're given."

"I would."

Desòchu smiled and clapped him on the shoulder. "I know, little brother, and your day will come. Just a bit longer."

Pidòhu whimpered as he slumped to his knees. Air ripped past Rutejìmo as Gemènyo appeared next to Pidòhu. The tiny eddies of sand spun away as Gemènyo caught him and helped him back to his feet.

"No, no, little one. Just a few more steps."

"I-I—" gasped Pidòhu, "I can't."

"Of course you can," Gemènyo said compassionately, "just take one more step."

Pidòhu whimpered as he took another step, then a second.

Rutejìmo and Desòchu followed mutely behind the two. The scuff of sand shifted underneath Rutejìmo's feet. He almost slipped, but knowing the clan was watching, he wrenched himself back into place. A blush burned on his cheeks, and he fought the urge to gasp for air.

"Rutejìmo," Desòchu said in almost a whisper.

Rutejìmo looked up, surprised. "Y-Yes?"

"You should help Pidòhu with the cooking tonight."

"Why?" he grumbled. "He came in last."

"He's clan. And he is struggling. He could use a friend."

Rutejìmo watched as Pidòhu staggered into the center of the camp near the fires. Gemènyo stepped back as the frail boy dropped to his knees and dug into his bag. Pidòhu's back was covered in sweat, and tiny rivulets ran down to his arms before dropping off. Droplets hit the sun-heated sand, and tiny curls of steam rose up from the impact.

Desòchu clapped Rutejìmo on the back. "Good run, little brother. Just think about what I said. No matter how much you don't like him, clan is everything."

"Yes, Great Shimusogo Desòchu."

Desòchu gave him a smile and jogged over to talk to Gemènyo and Hyonèku.

Rutejìmo stopped at the rocks across from Karawàbi and Tsubàyo. He glanced over to the other teenagers, who glared back.

Tsubàyo stood up and shoved himself off. "Couldn't keep up, huh?"

Bristling at the comment, Rutejìmo balled his fists and took a step forward, but then he felt attention on him. Peering around, he saw both Hyonèku and Gemènyo watching him warily. He let out a hiss of annoyance and forced his fingers to relax.

Smirking with triumph, Tsubàyo gestured for Karawàbi to follow and headed toward the adults.

Rutejìmo watched him leave, hating that he couldn't beat Karawàbi into the ground like the smug bastard deserved. He peeked back and noticed Gemènyo was still watching. With a sigh, he took a step toward Pidòhu, but stopped as Chimípu knelt down next to him.

Without saying a word, Chimípu helped Pidòhu finish gathering up the cooking supplies and carried them over to the fire pit.

Pidòhu followed a few steps behind. "Thank you, Great Shimusogo Chimípu."

She nodded and pulled out the cutting board from Pidòhu's arms.

Rutejimo stepped back. He didn't want to be near Chimípu at the moment, not after struggling so much to keep up with the clan. He felt a dark cloud gathering over him as he turned his back on the two and headed to the shadows of the Wind's Teeth and away from everyone else.

Chapter 8

The Morning Sun

The true nature of a woman cannot be found with simple questions or tests. It can only be found when her child is under the knife's edge or when she must choose between her husband and family.

— Yunujyoraze Byomími

"**W**ake up, Jimo!" Chimípu's voice cut through the side of his tent.

Rutejìmo groaned as he cracked open his eyes. His head hurt, and his legs ached from yesterday's run. He wanted just a few more hours to sleep. "Go away!"

He rolled over and closed his eyes.

"Now!" snapped Chimípu. There was a strange tone to her voice, a sharpness on the edge of panic. Rutejìmo had never heard her sound like that, and he felt a prickle of fear crawl down his spine.

He sat up sharply and looked around. Spears of sun bore down on the thin fabric of the tent, and the transient coolness from the night was quickly turning into a stifling heat. Not even a trickle of breeze ran through space between the flaps.

He peered out through the opening, but Chimípu was already striding away. Scratching his head, he pulled on a fresh pair of shorts and carefully rolled his dirty clothes into a tube before shoving them into his travel pack. Groaning, he dragged his pack out of his tent and stood up.

The sun was brighter than he expected. He shaded his eyes and peered up. Tachìra, the sun spirit, was a fist height from the horizon. "They actually let us sleep in?"

"No," snapped Chimípu as she spun around, "it means they left us in the middle of the night!"

Rutejìmo froze, the prickling along his skin turning into the buzz of a thousand insects. The world spun around him as he stared at her, wondering if he misheard. "W-What?"

"You heard me, sand-blasted incontinent! I said they left us."

"No, Desòchu would never do that. He would never..." Rutejìmo peered around but he didn't see the other tents. "...leave... me...?"

There were only four tents still set up: Rutejìmo's, Pidòhu's, Tsubàyo's, and Karawàbi's. He didn't know where Chimípu's tent had gone, and he wondered where she set it up. After a few seconds, he guessed that she already had packed her tent before she woke him up.

The concern cut into him as he scanned the camping area around the three rocks. His brother's tent was gone. So was Gemènyo's and Hyonèku's and all the others. In fact, if it wasn't for the dead fire pit in the center of the three rocks, there would be no sign the clan had spent the night.

Rutejìmo turned back and asked, "Where is everyone?"

Chimípu let out an exasperated sigh. "Do you really think I know the answer to that?" She scanned the horizon, no doubt looking for signs of movement.

"Why not, Chimípu? You know everything else."

"That's because you're an idiot with sands for brains."

Tsubàyo groaned as he came up scratching his ass. "So? They left you behind also, Mípu."

Chimípu glared at him and pointed her longest finger at him. "Listen, shit for brains, I don't have time for your crap or posturing. I'm going to jog out to that dune"—she pointed to a taller ridge of sand—"and see if I can find them. Don't do anything stupid."

Tsubàyo shrugged and scratched the scars on his face and throat.

Chimípu made an exasperated sound and started across the sand. Rutejìmo followed her with his eyes. He was stunned how fast she lost her calm and wondered if he shouldn't be more worried himself. Chimípu was always collected and smug. Rutejìmo wasn't sure if he liked the change.

"Damn the sands, it's late," grumbled Karawàbi as he staggered up. "What is going on?"

Rutejìmo kept his gaze locked on Chimípu as she accelerated into a run. The sand kicked up behind her as she disappeared behind a smaller dune.

Tsubàyo grunted and gestured to the empty site. "The clan ran off without us."

Karawàbi looked surprised and then turned around. For a long moment, he stared at the empty campsite before he turned back. "When did that happen?"

"Last night."

"Why didn't we hear them?"

Tsubàyo reached over and smacked Karawàbi on the shoulder. "Because I couldn't hear anything over your snoring, idiot."

"Oh," came the reply. Karawàbi toed the ground for a moment. "I'm hungry."

Tsubàyo shook his head slowly before pointing to Rutejìmo's and Pidòhu's tent. "Then get Dòhu up and have him make us breakfast."

"Okay, Bàyo." Karawàbi turned on his heels and walked toward the tent. His feet scuffed against the sand.

"Jìmo...," started Tsubàyo.

Rutejìmo turned to focus on him. "Yes?"

"You going to obey the uptight bitch or me?"

"What?" Rutejìmo shook his head in confusion.

Tsubàyo stepped forward and gestured in the direction of Chimípu. "That girl has rocks jammed up her ass. If the clan really abandoned us, she's going to insist on being in charge. She is always lording over us, and that won't change out here. You know that, right?"

There was no question Chimípu was already taking charge when she woke Rutejìmo up. He let out a long sigh. "Yeah, she will."

"Do you really want to run in her shadow for the rest of your life?"

Rutejìmo shook his head.

Tsubàyo smiled triumphantly. "Good. I knew you'd see it my way."

Rutejìmo felt uncomfortable at Tsubàyo's declaration, but he said nothing.

"Now"—Tsubàyo clapped Rutejìmo on the shoulder—"I'm hungry. Dòhu! Where's Dòhu?"

Rutejìmo looked around, but didn't see Pidòhu.

Karawàbi headed straight for Pidòhu's tent and peered inside. With a chortle, he reached in and pulled Pidòhu from inside.

The frail teenager kicked and lashed out, both uselessly, as the much larger boy set him down on his feet.

CHAPTER 8. THE MORNING SUN

Pidòhu shook his arm free from Karawàbi's grip. His eyes were sad but not surprised as he looked around at the empty site. Instead, there was despair in his expression.

Karawàbi grunted. "I'm hungry. Go on, make breakfast for us, boy." He stepped over to Pidòhu and shoved him to where the fire used to be.

The slender boy stumbled forward and dropped to his knees. The sand rolled away from him as he looked up at Rutejìmo, Tsubàyo, and Karawàbi standing over him.

"With what?" Pidòhu gestured to the empty site. "The only thing we have is the food in our packs."

"So?" grunted Karawàbi.

"Rations don't need to be cooked, Wàbi," Pidòhu gave Karawàbi an annoyed look.

"I don't care." Karawàbi balled his hands into fists, and the sound of cracking knuckles snapped through the air. "I'm hungry. Find something, Dòhu."

Pidòhu sighed and shook his head. "Give me a few minutes."

"Hurry up, runt."

Tsubàyo gestured to Karawàbi, and the larger boy headed that way. Tsubàyo cleared his throat and gestured for Rutejìmo to also follow.

Rutejìmo looked back and forth between Tsubàyo and Pidòhu. The frail boy was digging through his travel pack, pulling out a few kindling sticks and a sparker. The device was a flint wheel attached to a long coil of wire. When pulled, it would create a shower of sparks to start a fire. He padded over to the pit and brushed away the sand to get to the ash beneath. Heat rose in shimmers around his fingers as he jammed the kindling into the ashes and set the device next to it. Grabbing a wire on the top, he planted his hand and yanked it. A shower of sparks poured out but the kindling didn't catch. He rewound the wire and tried again.

"Jìmo," called Tsubàyo.

Rutejìmo glanced back to the two boys, but then Desòchu's words came back. He shook his head and took a cautious step toward Pidòhu. When Tsubàyo didn't say anything, he headed over and squatted next to Pidòhu; the similarity to Chimípu wasn't lost on him, and he tried not to think about it. "What can I do, Dòhu?"

Pidòhu looked surprised. "I-I—" He glanced over to Tsubàyo and then back to Rutejìmo. He pointed to the side of one of the towering rocks. "Over there, there should be a food bag hanging on a ledge. Assuming they didn't take it. Could you find it?"

Rutejìmo jogged to the rock and looked around. When he didn't see anything, he paced back and forth and scanned the ragged rocks with a sinking feeling. He continued to circle the rocks but his mind began to wander.

Desòchu must have known about this as the leader, but Rutejìmo's older brother would never leave them alone. It was dangerous out in the sun. No shelter, very little water, and after three days of hard running, none of them had the energy to do anything.

Rutejìmo scanned the horizon, looking for Chimípu. She was just a black dot a few dunes over, running along one of the many ridges that crossed the desert. Chimípu had more energy than anyone else. She was a better runner and warrior. Jealousy rose up in him, and he wished he was as good as she.

"Damn the sands," he muttered, and gave up looking for the bag. "My own brother abandoned me."

He didn't want to go back to Pidòhu without the bag, or go near Tsubàyo. With a long sigh, he kicked the sand and headed for the farthest rock.

Rutejìmo stopped in the shade and slowly raised his gaze up the towering stone to focus on the sharp point sticking high in the air. It was easily over a chain in height, and in a happier time, he would have climbed it in a heartbeat. But now, abandoned by

CHAPTER 8. THE MORNING SUN

his own clan, left to die in the cruel desert, he didn't know what to do.

"Damn my brother."

"Jìmo!" yelled Tsubàyo. "Where did you go!?"

Rutejìmo looked across the endless waves of the desert and shook his head. "Damn my brother," he repeated and headed back.

He made it only a rod before movement on the rock caught his attention. He stepped back and shielded his eyes to peer up the towering Wind's Tooth. It was the food bag, but it was halfway up the backside of the rock, about thirty feet off the sands.

"Jìmo," called Pidòhu as he came around the rock, "did you find it?"

Rutejìmo mutely pointed to the bag.

Pidòhu looked up, then did a double take. "How did it get up there?"

Rutejìmo shrugged helplessly.

"Can you get it, Jìmo?"

Nodding, Rutejìmo padded up and inspected the rock. It was rough with sharp edges. He didn't want to climb up the face, but both of them knew who was better at scaling rocks. He tried to calm his quickening breath. "Give me a second."

"Thank you, Jìmo."

"For what, Dòhu?"

"For helping."

Rutejìmo peeked over at the slender boy before turning his attention to the bag. He mapped out the rocks, trying to find a place to climb. "Did you know this was going to happen?"

A sharp intake of breath answered his question.

"Was it planned?" He felt a strange sense of euphoria and betrayal tightening his throat. His brother would never abandon him.

"I'm guessing yes."

"Why?"

Pidòhu turned to him. "Didn't you think it was strange we had so many adults in this group?"

"No...." Rutejìmo hated being reminded that Pidòhu saw something long before he did.

"It's a trial."

"I know, this is Chimípu's—"

"No, it's a rite of passage for all of us."

Rutejìmo froze, his eyes not seeing for a painful minute. "F-For all of us?"

"Yes, that's why there was so many adults. I didn't think they were going to just leave us here, but this entire trip was for more than just—"

"What," snapped Tsubàyo as he came around the rock, "is going on?"

Pidòhu clamped his mouth shut.

"Well?" growled Tsubàyo as he stopped in front of Pidòhu. Karawàbi strolled behind him, scratching his ass.

Rutejìmo cleared his throat. "Pidòhu thinks this is a rite of passage for all of us."

Tsubàyo scoffed and glared at Pidòhu. "You aren't a man and will never be one. They are letting the sands take us because none of them want to be kin-killers."

Pidòhu stepped back, holding his hand.

Rutejìmo said, "No, he thinks that is why they brought so many on the trip." But Rutejìmo still didn't believe that is why they were in such a large group. He thought about the unexpected member also with them—Jyotekábi, the strangely dressed woman from Tateshyúso clan. The Tateshyúso never left the valley.

"Oh," drawled Tsubàyo as he took a step toward Pidòhu, "you knew this was going to happen?"

Paling, Pidòhu held up both hands. "I-I didn't know, I just guessed."

CHAPTER 8. THE MORNING SUN

Tsubàyo growled and took another step closer. Pidòhu tried to step back, but Tsubàyo followed him. "You knew they were going to abandon us? And you didn't think it was important to say anything? Are you working for them? A spy?" As he spoke, his voice grew louder and angrier.

"No, Tsubàyo, I didn't know. It was just an idea. I would never—"

Tsubàyo struck Pidòhu with his open palm, the crack of flesh on flesh echoed against the rocks. Rutejìmo jerked violently at the sound. Pidòhu spun once before he crumpled to the ground.

"I'm your better, boy," screamed Tsubàyo, "and don't you forget it! You call me great or don't speak!"

Pidòhu whimpered as he held his face with his hand.

Tsubàyo kicked sand on him. A few rocks bounced against Pidòhu's face before landing on the ground with little dull thumps. "Now, make my sand-damned breakfast."

Uncomfortable, Rutejìmo turned to the rock and steeled himself for climbing.

"No, Jìmo, let Dòhu do that."

Rutejìmo stopped at Tsubàyo's command. He turned slowly back to the scarred boy.

Tsubàyo gestured angrily at Pidòhu, who was getting to his feet. "He probably put it there just to see someone fall. Let him climb up."

"But—"

"I said," growled Tsubàyo, "let him"—he stepped toward Rutejìmo—"climb up there and get his own damn bag."

"Dòhu doesn't climb that well."

"Like shit he doesn't. I bet it was just one more lie, right?"

"No," whispered Pidòhu, "I—"

"Climb the damn rock!"

Rutejìmo and Pidòhu jerked at Tsubàyo's shout.

Tears glittering in his eyes, Pidòhu slowly made his way to the rock. He stared up at it with trepidation, and Rutejìmo could see him trembling.

Rutejìmo stepped forward, but hesitated when Tsubàyo let out a hiss. He wanted to help, but couldn't.

"Let him climb, Jìmo."

Rutejìmo pressed forward.

"I said—"

"I'm giving him my gloves!" he snapped. As soon as he said it, he was shamed he didn't say what was on his mind, that he wanted to do it for Pidòhu. Committed to his new lie, he peeled off his gloves and handed them to Pidòhu. He whispered to the slender boy. "I'm sorry."

Pidòhu nodded. "Thank you, Great Shimusogo Rutejìmo."

Rutejìmo turned away with a flush of embarrassment. He didn't deserve being called "great" anything; that was reserved for those who deserved respect. He walked from his own failure, but only a few rods before turning back to watch.

Pidòhu slowly picked his way up. He strained to reach the rocks, and when he pulled his trembling frame up, he grunted with exertion. He struggled to remain in place as he reached up for the next handhold.

"Move, boy," said Tsubàyo. "I'm hungry."

"I'm trying."

"Try harder."

Rutejìmo looked away but listened to Pidòhu climbing the rock. It took long, painful minutes, and Rutejìmo was reminded he could have done it in half the time. Even the idea of looking at the ground thirty feet below scared him, but he couldn't imagine what Pidòhu was thinking.

"Finally!"

Rutejìmo glanced up to see Pidòhu easing the bag off the ledge. Surprised, Rutejìmo let out his held breath before he realized he was holding it.

"Hurry up, boy," snapped Tsubàyo.

To climb down, Pidòhu worked blindly as he felt for the toeholds and tested each one before putting his weight on it. Rutejìmo could see him shaking with the effort to keep from falling. The bag swayed back and forth with every movement, threatening to fall.

A pebble bounced off the rock next to Pidòhu. It clattered down the Tooth before hitting the ground with a thud.

Rutejìmo gasped and looked to where Karawàbi was hefting another rock with a grin on his face. "Wàbi!"

Karawàbi shot Rutejìmo a glare and flicked a larger rock. It bounced a few links from Pidòhu's hand. Pidòhu gasped and flinched away a moment later. He would have been too late to avoid being struck, if it hit him. His lower foot scraped against the stone with renewed attempts to find a foothold.

Rutejìmo stormed forward. "Stop that, Karawàbi!"

"What?" Karawàbi threw another rock, and it hit the stone near Pidòhu's feet. "I'm not going to hit him."

"He's twenty feet off the ground!"

Another rock. This one struck the stone near Pidòhu's shoulder, and flecks of sand poured down. "The sand is soft. He won't get hurt."

Rutejìmo halted in front of Karawàbi. He was a link shorter than the larger boy and couldn't tower over him. "He is clan."

"Not for long," chuckled Karawàbi. He drew back and threw the rock. It whistled past Rutcjìmo's ear.

Rutejìmo balled his fist to strike Karawàbi, but then he saw Karawàbi's face pale. Rutejìmo spun around with a feeling of dread clenching around his heart.

Pidòhu was clawing at the rocks with one hand as he fell back. One foot was flailing in the air, and the rapid thumping of his toes striking the stone was a drumbeat that matched Rutejìmo's own sudden pulse. The sound of fingernails scratching against stone filled the air as Pidòhu's weight snatched him from the stone cliff.

At first, he moved with sickening slowness as he fell back, but he quickly accelerated as he peeled off the stone wall and plummeted to the sand below. Over the thump of his body hitting the ground, Rutejimo heard the sound of cracking bone, and it sent a pang of fear through him.

Chapter 9

Blood and Bone

Actions made in a moment of unconscious reaction are worth more than a thousand lectures of note.

— Yunujyoraze Byomími

For a long moment, no one said anything. A few rocks bounced off the Wind's Tooth and hit the ground with heavy smacks. One of them, slightly larger than Rutejìmo's fist struck Pidòhu in the back. The meaty thud only brought a shudder before it rolled off into the sand. It left a blood-flecked wake before it stopped a few links away. The wind had quieted, and nothing obscured the sound of Pidòhu's groans.

Rutejìmo stared at Pidòhu's limp body. He had never seen someone seriously hurt before. He kept replaying the sight of his body plummeting to the ground and the sound of impact. He tried to step back, to run away, but his legs refused to move. A whimper rose up, and he realized it came from him. Helpless, he glanced over to Tsubàyo in hopes that the older boy would do something Rutejìmo could follow.

Tsubàyo had a look of stunned shocked on his face. Sweat glistened on his brow and his dull green eyes were shimmering. He started to turn away, but his look never wavered from Pidòhu's body.

Pidòhu moaned, a broken, wet noise. "H-Help...?"

Rutejìmo choked back sobs. He didn't know what to do. He knew he should rush over to Pidòhu, should have already done it, but he was afraid Karawàbi would stop him or berate him. Silently, he prayed Tsubàyo would step forward, turn around, or even give a command.

Pidòhu reached up from the shadows of the rock. His hand was bloody, and bits of sand and rock clung to his lacerated palm. "H-Help me."

Rutejìmo looked back at Tsubàyo and then to Karawàbi.

Karawàbi seemed unfazed by Pidòhu's fall. Instead of shock or horror, the corner of his mouth had curled up in a smirk. He turned to see Rutejìmo looking at him and took a step toward him. "What? You have a problem?"

Whimpering, Rutejìmo stepped back. The sand swallowed his foot, and he almost lost his balance. He stumbled back, his eyes locked on Karawàbi, but the larger teenage boy didn't come any closer.

"I can see bone," sobbed Pidòhu, "and there's blood everywhere. Please, help?" His voice was ragged and gasping.

Rutejìmo felt sick to his stomach. He clutched his belly as he looked at Tsubàyo hopefully.

Tsubàyo spun on his heels and sprinted away from the accident.

Karawàbi chuckled dryly and dug his hands into his pockets. "Come on, Rutejìmo, it's time to go." And then he strolled after Tsubàyo while whistling cheerfully.

Rutejìmo turned back to Pidòhu but he couldn't force his legs to move. His mind screamed to run way with Tsubàyo, but something held him in place.

"Jìmo?" Pidòhu sobbed as he lifted his head. "Please help me."

Rutejìmo couldn't move.

"Where did Bàyo and Wàbi run to, Jìmo?" Chimípu's voice drifted through the wind behind him. She didn't seem concerned or worried; she must not have seen Pidòhu.

The urge to run away doubled, and Rutejìmo managed to get a foot out of the sand before setting it down heavily. He looked guilty at Chimípu as she walked up.

A few strands of her dark hair whipped in the wind that stirred the sands around her. A small plume of dust was dissipating behind her as if she were running.

"Mípu?" called out Pidòhu.

In a flash, Chimípu's curiosity turned to concern and then to anger. She rushed forward. Rutejìmo was in the way, but she shoved him hard to the side. "Where is he!?"

Rutejìmo stumbled back, his eyes locked on her.

Her eyes widened and she gasped. "Dòhu!?" She sprinted over to him before dropping to her knees next to his prone form. "What happened!? Where are you hurt?" She gingerly felt along his arms, no doubt looking for more broken bones.

"I-I fell. And hurt myself."

"Tachìra's left nut. You didn't do this yourself." She glared at Rutejìmo. "What did you do to him!?"

Rutejìmo gulped, fighting the overwhelming desire to run away. He held up his hands. "I-I didn't...." He couldn't finish the sentence. He didn't do anything, but he could have. A thousand different things flashed through his mind, and the guilt tore at him.

Chimípu glared at him. He saw disgust and anger burning in her green eyes. She turned away. "Just... just go away." She shifted to her other knee and started to inspect Pidòhu's wounds closely.

It was the hardest thing for Rutejìmo to step closer. It wasn't only curiosity that drove him, but an unfamiliar sense that he needed to do something. He didn't understand it, but seeing Pidòhu splayed out on the ground gave him a sick feeling. But, as much as he wanted to run away, he couldn't do anything but inch closer.

Tears ran down Pidòhu's face. Shaking, he clutched Chimípu's thigh and dragged himself over until his head rested on her leg. There was a strange sense of familiarity between them as Chimípu stroked his hair and whispered softly. He looked up but said nothing.

Together, they lifted their heads to look down at Pidòhu's right leg. The jagged ends of both bones stuck out of his leg, the four cracked ends dripping with blood. The wound soaked the fabric of his trousers and dripped to the ground in a rapidly growing crimson stain.

Rutejìmo dropped to his knees as he threw up. The acidic taste burned in his mouth, and he wished it would burn away his memories.

"Jìmo!" snapped Chimípu.

Rutejìmo jerked and looked up guiltily.

"Get my pack," she ordered.

He was relieved to get an order and direction. Turning around, he willed himself to move and headed back the way Karawàbi and Tsubàyo had run.

"Hurry!" yelled Chimípu from behind him.

Jogging, he ran around the rocks. When he saw Tsubàyo pawing through Pidòhu's bag, he slowed to a stop. Pidòhu's supplies were spread out along the ground, carelessly tossed aside. Some of his clothes were already buried by the blowing wind.

Karawàbi stood near Tsubàyo, hands in his pockets and a cruel smile on his face. He had two packs slung over his shoulder, Tsu-

CHAPTER 9. BLOOD AND BONE

bàyo's and his own. Their tents were already strapped to the side.

As Rutejìmo approached, Tsubàyo stood up. "How bad is it, Jìmo?" His voice was calm and calculating.

Rutejìmo swallowed back the bile. "Not good, Bàyo. He broke bones, and they are sticking out. I... I can see blood everywhere."

Tsubàyo reached into Pidòhu's pack and pulled out a small leather book. He looked at it briefly before throwing it over his shoulder. He grabbed the nearly empty bag and bunched it close before straightening back up. "Pity. We'll just have to go on without him. Come on and take this, I've gotten rid of the useless stuff." He held out the bag for Rutejìmo.

The sick feeling redoubled. Rutejìmo almost bent over as he felt it burning his throat, choking him. "I-I have to get Mípu's bag."

"Why?" Tsubàyo shook his head and held out his hands. "Dòhu isn't going to survive with a broken leg."

"B-Because, she... told me to." Rutejìmo couldn't look Tsubàyo in the eyes.

"You're pathetic, worm-rotted pile of diseased crap. Are you incapable of doing anything on your own?"

Rutejìmo's cheeks burned at the insult. He felt ashamed for abandoning her but also for not following Tsubàyo. He didn't know which one he should obey.

"Jìmo!" Chimípu's call echoed off the rocks.

Rutejìmo gulped and grabbed her bag. "I have to get this."

"Go on, boy, run to your mistress." Tsubàyo kicked sand at Rutejìmo's face. "Like a good puppy."

Choking on his response, Rutejìmo dropped Chimípu's bag. He scrambled to pick it up before Karawàbi could step on it. His finger caught Pidòhu's leather book in the sand. After a moment's hesitation, he grabbed it and Chimípu's pack and backed away from the two.

Karawàbi snorted with disgust, and that was enough to spur Rutejìmo to run back to Chimípu and Pidòhu.

On the far side of the Wind's Tooth, Chimípu had stripped off her shirt and was using the fabric to blot the blood oozing out of the wound. Her dark skin glistened with sweat, except where she had a long, white cloth wrapped around her breasts. She glanced at Rutejìmo as he sank to the ground next to them.

"Took you long enough," she snapped.

"Sorry."

"Put your hand here." She pointed to a bloody spot on the cloth. "And put pressure on it. But, don't touch the bone itself."

Rutejìmo almost threw up again as he looked at the gaping wound. He clutched the book tighter.

"Now!"

Closing his eyes, he gingerly reached out to obey.

Chimípu grabbed his wrist and yanked him closer.

Rutejìmo lost his balance and shoved his hands forward. He slammed into the sand between Pidòhu's legs. Gasping, he opened his eyes to see himself only inches away from the blood wound.

Chimípu yanked his hand from the ground and jammed it against the sticky, hot fabric. "Pressure, now. I won't lose Dòhu because you can't handle some blood."

She grabbed her pack and dug into it.

Underneath Rutejìmo's hand, Pidòhu shook violently. His face was pale and drawn. Pidòhu jerked as a shirt landed on his hand, and Rutejìmo felt bones scraping.

Pidòhu clenched and then let out a wail of pain.

"I'm here, Dòhu. And you'll be all right. Just give me a second." Chimípu's voice was compassionate and caring when she spoke to him. Not like the sharp orders she just gave Rutejìmo. She let out a grunt of triumph as she pulled out a leather roll from her pack. With a snap of her wrist, she unrolled it along the ground to reveal a field kit. One end had a collection of knives, needles,

CHAPTER 9. BLOOD AND BONE

and awls. The other had small pouches that would contain herbs, string, and other items used for wounds and repairs.

She looked up at Rutejìmo and Pidòhu. "Jìmo, use both hands and more pressure, it's leaking."

Rutejìmo looked down to see blood trickling from underneath the fabric. He gulped and sat down the leather book before gingerly pressing both hands on the blood-soaked fabric.

Chimípu pulled out two bunches of leaves. She crawled around Pidòhu, dragging the roll, and settled into place opposite to Rutejìmo. Her hand was steady as she pressed the leaves to his lips. "Get a lot of saliva in your mouth, and suck on these. Don't swallow, though. These will help with the pain."

Pidòhu groaned. "I know, I helped you pick them, remember?" He opened his mouth and accepted the herbs.

She smiled weakly. Turning away, she started for the field kit but stopped sharply. "Jìmo, why did you bring that?"

Rutejìmo peered down to see that she was pointing to Pidòhu's book. "Um, Karawàbi is... going through Pidòhu's bag. They're leaving."

Chimípu stared at him incredulously. "Seriously? Here? Now? But what about Dòhu?"

He didn't want to say the words. He looked away from both her glare and the wound.

She jammed her finger into his side. "Don't they know he's hurt?"

He could only nod.

Chimípu stood up sharply. "What is wrong with all of you!? They can't leave. We can't split up the clan, not here, not now!" Her shrill voice echoed against the rock. She dropped the other leaves on Pidòhu's stomach. "Dòhu, Tell the daft idiot how to pack the wound, I have to stop them."

Rutejìmo followed her as she ran after Tsubàyo and Karawàbi. When Pidòhu moaned, he turned back. "I-I... what do I do?"

Pidòhu pushed the sodden herbs into the side of his mouth before he answered. "Pull back the shirt and pack these"—he scooped up the herbs from his stomach—"where it is bleeding. It will stop the flow and prevent poisoning."

Looking down at the herbs, Rutejìmo shook his head. "Dòhu, I don't think I can do this."

Pidòhu said nothing, but there was a pale, frightened look on his face. Tears still ran down his cheeks. "It really hurts."

At the sound of Pidòhu's cracked voice, Rutejìmo sighed and wiped the tears from his eyes. "I'm sorry. I... I didn't... mean—"

"I know," whispered Pidòhu.

Gulping, Rutejìmo steeled himself. He tugged back the fabric. It clung to the wound, and he pulled harder. As it peeled off, a fresh spurt of blood blossomed in the gaping wound around the bone.

Pidòhu whimpered. "Hurry, please?"

Rutejìmo squished the sodden leaves in his palm. Gulping to fight the bile rising in his throat, he steeled himself to help. With a shaking hand, he gingerly shoved the herbs into the torn flesh.

Pidòhu hissed in pain and Rutejìmo yanked his hand back.

"No, keep doing that. Hurry."

Rutejìmo tried again and shoved the herbs into the wound, focusing on the areas that had blood pooled against the skin.

The injured boy let out a cry when Rutejìmo accidentally scraped against the ragged end of bone.

"It isn't working." Rutejìmo felt helpless, "Do I need more?"

"Just give it a few seconds," gasped Pidòhu. "Just a few seconds."

"There is so much blood." Rutejìmo hated that he was whimpering himself, but he couldn't move his gaze away from the blood filling the wound. The bare ends of the bones, four ragged spears of splintered white, twitched with every beat of Pidòhu's pulse.

CHAPTER 9. BLOOD AND BONE

Tenderly as he could, Rutejìmo dabbed at the blood with the corner of the fabric. The cloth quickly grew hot and sticky, but he hoped he was helping instead of making it worse.

Pidòhu let out a sudden gasp. "Oh, it's working."

Rutejìmo glanced down and realized the bloody wound was crimson, but blood no longer flowed out from the ragged ends of skin. He gulped at the nausea that slammed into him. "W-What do I do now?"

Pidòhu's eyes were glazed over as he glanced down. His cheek moved as he swirled the pain herbs in his mouth. With a nod, he pointed to one of Chimípu's shirts spilled out on the sand. It was her white ceremonial top, imported from the northern regions and very expensive.

"A-Are you sure?"

He nodded and moved the herbs to the side to speak. "It will soak it up. I'll buy her a new one, I promise."

"I—" Rutejìmo stopped speaking and grabbed it with one hand. He shook it free of sand, then carefully pushed it past the broken bone and into the wound. The bright white fabric turned crimson almost immediately.

Pidòhu jerked when Rutejìmo accidentally scraped the bone.

"I'm sorry!"

"J-Just hurry up, please? Don't move my leg, but try to staunch as much as you can."

Following Pidòhu's instructions, Rutejìmo carefully stuffed part of the shirt into the ragged wound. As he did, he could see how the sodden fabric helped bind the bones together and prevent them from ripping the skin further apart. When Pidòhu told him to wrap it tighter, Rutejìmo hesitated but obeyed. More blood oozed out of the wound, but Pidòhu gave a sigh of relief when Rutejìmo finished tying the limb and immobilizing it.

"Like that, Dòhu?"

When Pidòhu didn't answer, Rutejìmo looked up with concern. Pidòhu was slumped back, breathing shallowly, but his eyes were rolled into the back of his head.

Terrified Pidòhu had somehow died, Rutejìmo reached up and rested his hand on Pidòhu's chest. The rapid rise and fall gave him comfort. "I'm sorry, Dòhu."

The scrunch of sand tore his attention away from Pidòhu. He looked up as Chimípu dropped to her knees next to him. She pressed a hand against Pidòhu's throat and cocked her head.

Rutejìmo noticed she had a bruise forming over her eye and her knuckles were scraped. Part of her lip was also split, and she licked away the blood welling up.

Chimípu glanced at him, then back to Pidòhu. "Tsubàyo and Karawàbi are going their own way. If you want to go with them, I recommend you pack up and get the sands out of here."

Her voice was harsh and bitter. He trembled at the noise of it. He looked back at the rocks and then to Pidòhu. "Is he... going to live?"

"I will do everything I can to save him." She glared at him. "Unlike Tsubàyo and Karawàbi, I don't pick who is in my clan. That's Shimusògo's decision, not yours."

"I didn't...." But the words wouldn't come. He shivered from the intensity of Chimípu's look. Turning away, he swallowed to ease his tight throat. "I wasn't choosing."

"Dòhu?" Chimípu whispered, but it was soft-edged and compassionate. Rutejìmo glanced over to see her leaning over Pidòhu and stroking his sweat-soaked hair. "Just hold on, okay? As soon as the incontinent piles of horse crap"—her eyes flickered toward Rutejìmo—"go away, I'll get something for you to eat."

Rutejìmo got on his feet, but didn't stand up. Crouching, he watched as Chimípu focused on Pidòhu. It felt as though she was just counting the seconds until he left. "Chimípu?"

Slowly, she turned toward him. "Make a choice, Rutejìmo, if you can. Either stay here and be useful or just leave."

As he stood up, the sick feeling grew in his stomach. It was a burn that threatened to rise up in his throat. He glanced down at his blood-stained hands. "Mípu... I'm sorry."

"Go away, Jìmo." She didn't look at him again. "Just go away."

He saw a tear roll down her bruised cheek before she turned away from him.

Chapter 10

Separation Anxiety

> Inspiration rarely comes when waiting for it.
> — Marfun Golem, *The Failure of Innovation*

"I can't believe that bitch!" Tsubàyo led the way along a dune. He was in high spirits, despite the fresh bruises on his arms and a scratch that bisected his scar tissue. He swung Pidòhu's bag in his hand as he headed along a route only he could see.

Karawàbi followed closely behind. He had Tsubàyo's and his own pack on over one shoulder and Pidòhu's over the other. He didn't have any bruises or scratches, but Rutejìmo noticed a faint limp when he hit the ground at the wrong angle. The large teenager moved in relative silence, only grunting when Tsubàyo asked a question.

Rutejìmo could only imagine that both of them took on Chimípu while Rutejìmo was trying to stop Pidòhu's bleeding. None of them talked about it, but he could see it in their injuries and the way they avoided referring to what happened with Chimípu.

He wasn't sure why they had fought her or why they insisted on leaving, other than Chimípu's saying they had to keep together. His brother used to say something similar, that the clans cling to themselves at night for safety. He tried to tell himself that he had to choose sides and that Chimípu had rejected him. It didn't ring true and he remained silent, lost in guilty thoughts and regret.

It was a few hours after noon. The sun bore down on them, and Rutejìmo could feel it searing along his skin. There was a breeze, but it was hot and thick with sand. It left a foul taste in his mouth, and he had to pretend it wasn't from leaving behind two clan members in the shadows of the Wind's Teeth.

He peeked over his shoulder. The rocks were only a dark dot on the horizon. Their path was almost hidden with the searing winds that blew across the dunes. To his right, the air hazed over with the heat.

"Don't give her another thought, Jìmo."

Tsubàyo stood on top of a ridge and watched him with a dark look in his eyes. The scars from his childhood injury gave his face a rippled pattern not unlike the dunes they had been climbing for the last few hours.

Rutejìmo licked his lips, feeling the cracked edges with his tongue. "What about Pidòhu?"

Karawàbi shrugged. "He's dead, he just doesn't have the sense to know it."

Tsubàyo nodded in agreement.

Rutejìmo glanced back the way they had come.

"Jìmo," warned Tsubàyo, "I said stop thinking about it."

"Did we do the right thing?" Rutejìmo knew the answer before Tsubàyo opened his mouth.

"Got rid of dead weight?" Tsubàyo mimed thinking as he tapped his forehead. "Yes, we did. Now we don't have to deal with

CHAPTER 10. SEPARATION ANXIETY

a worthless runner and a stuck-up bitch that thinks she knows everything. We are better off."

Rutejìmo didn't have the same confidence.

"Come on, we have another good hour and we can set up camp by that rock." Tsubàyo pointed to the south where rocks stuck out from the sand like shattered toenails.

Rutejìmo almost looked back again, but caught Karawàbi watching him. Blushing, he forced himself to trudge forward.

"You know what?" Tsubàyo declared, "We're Shimusògo, let's run." Without waiting for a response, Tsubàyo jogged down the dune.

Karawàbi groaned, and both he and Rutejìmo ran after Tsubàyo to catch up. With their physiques and endurance, their run quickly became a line with Karawàbi following right behind Tsubàyo and Rutejìmo struggling a few rods away. And he felt more alone than he had ever felt before.

He missed Pidòhu. No matter how slow Rutejìmo ran, he knew he would beat the slender boy. It was different being the slowest runner, and he felt a bit of sympathy for Pidòhu.

As he stumbled down one of the slopes of sand and rock, he caught movement in the corner of his eye. He stopped and looked, but he saw nothing but the dark swirls of sand on sand. He turned in the other direction but there was nothing.

"Jìmo?"

Rutejìmo shook his head. "Thought I saw something."

"Probably just a snake," said Tsubàyo. "Hurry up."

Shaking his head again, Rutejìmo returned to jogging. He struggled on the upward slope of the next dune. By the time he reached the top, he was sweating and gasping for breath.

Karawàbi and Tsubàyo were already ahead of him, and he let out a groan before chasing after them. His legs hurt from the effort but he knew there was no way they would slow down for him.

Annoyance prickled along his thoughts as he glared at Tsubàyo's back.

He caught a hint of movement again. This time, he didn't stop but glanced over without slowing.

It was a bird racing him, just a few paces ahead of him and to the right. The avian glided across the sand on long legs. Its three-toed claws didn't leave a trail behind it or disturb the sands with the breeze of its passing. It kept its short wings tight to its body as it ran. A brown-and-white speckled pattern ran from its crest down to the end of the long feathers that formed the tail. It was a shimusogo dépa, the dune-runner bird Shimusògo took his name from.

Startled, Rutejìmo slowed down, and between one step and the next, he lost sight of the bird. Desperate, he tried to maintain his speed while looking around but the dépa was gone. He slowed down further, peering over his shoulders for the bird.

As he came to a stumbling halt, all the joy fled out of him. In one moment, he was experiencing a high and in the next it was gone. It wasn't until it was missing that he realized he was experiencing it. In its wake, a longing burning inside him. He wanted to run, something he had never felt before, and the urge sang through his veins.

Rutejìmo frowned and turned in a circle. The dépa was gone and Tsubàyo and Karawàbi were quickly outpacing him. The need to run burned hotter. In the back of his mind, he knew that if he just ran fast enough, the dépa would return. The knowledge, however, frightened him since he never had an urge to run before nor did he ever see a dépa while running.

The other two distancing him finally pushed him to take the next step. He did and the longing burned brighter. He stumbled before moving into a jog, but it wasn't enough. He needed to run, it was a foreign craving that screamed to move faster. Disturbed and frightened, Rutejìmo gave into his needs and threw himself

CHAPTER 10. SEPARATION ANXIETY

into a full sprint.

Between one step and another, the dépa rushed past him and settled into place a rod before him. He found his rhythm and chased after it, but the bird continued to run just ahead of him. With every step, he felt a bubbling excitement stretch up his legs. It wasn't the burn of effort but something else, a drug that came from chasing a bird that didn't exist.

The sound of feet on sand drew his attention away from the dépa. In his attempts to catch it, he had caught up with Karawàbi. Rutejìmo wondered if they had slowed down, but both of them appeared to be running as fast as before.

He stumbled over a rock and came to a halt. As he did, the dépa disappeared before his eyes. Panting, he watched as Tsubàyo and Karawàbi continued to race ahead, neither looking back for him.

Rutejìmo started to jog after him. This time, he concentrated on the fleeting sensations inside him. With every step faster, the excitement returned and encouraged him to run faster. He pushed himself and the thrill of anticipation was almost as strong as the euphoria he felt when the dépa reappeared. The aches and pains of running for days faded away, leaving only a rush of excitement and a wind in his face

For the briefest moment, he felt a connection to something incredible, a wordless sensation of being part of a force far larger than himself. It was a connection to the unknown and every step brought him closer.

As the epiphany was about to reveal itself, he tripped.

Rutejìmo gasped as he landed face-first into the searing-hot dune. The sun-baked sand burned his chest, throat, and arms. He choked on it as he struggled to his knees. Automatically, he looked for the dépa but it was gone. He sighed and got back on his feet.

He started forward again, racing for his new-found rush and the appearance of what he assumed was his clan spirit, Shimusògo.

Chapter 11

Standing Alone

Time alone gives a man a chance to consider the mistakes he made.

— Heyojyunashi Gutèmo

They came to a gasping halt at a pile of rocks. The stones didn't tower over them like the Wind's Teeth, but the outcropping gave some shelter against the wind kicking up sand from the west. It was near the end of the day, and the shadows formed by the setting sun sent long fingers of shade across the red-tinted sands.

Rutejìmo leaned against the rock and panted for air. Sweat trickled down his entire body and his legs trembled, but elation burned brightly in his veins. He had kept up. For the first time since they started this accursed trip, Rutejìmo managed to run with the rest of the clan. Even if the clan was only three teenage boys. He wondered if, somehow, the others had slowed down for him. He glanced at Tsubàyo with a silent question.

The teenager scratched the scars on his face and caught the look. "What?"

"Bàyo, did you—" He cleared his throat and inhaled sharply before he said, "Were you running slower?"

Tsubàyo shook his head. "No, why would I do that?"

"Because... I...." He felt embarrassed talking about it. Rutejìmo stood up and shook his head. "Don't worry about it, I was thinking about something." He turned and headed around the far side of the rocks.

"Jìmo! Don't go too far. You'll need to get a fire started for dinner."

Rutejìmo tensed with annoyance. He had just spent the entire day running with the others. Despite chasing the dépa and feeling more energetic before, running was still exhausting and he felt the ache seeping into his limbs.

When he went with Tsubàyo, he never expected to be the one serving the others. It felt demeaning when Tsubàyo should have been glad that Rutejìmo had gone with him instead of staying with Chimípu.

Rutejìmo glanced at Karawàbi, but there was no compassion from the other teenager. The larger boy tossed down the bags and pointed to them. "Don't forget these too. Put my tent by the rocks."

Setting his jaw, Rutejìmo stalked around the rocks to get away from both of them. He continued to walk until he could no longer hear Tsubàyo or Karawàbi. Taking a deep breath, he tried to calm down and fight the sick regret building in his stomach.

The view of the desert was both familiar and strange at the same time. The sun was an angry red blob on the horizon, the edges wavering with the heat that rose up from the sun-baked sands. Dunes and patches of rocks spread out as far as he could see until they disappeared into the haze of sand and wind. It was the same thing he saw every time he went to the edge of the clan's valley. But the swells of sand and the piled rocks were in the wrong places. It wasn't home and it brought a pang of homesickness.

His mind drifted to the run. The dépa was real, but neither Tsubàyo nor Karawàbi had reacted to it when it ran between their legs. He wanted to ask either of them had seen it, but he didn't want to be mocked if they were ignoring it or if they thought he was seeing things.

Chimípu wouldn't have been much better. She always acted superior to him, both in her attitude and the casual way she excelled at everything. It was different than Tsubàyo's overbearing command, but Rutejìmo wasn't sure if he had made a mistake by leaving them or if he was simply choosing who would humiliate him.

To his surprise, Rutejìmo worried about Pidòhu. When Pidòhu had quietly explained how to bandage his own broken leg, Rutejìmo was surprised at his strength of will. If Rutejìmo were in his place, he would have been screaming and sobbing far more than Pidòhu's quiet cries.

There was more to Pidòhu than Rutejìmo even imagined, but there would never be a chance to find out more about him. Looking back, Rutejìmo realized he had abandoned Chimípu and Pidòhu just like the rest of the clan did. His thoughts grew dark as he recalled the events of the day, seeing the endless places he made a mistake. But, among all of that, he would have never considered that his own brother would have abandoned him.

He sighed and let his head swing back. It struck the rock with a little burst of pain, but it was nothing compared to the ache in his legs. "Why couldn't this be easy?"

No answer came except for the wind sending grains of sand bouncing against his skin. He breathed in the dusty, arid air. A moment later, he caught the scent of wood smoke. Frowning, he lifted his head and looked back to where Tsubàyo and Karawàbi were. There was no smoke, and none of them carried wood to burn; it was too heavy. The Shimusògo used travel fires, tins filled with an alchemical substance that was far lighter and less precious than wood.

Turning in a slow circle, he scanned the horizon for the source of the smoke. He turned around twice before he gave up as a product of his imagination. But, as he was coming back around to leave, he spotted a flash of light in the distance. It came from one of the long shadows formed by distant mountains and the setting sun. He focused on it, watching as it flickered. A moment later, he identified it; it was a campfire.

The clans of the desert were rarely friendly. When they met in the middle of the sands, it frequently began with tense words, and if someone wasn't careful, it ended in bloodshed and violence. Only efforts on both sides could allow such an encounter to end peaceably.

Rutejìmo turned away from the fires and let his thoughts return to his self-doubt and confusion. He slid down to the ground and watched the last of the sun dip behind the horizon.

"Jìmo, start the fire." Tsubàyo's command preceded the teenager as he came around the curve of the outcropping. He tossed the brass container with the alchemical fire at Rutejìmo's feet.

Rutejìmo glanced at the distant lights. He counted at least six fires since he first noticed them. And if he could see them, then they could see any fire he created. He shook his head. "I-I don't think we should."

Tsubàyo stepped closer, towering over him. "Call me Great Shimusogo Tsubàyo. I'm in charge here, boy."

Rutejìmo dropped his far hand behind his thigh as he clenched it into a fist. He wanted to lash out at Tsubàyo, to teach

CHAPTER 11. STANDING ALONE

him a lesson, but they were all tired, and he had no doubt that Karawàbi would join in just to beat Rutejìmo into submission.

His chest muscles spasmed with stress and sullen anger. "Great Shimusogo Tsubàyo. But, what about those fires?" He felt sick to his stomach as he pointed across the sands to the other clan. "Do we really want to get their attention?"

Tsubàyo frowned and peered across the darkening world. For a long moment, he said nothing, but then he sighed. "Fine, get the salted meat out for us. I'm hungry." With a kick that caught Rutejìmo in the hip, Tsubàyo spun around and marched back around the rock.

Groaning, Rutejìmo grabbed the brass box and staggered to his feet. Giving the other camp one last look, he followed after Tsubàyo.

While Rutejìmo was on the other side of the rocks, neither Tsubàyo nor Karawàbi had set up the tents or brought out the food. Instead, the four packs were piled in mute testimony that spoke volumes. Feeling his muscles growing tight with suppressed anger, Rutejìmo knelt down at the packs and began to dig into them.

He started with Pidòhu's bag, partially out of curiosity. It was a mess after Tsubàyo pawed through it. He pushed aside the clothes and felt around the bottom. A carved rock bounced on his fingers. Glancing up to ensure neither of the others were looking, he chased it out of the bag and into his palm.

It was a rock of a color that Rutejìmo had never seen around the valley. On one side, it was polished to a mirror smoothness. On the other, Pidòhu had somehow mounted a metal gear. Rutejìmo ran his finger along the bottom and felt the faint ridge where stone stopped and metal started.

He was about to toss it away when he saw three others in the bottom of the bag. With a start, he realized what they were: voting stones. As teenagers, neither Pidòhu nor Rutejìmo could vote in the clan affairs, but that didn't stop them from gathering the rocks they planned to first toss into a bowl. He had no doubt that Tsubàyo and Karawàbi had rocks of their own, but it was considered back luck to reveal it before they were acknowledged as an adult.

Rutejìmo felt as though he was prying into Pidòhu's private life. He gathered up the remaining stones from the bag. If the others saw them, they would no doubt toss them into a fire or desecrate them in some way. He opened his own pack and set them in with his own, secreted in a small pouch at the bottom.

He might never see Pidòhu again, but at least his legacy would remain untouched by their cruel jokes.

A blush on his cheeks, Rutejìmo continued to work his way through Pidòhu's pack. He found water and supplies, which he set aside. He also found a thin, cloth-bound book, but a quick glance showed lines of Miwāfu script that Rutejìmo couldn't read.

"What's that?" grunted Karawàbi. The larger boy strode over and snatched the book from Rutejìmo's hand.

Rutejìmo reached out for it, but stopped when Karawàbi glared at him.

"Give that to me, Wàbi," Tsubàyo said. When Karawàbi obediently handed it over, Tsubàyo opened it and read a few pages. A slow smile crossed his lips. "Listen to this: the day sun warming, dancing off the sky, no more crying now."

Karawàbi rolled his eyes. "Poetry? Why is he bothering?"

Tsubàyo flipped through a few more pages. "Mostly togomakēnyu it looks like. Poetry for a dead boy."

Rutejìmo held out his hand. "Could I have it?"

"Give it to me, Bàyo." Karawàbi stepped closer.

Tsubàyo shot a cruel smile at Rutejìmo and handed the book over to Karawàbi. The larger teenager took it and headed around the rock. A few seconds later, the sound of urine splashing on the pages filled the air.

Rutejìmo bowed his eyes, glad he had hidden Pidòhu's stones from their attention. He finished digging into the packets and found the salted meat. Sitting down on the ground, he opened up the brass box with the alchemical mixture. He dipped his finger in the dark gel and brought out a glob. Carefully, he smeared a thin layer over the hunks of meat before closing the box. Wiping his hands on the sand at his feet, he set the meat on the rock and took a deep breath. Pursing his lips, he breathed hard on it. The gel ignited under a combination of humidity and the moving air. A heartbeat later, a translucent flame enveloped the meat. He added dried vegetables, some powered fruit, and a bit of salt to each before delivering a plate to the others.

All three ate in silence.

Rutejìmo remained with his back to the others, not wanting to attract their attention and wondering, once again, if he had made a mistake by following Tsubàyo.

Chapter 12

Investigating the Night

> The desert folk have a quaint legend that the sun, as personified by the spirit Tachìra, is in constantly rivalry with the moon, named Chobìre, for the affections of the desert, Mifúno.
>
> — Kalem Ratenbur, *Primitive Legends of the Mifúno Desert*

As the sun sank below the horizon, darkness flooded the camp.

Rutejìmo pulled out a handful of glow eggs from the various bags and set them up around the camp. Each egg was carved out of rock with a glass globe blown inside. Inside, there was a clockwork mechanism attached to a metal spike poised over a crystal mounted in the middle. Rutejìmo wound a key in the bottom and released it. The spike began to tap rapidly on the crystal which created a tiny flash of bluish light. It flickered in the corner of his vision, but it was sufficient for his remaining duties.

Neither Tsubàyo nor Karawàbi helped help pitch the tents, but

Rutejìmo wasn't expecting them to. It was clear he was the weakest member in the group of three and it was his duty to do the servile tasks. It rankled, though, and he wondered if Pidòhu felt the same thing when forced to make dinner for the other clan members.

He dragged his bag and Pidòhu's to his tent. He tied the flaps shut before picking up the abandoned plates and heading some distance from the campsite to clean them. Without water, he used a handful of coarse sand to scrape the plates clean. Then, he found a patch of finer sand to remove the sweat and grime off his own face and chest. It wasn't a satisfying clean, but it would keep him for the night.

As he cleaned himself off, he kept the glow egg against his bare chest and his back to the other clan's campsite. There was almost no chance that anyone could see such a dim light from such a distance, but the desert was filled with clans with remarkable talents. Just as his could run with speed, there were ones who commanded fire, horses, or even rock.

Duties finished, Rutejìmo was ready for bed. He hoped tomorrow would help ease the guilt tearing into him and the feeling that he had made a mistake. He wrapped a leather strip around the plates for storage and headed back.

"Jìmo?" Tsubàyo stopped him as Rutejìmo was walking past.

"Yes... Great Shimusogo Tsubàyo?" The muscles in his chest tightened.

"Why don't you, Karawàbi, and I go check out that clan?"

Rutejìmo looked at the fires in the distance. "I don't think...." He gulped as a feeling of discomfort rose inside him. "I don't think we should do that."

"Why not?"

"It's night. We can barely see. And what if they are clans of the moon? We could be in danger by attracting their attention."

CHAPTER 12. INVESTIGATING THE NIGHT

Tsubàyo rolled his eyes. "We're in the middle of the night. For all the moon crap, I really doubt they can see in the dark. Just a check. And maybe see if we can get supplies to head home."

"You mean buy? We don't have a lot of money."

"Yeah, sure, I meant buy. Come on, they are only a mile or so. It will take us an hour tops."

"A mile in pitch-dark, Bàyo." At Tsubàyo's glare, Rutejìmo corrected himself. "Great Shimusogo Tsubàyo."

"Well," Tsubàyo said as he stood up. "We're going."

Karawàbi grunted. "I'm staying."

Turning on his friend with a glare, Tsubàyo snapped out, "What?"

"I'm tired. I'm going to sleep." Karawàbi yawned as he staggered to his feet.

"Fine! It will just be me and Jìmo."

Rutejìmo gestured to the tents. "Can't I stay?"

"No."

"Why can Karawàbi stay but I can't?"

"Because he isn't a shit. Come on, boy."

Rutejìmo glanced helplessly at Karawàbi, hoping for help.

The larger teenager glanced at him, then made a shooing gesture with his hand.

Dismissed, Rutejìmo looked around before he headed to his tent.

"Where are you going, boy?"

"To get my pack."

"Why?"

"We always carry our packs. It is the Shimusògo way."

"Well," Tsubàyo said in irritation, "leave it. Karawàbi will watch it, and we'll be right back."

"But—"

"I said leave it. Come on, damn it, or I will have Karawàbi beat the crap out of you."

Rutejìmo gulped and glanced at Karawàbi, who froze as he crawled into his tent. The larger boy stuck his head out, and there was a cruel hope in his eyes.

Sick to his stomach, Rutejìmo shook his head. "I'm coming."

Karawàbi looked disappointed, and Rutejìmo let out a sigh of relief.

Rutejìmo hated himself as he turned and followed after Tsubàyo.

The walk to the other clan was long. Both Tsubàyo and Rutejìmo strode in a small pool of blue light from the glow eggs. Beyond a few feet in either direction, the pitch-darkness obscured everything. There were no landmarks, no dunes to look at. Rutejìmo couldn't prepare for the shifting sands or rocks until he was right on it. More than a few times, he tripped when he missed a dip or ridge that would have been obvious in the sun.

It was also cold in the darkness. The sand, while baking hot in the day, quickly lost heat. Within a few minutes of leaving, Rutejìmo's breath fogged in the air, and the tapping of his glow egg was only slightly faster than the occasional chatter of his teeth.

As they got closer, it was obvious that the other clan wasn't worried about anyone seeing them. At least a hundred people moved between silk pavilions, smaller tents, and sand sleds. The fires drew Rutejìmo's attention. The largest was in the center, and the roaring flames cast light and heat into a reddish haze. Four nearly naked people, three males and one female, transferred large logs from a wagon to the bonfire, tossing each one at a steady rate. The light made their dark skins look black.

There were eight other fires in the camp. They were smaller, but also fed by the constant supply of wood. Unlike the bonfire, each of the smaller fires were built up around a brass column that reached out of the light from the fires. The base of each column was covered with letters and names, but he couldn't read any of them from his distance.

"Bàyo? What are those things for?"

Even in the dim light, Tsubàyo's glare was obvious.

Impatient and annoyed, Rutejìmo corrected himself. "Fine, Great Shimusògo Tsubàyo, what in the sand-cursed winds are those columns for?"

"Probably something for the spirit. I don't care. Look"—he pointed to the far side of the camp—"they have horses."

Rutejìmo looked in the same direction. Horses milled in a herd a few chains from the rest of the camp. He had missed seeing them since they weren't near one of the strange columns or fires. Instead, their black bodies were almost invisible in the darkness except for the green reflections of their eyes. He shivered at the sight of them; black horses were one sign of the night clans.

Even though there were easily two dozen horses, there were only two clan members attending them. Both were slender and short and female. They said nothing as they ate from wooden boards while perched on a rock. One looked out over the horses, and the other watched the people.

Rutejìmo leaned into Tsubàyo. "So? We are Shimusògo, we don't need horses."

"They would make it easier to head home," said Tsubàyo. He licked his lips as his eyes glittered. "And there is only one of them watching. We can take both of them."

"They are probably horse lords and don't need to see their horses. What do you think you'll do, just wander over and purchase three of them? I don't know about you, Great Shimusògo Tsubàyo, but I left my riches at home."

Tsubàyo gasped and grinned. "We'll steal them! And then ride away from all of this crap."

Rutejìmo interposed himself between Tsubàyo and the horses. "Are you insane!?" he whispered sharply. "Do you know what they do to people who steal horses? They gut them, attach their intestines to a horse, and yank. I don't know about you, but I really don't want to see how long my guts stretch across the sand!" His voice threatened to rise above a loud whisper, but Rutejìmo couldn't help it.

Tsubàyo's eyes glittered as he glared at him. "I know what I'm doing, boy. And I'm in charge. I say we steal them."

"No," Rutejìmo said with a shake of his head. "No, I won't ride a horse."

"Then we'll only have to steal two of them."

Rutejìmo continued to shake his head. He stepped away from Tsubàyo, the sick feeling rising in his throat. "No. I'm Shimusògo, and we don't ride."

Tsubàyo glared at him and whispered loudly, "Shimusògo abandoned us. The clan left us in the middle of the night. I don't really care what they want or what they say. I'm going to take those horses and head straight for Wamifuko City."

"I thought we were heading home."

"Curse them to sands." Tsubàyo pushed Rutejìmo aside and headed toward the horses. "Are you coming?"

"N-No." He gulped and repeated himself. "No." He felt a little better than the last time.

Tsubàyo's eyes glittered, and there was a knife in his hand. "You better not be in camp when I get back, boy. If you are, I'll kill you."

Rutejìmo stared at the blade in surprise. "Where did you get that?"

"I've always had it."

"You'd pull a knife on clan?"

"A clan that abandons us is no clan for me." Tsubàyo's voice was a growl. "Go on, head back. Go back to Mípu and Dòhu. I'm sure their weak spines will match your own." He stepped back toward the horses. "And we better not meet again, Jìmo, or you'll regret it."

Rutejìmo wanted to stop him, to try convincing Tsubàyo not to steal, but as he reached out for his clan brother, a yell rose up from the camps. Terrified that someone had caught them, Rutejìmo spun around and looked back at the camp with a sinking feeling.

One of the columns was crumbling in the fire. Clan members yelled out frantically as half of them ran away from the fire and the other half sprinted toward it. With sick fascination, Rutejìmo watched as the metal snapped and the column folded in half.

But, instead of simply falling to the side, a second part of the column fell out of the darkness and slammed into the ground. The other seven columns suddenly tilted toward the fallen one, and the sky above the bonfire lit up.

Rutejìmo held his breath as he stared at a large, curved glow of something towering over the massive fire. It stretched across all of the fires, and Rutejìmo realized that the columns were actually legs to some mechanical creature.

The yelling continued as people ripped the tents from the ground and dragged them away. Others grabbed lights and ran toward the darker parts of the camp. A few second later, they brought out a ladder. They set it against the side of the mechanical creature and quickly climbed the rungs.

Rutejìmo lifted his head as he watched them reach the bottom of the massive vehicle and crawl over it like flies on a corpse. The lights they carried were tiny motes against the brass-and-steel surface, but he could clearly see two large pincers and a curved tail reaching high into the darkness.

It was a scorpion and larger than anything Rutejìmo had ever seen. It would have dwarfed the Shimusogo Valley and would have reached his grandmother's cave even if it stood on the floor of the valley.

Something began to quake inside him. He was frightened, more scared than he ever had been. It was too large, too terrifying for his mind to comprehend. He looked around for Tsubàyo, but the other teenager was gone. Rutejìmo didn't know if he had headed back to their camp or for the horses. He didn't know anything but the fear that clutched his belly.

A groan of metal pounded in the air. A whimper rose in Rutejìmo's throat as he watched the mechanical scorpion come to life. Steam poured out of the crumbled leg, but the others gained a sudden rigidity, and the vehicle straightened as the seven feet sank into the ground.

Ruby light flashed across the desert. Rutejìmo flinched, but it wasn't an attack. He stared up at the vehicle and saw that it now had five glowing eyes on the side. One of the eyes was much larger, and there was no doubt there was a matching set on the far side.

Rutejìmo backed away from the chaos. He couldn't stay. As he stared wide-eyed at the people running around, he saw a woman leading a line of horses to the wood wagons. It was one of the two who watched over the horses. She was wearing a dark outfit, much different from the others. A curved blade flashed at her side. Her arms and back were bared, but almost every inch of her skin was covered in black tattoos.

The fear peaked, and Rutejìmo turned on his heels. He sprinted away, heading back to the camp. He didn't want to be found when they pulled the tents and pavilions away from the massive scorpion, nor did he want to be near it in case it fell to the ground.

The din quieted quickly as he ran blindly into the darkness. The glow egg gave only the faintest of lights, and he slammed into the side of a rock. Pain tore through his senses, and he spun as he hit the ground. Sobbing underneath his breath, he crawled away from the noise and light.

An earthquake ran through the sand. With grains pouring across his hands, he glanced back in fear that the scorpion was following. But the massive vehicle was stepping away from the fires and settling down with the crumpled leg stretched out across the sand.

Rutejìmo turned back and scrambled to his feet. He ran ahead, wishing that the dépa would return so he could follow it. But, it was his own plodding limbs that dragged him across the sand and into the choking darkness of an unlit desert.

Chapter 13

Breaking Up

> Desert spirits cannot be first heard during happiness. Pressure is needed to open up the gates of power.
>
> — Mifukiga Chobāni

Rutejìmo woke up huddled against a rock. The morning sun had not reached the horizon, but the false dawn gave his aching eyes a chance to focus on something besides ever-present darkness.

It had been a night of hell for him. He only dozed and shivered. Every time he started to drift to sleep, the fear that something was going to rush out of the darkness kept him awake. Every wind, every prickle along his skin, and even the pounding of his heart refused to let him close his eyes for long.

He yawned with exhaustion. As soon as he could distinguish the ground from the sky, he staggered to his feet. Pain radiated from his leg, and he looked down to where he had slashed open his trousers on the rock he used as shelter. The long gouges were bloody, but he had managed to keep them covered long enough for a thin scab to dry over the top. His hands were smeared with his dried blood. Disgusted, he used some sand to scour them clean before crawling up on the rock.

His entire body ached from the effort, but he couldn't survive another night alone in the desert. Shielding his eyes, he turned in a slow circle in hopes he could see the camp.

To the one side, he saw smoke billowing up in a lazy cloud. It was too large to be his camp, and he shivered at the nightmare of the immense brass vehicle towering over the campfires. Turning his back, he tried to imagine the route they walked and peered along the horizon.

He couldn't see anything, and despair gripped his gut. Around him, the wind kicked up sand, and the dry grit scraping against his bare skin encouraged him to move. He yawned again, found a place to relieve himself, and made up his mind to start moving.

One lesson was drilled into him from the moment he could walk. If he was lost, he was to head for the tallest rock. For many places, it would be the Wind's Teeth, but at least it gave him a direction. He looked around again and saw a pair of rocks sticking out. It was in a different direction than the scorpion and the clan, and he considered the distance with trepidation. It was over a mile away, but he didn't know how long he had been running in the dark. He could be a hundred chains away or a number of miles from his tent.

Rutejìmo promised himself he would never run in the dark again. Groaning at the aches and pains, he started walking toward the rocks. It was going to be a long day, but he had to do something to avoid thinking about the very possible future that he would die alone on the sands because of Tsubàyo and his own stupidity.

An hour later, the sun baked his skin, and he was sweating.

CHAPTER 13. BREAKING UP

Rutejìmo stripped off his shirt and draped it over his shoulders. He trudged along the top of a ridge, forcing each step through the sand that enveloped his feet. He ached and he was tired. His stomach gurgled uncomfortably, but there was nothing to eat.

He regretted leaving his pack in the tent. He berated himself for following Tsubàyo, leaving Mípu and Pidòhu. He also wished he had never watched the clan meeting that set them off on the trip. Everything would have been better if he had just remained an innocent boy.

Lost in dark thoughts, he almost missed the dépa racing across the ridge.

Rutejìmo gasped and trailed the bird's footsteps, but the bird was already gone. Frowning, he turned around, but he couldn't find where the dépa could have disappeared. The wind erased its trail, and he was once again lost.

He took a careful step forward, then another. When the dépa didn't reappear, he sighed. Unsure, he started to walk along the ridge again. This time, he kept his eyes out for the flash of feathers or the trail of the bird.

A flutter caught his attention.

He spun around as the dépa raced past him. He lost his balance and dropped to one knee. The scab along his leg tore open, and hot blood dribbled down from the scratch. Clutching his wound, he looked up to see the dépa standing only a few yard away from him.

The feathered bird cocked its head. Tiny feet danced along the grains of sand as it stared at him.

Rutejìmo groaned and tried to stand up, but the pain slammed into him and he dropped back to his knees. "I can't."

The dépa took a step back, then forward.

"What do you want?" He felt foolish talking to the dépa, but it was something besides himself. Blood trickled through his fingers.

Moving sharply, the dépa spun around and raced a rod away before stopping. It turned around and cocked its head again.

Rutejìmo didn't move.

The bird paced back to him and chattered. A moment later, it spun and raced back to the same spot and stopped.

"You," Rutejìmo's lips were dry as he spoke, "want me to follow?"

With a blur of movement, the dépa ran another rod and stopped.

Groaning, he pushed himself up to his feet. "What am I doing? How can I follow you? You're a bird!"

The dépa ran back and then away, repeating its movement.

He took a step and swayed from the pain. Fresh blood ran down his leg. He stopped. "No, I can't."

The bird took a step, and then it was gone.

Rutejìmo gasped and looked around, but he couldn't find it. "Wait! Where are you!?"

His voice was alone in the desert.

Rutejìmo whimpered and stared at the spot where the bird had been standing. Except for the little pits on the sand from its feet, there was nothing to indicate it had been before him. There was something about the bird that drew him forward. It was more than the dépa being named for his clan. It was more than just a tiny creature standing in front of him.

He took a hesitant step after the bird's trail. Nothing changed, but it felt right. He stripped the shirt off his shoulders and tore off a long piece. He wrapped it around his leg as a bandage. He tied the remains back around his waist. With a deep breath, he took a step after the bird, then another.

The dépa didn't reappear, but Rutejìmo knew it wouldn't. He wasn't going fast enough, but the pain in his leg slowed him down. Whimpering, he forced himself to run faster, stumbling over the rocks as he struggled for enough speed to summon the bird.

He found his pace, far slower than anyone else in the clan except for Pidòhu, but he kept on running. Doubt warred in his mind, mixing with the humiliation and embarrassment. He struggled with the urge to stop. His feet struck the sand with a steady rhythm, but each step was harder than the previous one.

And then the dépa was there; one moment, he was struggling to run alone, and the next the bird was a few paces ahead of him, matching his speed. It left no trail but he could follow it easily. The quiet scuffing of the dépa's feet was a contrast to the thudding of his soles.

He listened to the sound of the dépa. It had a rhythm to it footsteps. It was peaceful and encouraging. As when he ran the day before, his mind drifted and he lost himself in waves of euphoria. He stopped caring about his gasping breath, the stitch in his side, or even the wound in his leg. All that mattered was the running and keeping up with the nearly silent bird that was always a few steps ahead.

Before he knew it, he was running toward a familiar rock outcropping. Seeing the three tents in the morning light gave him hope, and he headed straight for it.

The dépa continued to pace right before him until he reached the rocks. When he slowed down, it did the same before disappearing between one step and another.

Rutejìmo came to a stop over a chain from the camp and looked back. He could see only one trail in the sand, but one stopped where the dépa disappeared. He glance back up at the camp, then bowed toward the end of the dépa's trail. "Thank you, Great Shimusògo."

He didn't know if it was actually the clan spirit, but there was no doubt that the dépa was more than a simple bird. But, he didn't want to disrespect what could be the clan's spirit. He felt foolish bowing, but held it for a long count before straightening. There was a blush on his cheeks when he walked back into the campsite, his imagination already preparing him for Tsubàyo's sharp words or Karawàbi's insults.

As he circled around the nearest tent, he spotted Karawàbi sitting in front one tent. The larger boy was drawing circles in the sand with his fingers. Judging from the squiggles and marks, he had been doing it for a number of hours.

Rutejìmo looked around, but didn't see Tsubàyo. "Wàbi, have you seen Tsubàyo?"

Karawàbi looked up sharply. "Jìmo? Where have you been?"

"I got lost out in the desert all night."

"Took you long enough to get back." Karawàbi scrambled to his feet. "Well, might as well start making breakfast. I'm hungry."

Rutejìmo came to a shuddering halt. "Excuse me? I just spent the entire night sleeping in the desert. Look at this!" He brandished his bandaged leg.

With a yawn, Karawàbi shrugged. "Don't really care what you've been doing. I'm hungry. So"—he cracked his knuckles—"either you start making food, or I'm going to beat the crap out of you."

Rutejìmo's stomach clenched. Balling his hands into fists, he turned and headed straight for the tents. He knelt heavily at the entrance of his tent, yanked open the flaps, and began to pack quickly.

Karawàbi's footsteps crunched on the ground. "What are you doing, Jìmo?"

"I'm going to back to Mípu and Dòhu."

A heavy hand landed on his shoulder. The thick fingers dug into the sensitive part of his shoulder, and Rutejìmo winced at the pain.

Karawàbi turned him around. "I don't think so. We aren't going anywhere until Tsubàyo comes back."

"He's not coming back! He tried to steal a horse."

Karawàbi shrugged. "So?"

CHAPTER 13. BREAKING UP

"We're Shimusògo! We don't ride horses."

"I don't see why not. They have four legs and big backs. Probably easy enough to get on one. They're animals and stupid." Karawàbi didn't seem upset or even concerned about Tsubàyo's theft.

Rutejìmo tried to pry Karawàbi's fingers from his shoulder. "Let me go."

"No." Karawàbi leaned forward. "You've been whining ever since we left the valley. I'm getting tired of it. Either you shut up and start doing what you're told, or I'm going to beat you until Tsubàyo comes back. And then"—he chuckled, and Rutejìmo winced at the hot breath washing across his face—"I'm going to keep beating you until he stops laughing."

Rutejìmo's arm grew numb as Karawàbi squeezed down. He whimpered and squirmed, but there was no escape from Karawàbi's grip. "Wàbi, let me go."

Karawàbi's fist caught him in the stomach. The impact was a dull thud that shook Rutejìmo to the core. With a chuckle, Karawàbi released his shoulder.

For the briefest of moments, Rutejìmo gaped in shock. And then pain exploded across his senses. It felt as though his insides had been ruptured from the blow. With a gasp, he bent over in agony and then dropped to the ground. His knees slammed into the sand. More pain shot up his legs. He slumped forward before catching himself with his good arm.

"Now, make my breakfast."

Rutejìmo sobbed with tears rolling down his cheeks. His stomach was in agony and his body on fire. The exhaustion of the previous night only added to his pains. He could barely focus on the sand underneath him and the wet patches wavered with every blink.

Through the agony, he realized that Karawàbi wouldn't stop. Now that he had attacked Rutejìmo, the brutality and bullying would continue. It would make his life hell.

He closed his mouth and struggled to calm his sobbing. Peering up, he saw the two packs by the tent. His was filled and closed but Pidòhu's remained open with its contents half spilled out across the ground.

Determination filled him. He planned his actions: grab the two packs and start running. It would be simple, and he could move faster than Karawàbi could respond, if he could move fast enough for the dépa to appear. He had no doubt that he could outrun Karawàbi.

Rutejìmo took a deep breath and launched himself off the ground.

Karawàbi's foot caught him the ribs. The impact picked him off the ground. He continued stumbling forward, body in agony, and slammed face-first into the side of his tent. The thin fabric wrapped around his body, and he struggled to free himself before Karawàbi could kick him again.

He gasped for air and managed to pull himself out. The collapsed tent caught his foot, and it took precious seconds to rip himself free. Frantic, he scrambled to his feet, spun around, and held up his arms in preparation to defend himself.

"Thought you'd be going for that," said Karawàbi with a chuckle. He hooked Rutejìmo's bag with his foot and tossed it aside. The pack landed a few yards away in the middle of the sand. He gestured for Rutejìmo to come closer. "Come on, limp dick. Get ready for your beating."

Rutejìmo lunged over the tent with a snarl.

Karawàbi's backhand caught him across the face. The world exploded into sparks of pain as Rutejìmo staggered back. He tripped on the tent again and he fell. With a whine, he wrenched himself to the side and felt muscles tearing along his side and ribs. He slammed hard on the ground, and the impact left him dizzy.

"Idiot," muttered Karawàbi as he stalked closer. "You haven't beat me in a fight since… well, ever. You might have grown some balls last night, but the rest of you is still a pathetic wimp."

Rutejìmo tried to crawl away, but his body wasn't responding. He was dizzy and nauseous from the blow. He clawed at the ground until he could get his hands and knees underneath him. Feeling Karawàbi walking closer, he dragged himself over the tent. The tent ropes tugged as his arms and legs as he made his way across the thin fabric. On the far side, his outstretched fingers slammed against a tent spike, and he pulled back his bruised hand with a hiss.

Karawàbi's shadow loomed over him. "Say good-bye, Jìmo."

Rutejìmo rolled over and looked up at Karawàbi. The other teenager's hands were balled into fists. His face was a mask of anger and cruelty, the same look Rutejìmo saw when Karawàbi was throwing rocks at Pidòhu. Deep inside, Rutejìmo knew Karawàbi wouldn't stop at a few bruises. He was going to hurt or even kill him.

Desperate, Rutejìmo grabbed the tent spike. His fingers cracked as he gripped it tightly and yanked it from the ground. With a scream, he sat up and slammed it down into Karawàbi's foot. The spike pierced flesh with only a token resistance. He didn't expect how easily it was to drive the spike clear through the foot; before he knew it, his hand smacked against his opponent.

With a gasp, Rutejìmo yanked his hand away from the spike. He glanced up at Karawàbi and then down at the spike. At first, nothing happened. And then crimson seeped up from the junction of metal and flesh. It pooled in the indention and then coursed down both sides of his foot before soaking into the sand beneath.

Karawàbi let out a long, gasping whine.

Trembling, Rutejìmo stared as a storm of emotions painted

themselves across Karawàbi's face. For a moment, it looked as though the teenager was consumed with pain, but then rage took its place.

"I'm going to kill you!"

Crying out, Rutejìmo crawled backward and then stumbled to his feet. He sprinted for his bag, caught the leather strap in his palm, and then threw it over his shoulder. He glanced back, just in time to see Karawàbi lunging after him, the spike still sticking out of his foot.

With another yelp, Rutejìmo spun on his heels and ran off into the sand. "Please," he gasped, "Shimusògo, help me!"

The wind blew into his face, blinding him as he ran up one dune. Reflexively, he turned and followed the ridge, hoping to get away from Karawàbi. He had to go back, even to Mípu. "Please, to Mípu and Pidòhu, please!"

The shimusogo dépa raced up next to him, heading north along the sands. He didn't know if the bird knew where to go, but it wasn't in the same direction as Karawàbi. Praying he was following the clan spirit, Rutejìmo raced after the bird.

Chapter 14

Coming Back

It takes a strong man to admit a mistake to a strong woman.

— Kosòbyo Proverb

Even following the dépa, Rutejìmo didn't think he would ever make it back to Chimípu and Pidòhu. Alone in the desert with the sun baking down and body aching from head to toe, every step was a struggle. But, if he dared to slow down, the dépa disappeared and he was forced to run bereft of the bird's company. Only when he push himself to run near his limits would the bird appear.

When he saw the Wind's Teeth, he almost sobbed with relief. It was early afternoon as far as he could tell, but he couldn't stop to look at the sun. Every stop meant he had to struggle to move fast enough to summon the dépa again. He bore down, pushed past the exhaustion, and drove himself toward the tiny, dark marks that would grow into the towering rocks.

He recognized his approach as he crested the dune. It was the same route they took the first time they approached the Wind's Teeth. But then Desòchu and the rest of the clan ran with him; now he was alone. The contrast of the two days was painful and Rutejìmo wished he was still struggling to catch up instead of coming back to two people he abandoned.

Coming to a stop a few rods away from the Tooth, he called out, "Hello?"

There was no answer.

Panting for breath, Rutejìmo headed straight to where they had set up the tents two nights before. His feet scrunched against the sand blown up against the rocks, and the wind teased his face. As he walked, he felt the muscles in his neck and chest tightening, not from his run but from the anticipation and fear.

He hurried over to where the tents had been. The rocks prevented the wind from erasing the tracks. He could see his own faint footsteps when he took down his tent, a swirl from where the others fought, and even a fresher trail going back and forth from Chimípu's tent and toward the rock where Pidòhu fell.

Rutejìmo stared down at the last trail. There was evidence of more than a few trails back and forth. He followed the paths, keeping his eyes on the footsteps precariously imprinted on the shifting sand. He didn't know what he would do if there was no tent or—his stomach lurched at the thought—Pidòhu didn't make it through the night and he was walking toward a corpse.

Doubt burned brightly, and he clutched his stomach from the pain. He was afraid of everything he would find around the corner: blood, death, or even Chimípu accusing him of abandoning her. He wanted to run way, to grab his small pack and just start running. But, there weren't enough supplies to make it to the Shimusogo Valley or Wamifuko City.

CHAPTER 14. COMING BACK

He came around the edge of the Tooth and saw Chimípu's tent. It was pitched against the rock with one stake caught in a crack a yard above the ground. A small alchemical fire burned a few feet to the side, with smoke rising up from four small birds cooking over the flames. A cloth was spiked to the ground with a rock in the middle; he knew there would be fresh water collecting underneath it.

Next to the fire sat Pidòhu. The young man was huddled underneath one blanket and had another neatly wrapped around his legs. Three sticks—the rods from Chimípu's tent—ran along his leg; Rutejìmo could see them peeking out of the folds. A large stain centered over his injury, but there was no blood dripping to the sand below.

As he stood there, Pidòhu's head jerked up and he looked around. Slowly, their eyes met, and Rutejìmo felt more ashamed than he had ever felt before. The hurt and betrayal in Pidòhu's gaze bore right to his bones, etching the guilt and shame into Rutejìmo's soul.

"Dòhu...." Rutejìmo stepped forward, holding out his hand. He didn't have the words to ask for forgiveness.

Around him, the wind kicked up and tore at his exposed skin. He blinked at the tears that formed in his eyes. It rose into a familiar howl, of a clan runner racing toward him. He managed to turn just as Chimípu's scream tore through the air.

"Bastard!"

Rutejìmo snapped up his arm in time to catch Chimípu's fist. The impact threw him back into the cloud of dust and sand that came with her charge. He choked on it and tried to stand up, but the dizziness caught him and he bent over.

Chimípu's kick caught him in his gut. The force knocked him into the air.

He landed hard and crumpled to the ground. Gasping, he planted his hands on the ground and tried to push up.

Her knee drove down on his neck, shoving his face into the rocks. The sharp edges cut at his cheeks and forehead.

Chimípu almost growled as she leaned over him. "Why shouldn't I kill you right now?" The scrape of a knife being unsheathed sent a sharp bolt of fear through Rutejìmo, but he couldn't get leverage to push her away.

"I didn't mean—"

"You abandoned us, you sand-cursed bastard! Your own clan!" The knife pressed against his throat, the sharp point digging into his skin. He stared at the bright blade. It was her mother's blessed knife, Shimusogo Rabedájyo, and the letters that named it shone in the sunlight.

"I-I—" He wanted to deny it, but he couldn't. With a long breath, Rutejìmo slumped down and stopped fighting. "Yes, Great Shimusogo Chimípu."

The point jerked, and he felt a pinch against his neck. Blood ran down his neck and he tensed with fear.

"Why," she said in a barely controlled voice, "did you come back?"

"Because...." He realized he didn't have a good answer.

She bore down on his neck. "Why!?"

"Because it was wrong!"

"What? Abandoning an injured clan to the sands," she said sardonically, "or knocking him off the rocks in the first place?"

"I didn't throw a rock."

"You were there!" The knife twisted, and more blood trickled down. "You could have stopped him!"

"I tried. I really did."

Chimípu yanked the blade away and used her foot to shove him onto his back. She took a step back. "You're pathetic, bastard. Weak-willed and soft of spine. I'd rather see you burn in the desert than stay here."

CHAPTER 14. COMING BACK

Rutejìmo started to crawl to his feet but stopped. He knelt down in front of her and bowed deeply. "I'm sorry, Great Shimusogo Chimípu."

"Stop that. I don't want your false respect." She stormed closer and brandished the weapon again. "By all rights, I should cut your throat right here and now."

Rutejìmo stared at the weapon, his body trembling with fear. He could still feel it against his throat, pricking the skin. A dribble of blood ran down his neck, and he felt the hot liquid soaking into the fabric of his shirt. By all accounts, she could have killed him seconds ago and he would have no chance to beg for forgiveness.

In the stories, the brave warrior would bare his neck and surrender his life to the person in front of him. It was the ultimate way to ask for forgiveness. When he was a little boy, he shuddered as he listened to the whispered tales around the bonfires. Most of the stories ended with a cut throat and someone's death.

Letting out a sobbing gasp, Rutejìmo forced his chin up. His body trembled, and every muscle, from his sphincter to his scalp, tightened in fear. Fresh tears ran down his cheeks as he lifted his head as far as he could, exposing his throat to her blade. "As," he choked, "Great Shimusogo Chimípu wishes." Unable to look at her, he closed his eyes and waited for the end.

For a long moment, the only thing he heard was the wind and his heart. He tried not to move. He imagined her pulling back the blade to slash at him and wondered what it would feel like. He had never seen anyone killed this way, but it sickened him to think that he would find out firsthand.

"Damn it," she whispered angrily, "put your neck down."

He didn't move until he heard her sheathe her dagger. Slowly, he opened his eyes to see Chimípu striding back to Pidòhu. She dropped down next to him, her back to Rutejìmo.

Shaking, Rutejìmo got to his feet and padded over to the fire. He knelt down and bowed to Pidòhu. "I'm sorry, Great Shimusogo Pidòhu."

Pidòhu waved his hand, the movement frail. "Forgiven, Rutejìmo."

Rutejìmo lifted his head and settled back.

Looking him over, Pidòhu frowned. "What happened?"

"I... I don't know where to start."

"Why are you back?" snapped Chimípu.

"Tsubàyo tried to steal a horse."

Both Pidòhu and Chimípu inhaled sharply.

Rutejìmo continued in a halting tale, telling them about the mechanical scorpion, the two clan members in black who were guarding the horses, and the other members. He told them about sleeping through the night in the dark, and Karawàbi's attempt to beat him into submission.

When he finished, Pidòhu asked in his quiet voice, "Where is Tsubàyo?"

"I don't know."

"And you left Karawàbi behind?" asked Pidòhu.

Chimípu grunted. "You do that a lot, bastard. Leaving your clan."

"At least," snapped Rutejìmo, "you didn't try to kill me."

Chimípu opened her mouth to respond. But then a smile curled the corner of her lip. She glanced down at Rutejìmo's pack. "Have you eaten?"

"Only trail rations last night. Nothing today."

"Idiot." She leaned over and plucked one of the four birds from the fire. She pulled out one of the boards and placed the meat on it. She bowed to Pidòhu before setting it down next to him.

Rutejìmo watched silently as she served herself.

To his surprise, she gestured for him to take the next one. "Eat both if you need to. You're probably starving."

His stomach gurgling, Rutejìmo fought the urge to snatch it from the flames. He picked it up and set it down on his board.

For a long moment, none of them touched their food, then Chimípu bowed her head and whispered a prayer to Shimusògo.

Rutejìmo joined in and, for the first time, he meant the words.

Chapter 15

A Quiet Conversation

Honest conversations happen when no one is listening.

— Badenfumi Shigáto

Rutejìmo sat in the darkness outside of the tent. He was exhausted, but it was his turn to stand guard while Pidòhu and Chimípu slept. He couldn't see more than a few inches past his nose in the dim light of the glow eggs, but he kept his ears open and listened for intruders. They didn't know if Tsubàyo or Karawàbi had followed him back, but Chimípu didn't want to take chances.

The cold wind of the desert nipped at his skin. The only thing keeping him from shivering was the heated rock between his legs. They used the last of the alchemical fire to heat six rocks for the night: four for Pidòhu, one for Chimípu, and one for himself. The latent heat would help a little against the cold, but as he sat in the darkness, he couldn't help but feel every frigid caress of the night winds.

He struggled to keep his mind from a spiral of depression. Chimípu had allowed him to remain, but she made it clear that she didn't accept him yet. She used insulting terms—boy, bastard, idiot—instead of his name. His anger prickled at it, but he kept it buried deep inside. He had bared his neck to her, trusted her, and she spared him. He could survive being called an idiot for that.

Next to him, Pidòhu moaned in pain and his leg shook. The blanket covering him slipped off and piled up against Rutejìmo's leg.

Working carefully, Rutejìmo eased it back over the boy's injured leg. His fingers accidentally brushed against Chimípu's thigh, and he snatched his hand back before she took off his hand.

"Jìmo?" asked Pidòhu in a croaked whisper.

Rutejìmo jumped in surprise, then leaned against the rock. "Yes, Dòhu?"

"How did you come back?"

When Rutejìmo considered telling Tsubàyo about the dépa, something had stopped him. But, when Pidòhu asked, there was no reluctance. Taking a deep breath, he crossed his arms over his chest before answering. "I followed a shimusogo dépa."

"A dépa?"

Rutejìmo nodded, then flushed when he realized Pidòhu couldn't see it. "Yeah. I was struggling to keep up with Tsubàyo as we... I left here. They wouldn't slow down or stop. But then I saw this dépa running near me. When I followed it, I could concentrate on keeping up with it. When I stopped I... lost sight of it."

"And today?"

"It led me here. It ran and I followed."

CHAPTER 15. A QUIET CONVERSATION

Pidòhu let out a pained gasp. "That's Shimusògo, you know."

Rutejìmo nodded. "I guessed. But why didn't any of the elders tell us what to expect? If I knew that it should show up when I ran faster, I'd... run faster, I guess."

"Being told how to see a spirit doesn't make it any easier to actually see them. Actually, they say your expectations make it harder for you to listen. So, if they told you, you would already have an expectation of what to see. And then you wouldn't be able to see it if it wasn't exactly the same way."

"You knew this was going to happen, right?"

A grunt.

"You knew what to expect."

Pidòhu groaned and started to sit up. After a second, he slumped back. "I had an idea, but I haven't seen Shimusògo."

"Has Mípu?"

"What do you think?" There was a wry tone in Pidòhu's voice.

"How long has she been seeing Shimusògo?" Rutejìmo glanced over toward Chimípu, but he couldn't tell if she was listening or not. He couldn't even see her.

"Oh, I'm going to say the run she went on when her mother died. She was crying when she left and when she got back... well, ever since she's had a new confidence. And she kept up with the elders far better than any of us."

Rutejìmo stared out, his thoughts spinning. "Then this was all for nothing? I thought we were doing her rite of passage."

"Actually, this trip is for all of us. Some of us, Tsubàyo and Karawàbi, I hope never make it. But, even if Shimusògo speaks to Chimípu, the elders still need to do this before they can accept it."

"Can't Shimusògo just tell them that he talks to Mípu?"

"Sometimes, you have so much sand in your head that you can't hear your spirits. It is just what it is. There are two parts to the rites: becoming a member of the clan and becoming a man, or a woman in Mípu's case. You and she both have talked to Shimusògo, you can hear him or see him, if you want. What you do with that power determines if you become one of the clan."

"Damn." Rutejìmo leaned back and sighed. "Why can't it be easy?"

"If it was easy, it wouldn't be worth it."

Rutejìmo chuckled. "True as sand."

Neither said anything for a long moment. The rock behind Rutejìmo was warmer than his skin, and he basked in the fading heat as he listened to the desert around him.

"Pidòhu?"

"Yes, Jìmo?"

"Do you think you'll see Shimusògo?"

A long sigh. "I don't know. Shimusògo runs and I cannot run right now. I keep looking for him, but I won't get speed on this trip. Instead, the only thing I see are shadows racing across the sands."

"What does that mean?"

"I don't know," Pidòhu said with a sigh. "I don't know if I'm just seeing things or they are actually there. Mípu can't see it. And, if I'm hallucinating, then I wished I knew why."

There was a long, uncomfortable silence. Rutejìmo toyed with his hand for a moment. Then he accidentally blurted out his thoughts. "Karawàbi peed on your poetry book."

"That," Pidòhu sounded sad, "was my father's."

"I'm sorry."

"I saw you didn't have my pack either." There was an unasked question in the air.

Rutejìmo sat up and reached out for his bag. He dug into the bottom and got out the stones he had transferred. Working blindly, he pulled out Pidòhu's. They were cold in his palm. He caught Pidòhu's hand and placed the rocks inside.

Pidòhu let out a sigh, and the rocks clinked together. "Thank you, Rutejìmo."

"I'm sorry I left."
"I already forgave you."
"I haven't forgiven myself, though."
"That," Pidòhu said with a chuckle, "can take a lot longer."

Chapter 16

Pushing Forward

> Revealing one's voting stones to the sun is a deeply personal decision that can never be taken back.
> — Ryugamiku Byotsúma

Rutejìmo yawned as he came back from answering the call of nature behind the far rocks of the camp. He was exhausted from the night, both from being awake during his watch and the uneasy sleep plagued with guilt. His feet crunched on the sand, and he wished he was back at home in the valley, ignorant of the last few days. If he had to do it again, he would try harder to listen to the lessons everyone had been trying to teach him. But, even as he walked across the sands, he knew he wouldn't. Just as he never woke up early to train after Chimípu humiliated him.

He stopped when he caught sight of Pidòhu. The frail-looking boy was huddled underneath blankets, wiping the sweat from his brow with a shaking hand. A second later, he did it again and stared at the droplets running down his hands with unfocused eyes.

Fear clutched Rutejìmo. He wondered if he was seeing someone die in front of him. He knelt in front of Pidòhu. "Are you okay?"

"I—" Pidòhu looked over Rutejìmo's shoulder, but when Rutejìmo glanced over expecting to see Chimípu, he saw nothing but sun-baked sand. "I keep seeing shadows. They are running across the desert, but they never get to me. I-I'm so cold." He shivered and clutched himself.

A frown marring his brow, Rutejìmo rested the back of his hand against Pidòhu's forehead. It was soaked with sweat and searing hot. The heat rolled off the injured boy, but it was a wet, sick heat instead of the burning dryness of the desert sun.

Pidòhu bit back a sob, tears shimmering his eyes. "All I see are shadows, Jìmo."

"I-I think I need to get Chimípu." Rutejìmo started to his feet, but Pidòhu grabbed him.

"No, Jìmo. Don't go."

Feeling himself on the edge of tears, Rutejìmo knelt back down. "Dòhu, I don't know what to do. I... don't know anything."

"I'm getting sick."

"Okay, that part I figured out." Rutejìmo rolled his eyes, "But what do I do with this? With you?"

Pidòhu frowned and then wiped his face. "I... move me. Take me home."

"We're days away. Won't it be safe to stay here?"

Pidòhu gave him a weak smile, his body swaying. "I think I know what happens if I stay. Don't you?"

Rutejìmo gulped. He'd heard stories about couriers dying, but it was always a dramatic death in delivering a final message. There was never a heroic story about a Shimusògo dying in the shadow of a rock, unable to move. Rutejìmo squirmed uncomfortably.

"Jìmo, I know we can't make it. But, if I stay here, I'm going to die. I'm going to get weaker. I don't want this to be my grave." He gestured up to the rock.

"We won't make it."

"Better to die on the move than in the shadows of a rock. But"—he gave Rutejìmo a weak smile—"I don't want to die. There is a chance to make it, to get home. I know I'll be okay if we do."

Looking into Pidòhu's pleading eyes, though, broke his hesitation. "I'll do it, Great Shimusogo Pidòhu." It felt a little easier to be respectful.

Pidòhu's eyes trailed to the side. "Shadows. All I see are shadows across the sand." He slumped back and closed his eyes. "Please, Jìmo," he said in a broken whisper, "just take me home."

Rutejìmo got up and eased the tent from around him. He pulled out the poles and began to lash them together into a narrow frame. Pidòhu was too heavy to carry and with his broken leg, he wouldn't be able to ride on Rutejìmo's back.

Pidòhu woke up after a few minutes. He gave short, gasping directions when Rutejìmo faltered.

He was almost done when Chimípu came running up in a cloud. Rutejìmo could almost see a dépa in the dust, jumping and sprinting ahead of her. As she slowed down next to him and the wind of her passing enveloped Rutejìmo, the dépa disappeared.

"What are you doing?" she asked angrily.

Rutcjìmo couldn't look at her. He continued working the remains of his pack, which he had torn apart and formed into a pad, between the ropes binding the rods together. "Taking Pidòhu home."

Chimípu tossed down two gutted snakes. She turned on Pidòhu. "Dòhu!" Her voice was brimming with frustration and exhaustion. "We can't move you!"

Pidòhu looked up, his eyes rolling slightly. "I'm not going to make many more nights."

"Then stay here with Jìmo. I'll run and get help."

"Even you know that lesson. Shimusògo never travel alone across the desert. An hour out, maybe, but never the long days alone."

"Damn that! You can't survive the trip!"

The wind kicked up around them, peppering Rutejìmo with tiny grains of sands. He saw a flash of movement, but when he spun around, there was nothing but sun and sand and rock.

Pidòhu wiped his brow again. "I might not survive the night. Mípu, please, at least let me die while moving."

She stood there, hands balled into fists. "Don't give up, Dòhu. We'll make it. I'll find something that will help, I prom—"

"I'm not giving up, Mípu. And that is why we're moving." A look crossed his face and he smiled. "Pretend I'm a package, if you want."

A tear ran down her cheek. "No, don't do that. Don't make me."

He smiled, the pale brown of his skin looking uncomfortably like a skull to Rutejìmo. "Shimusògo always delivers." It was the clan's motto on the job, a phrase Rutejìmo never understood until he heard Pidòhu speaking and realized he meant his body, alive or not.

Pidòhu dug into his pocket and pulled out a few pyābi. There were enough red coins to buy a sweet from a market but nothing else. The metal glinted in the sun. "Please, Great Shimusogo Chimípu. Don't let me die here."

Rutejìmo held his breath as he watched Chimípu shake her head. "No, I can't lose you."

"Please?"

She held out her hand. It shook violently. Her fingertips caressed the metal, and then she pulled back. "No, I will not take money from my clan."

Chapter 16. Pushing Forward

Pidòhu sighed.

Rutejìmo stood up, ready to take it.

"But." Her words were soft, but they stopped Rutejìmo with the force of a punch. "But, Pidòhu, I will borrow your money until we get home safely."

Pidòhu smiled and held up his change.

She dropped to her knees. Taking his hand, she kissed his palm as she took the money. "I promise, Pidòhu. You'll make it home, one way or the other. Not as a delivery but as clan."

Rutejìmo turned his back on them, his stomach twisting uncomfortably. He returned to the frame and tested each wrapping before moving to the next.

A minute later, Chimípu knelt down on the far side. She tossed a small bag of salted meat and a water skin at his feet. "Eat, boy."

"Chimípu...." Her red-rimmed glare silenced him. "Yes, Great Shimusogo Chimípu."

He ate in silence, watching as Chimípu finished up his work.

"We'll drag in shifts," she said in a terse voice. "Ten minutes, a half hour tops. Stop before it begins to hurt too much. We stop at the top of dunes when we trade off." She didn't look at him, and he felt a prickle of annoyance at her commands but shoved it aside. She wasn't giving orders for herself. They were for Pidòhu.

"What if we take each end?"

"Not over the sands, it is too hard to keep balance with three, and we might tip him. Do you remember the route you took?"

Rutejìmo nodded. "Yes, but what about Karawàbi?"

"We'll deal with him when we get there. But, you remember where there is shelter? Rocks, outcroppings?"

He thought back the last few days before. "I do, but we were only a day away."

Chimípu ran her hand down the padding of the frame. "It will take us two, maybe three, days to get that far. At least we'll know where we can take shelter."

Rutejìmo nodded, the food sinking into his stomach like a rock. He finished gathering the remains of the packs, using the ropes on the frame to secure their supplies.

Pidòhu caught his attention and he went over. Kneeling down, he stared as Pidòhu poured his voting stones into Rutejìmo's palms.

"Don't lose them," Pidòhu whispered.

Rutejìmo nodded. He pulled his own rocks from his pocket, which he had discretely transferred when he ripped his pack open. Blushing hotly, he held the two sets in his palm. His own voting stones were plain, a gray rock with an interesting pattern of white that looked like ribs of a bird. It was a stark contrast to Pidòhu's rocks with the embedded gears.

He knew he should keep his a secret. His choice of stones was intimate, a personal decision that had somehow been exposed to the sunlight. He gulped as he stared down at the rocks; it felt forbidden to show them to anyone before he earned the right.

Chimípu dropped three silver rings into his hand. Each one depicted in incredible detail a shimusogo dépa running in endless circles. He had seen them before—they were Chimípu's mother's voting stones. Surprised, he looked up at Chimípu.

She gave him a sad smile. "Keep them all together. Like a clan, we all come home or none of us do."

Speechless, Rutejìmo nodded. He crawled over to the frame and secreted the rocks and rings in a secure pocket. He doubled a spare shirt over the stones to ensure they wouldn't be lost even if the frame was upended.

He and Chimípu carried Pidòhu to the stretcher. When they set him down on it, Pidòhu hissed from pain and clutched at his knee.

"Sorry," Rutejìmo said.

"No, just continue."

"Lean back," ordered Chimípu.

When Pidòhu did, they bound him against the frame. They wrapped ropes around his chest and legs, careful to immobilize his broken leg as much as possible while giving him freedom to move his arms and head.

Pidòhu bore the discomfort in silence, a nervous look on his face. When Rutejìmo stepped back, Pidòhu gave him a thin smile. "Not so bad. I feel like a king with you two."

"Well, king," Chimípu said with a sly grin, "if you give too many orders, you can walk home."

It was a weak joke, but they all laughed anyways.

Rutejìmo pressed the full water skins into the crook of Pidòhu's arm.

Chimípu took the stretcher first, wrapping her hands around the ends and grunting as she picked it up. She gave it a hesitant tug. When it didn't move, she leaned into pulling it across the sand.

It made a loud scraping sound, but then began to slide.

She took a deep breath and bore down, dragging him up the dune.

Rutejìmo followed behind the two, to catch either if they fell.

Chapter 17

An Evening Run

> Every magic has a mechanism to activate. It could be precise rituals, prayer to a divine power, or dancing.
>
> — Kamanen Porlin

Rutejìmo trudged forward, focusing on digging each foot into the shifting rocks and lurching to pull the sled after him. His back and legs screamed out in pain, the ache burning clear up to his shoulders. He couldn't feel his fingers anymore; they had stopped bending hours before, and he panicked when he first saw the claw-like curve to them.

Pidòhu's stretcher pulled down, held down by weight and friction.

Rutejìmo let out a cry as he forced himself up, one step at a time. At the top of the dune was a rock with a broad shield against the sun and wind. It looked like a sand tick on the back of Mifúno, the desert, but it was shelter.

His eyes streamed with tears from the agony and staring into the burning red orb of the sun. It was sunset, and they had barely made a third of the route Rutejìmo ran the day before. It was painfully slow, which only made their efforts worse.

Chimípu jogged back down the sand, running along a shifting ridge. She held out her hands for the ends of the frame.

Rutejìmo shook his head and kept on trudging up.

"Damn it, Jìmo. Let me take the last rod. You've been dragging him for two hours now."

Rutejìmo gasped and shook his head again. His cracked lips worked silently for a moment. "You carried him through the high sun. For far longer than two hours."

"Yes, but I'm...." She closed her mouth.

"Better, I know. But I will"—he grunted and dragged himself farther—"do this!"

He expected her to shove him aside or to take the back end, but she didn't. Instead, she turned and walked next to him, keeping with his agonizingly slow pace as he dragged Pidòhu up the side of the dune and into the shade of the stone.

The shadows felt wrong to him, as if Tachìra's sunshine could no longer reach him. Frowning, he wiped the sweat from his brow and took a step back into the heated sun. The heat and light was a comfort, and he sat down heavily on the sand.

Pidòhu groaned and reached out for the rock above him. His fingernail scraped on the stone before he slumped back. "I like it. Homey." He said with a strained chuckled.

Rutejìmo smiled and stared down at his hands. The joints were locked in agony, curled around a handle that was no longer in his palms. He jammed his hands into the searing sand; the pain was nothing compared to ache of his frozen joints. He flexed, wincing as he worked at loosening his fingers.

"Can you find water, Dòhu?" Chimípu's voice was just as broken as Rutejìmo's, exhausted. Her body was soaked in sweat, and

CHAPTER 17. AN EVENING RUN

the fabric of her shirt clung to her skin.

Pidòhu peered around, scanning the sands.

Rutejìmo watched with surprise. He knew the basics for finding water, but Pidòhu wasn't simply looking for the lowest place. Instead, he was searching for something specific.

Bracing himself against the rock, Pidòhu pointed to a low spot with a dark patch of sand. "There. About three feet down. There are some rocks too, to brace the sides."

"Thank you, Great Shimusogo Pidòhu." Chimípu bowed and grabbed a set of spikes and the translucent fabric used to gather moisture. She trotted down to where Pidòhu pointed.

Rutejìmo turned to the pale boy. "Why there?"

Pidòhu chuckled and then shivered. "There are shadows pooling there. It feels... cool."

Chimípu was kneeling in a brightly lit valley between two dunes. There was no shadow or obstruction. "Shadows...? Where?"

"Yeah, I'm seeing them everywhere. A flit there, a breeze there. They flash across the desert like some bird..." He pointed up "...sailing high up there."

Rutejìmo was about to change the topic when he saw Pidòhu's attention shift. The injured boy was watching something moving across the sands. He turned to look. From the corner of his eye, he caught a flash of movement. He spun around, but once again, there was nothing but sand and sun.

Pidòhu chuckled. "Shadows in the corner of your eyes?"

The world tilted when Rutejìmo stumbled. Trembling, he turned back to Pidòhu. "What?"

"That's what you see? Shadows on the edge? Always fleeing before you can focus on them?"

Rutejìmo squirmed. "Maybe?"

"You've always been a lousy liar, Rutejìmo. Don't worry, they are real. I just can see them better now."

"W-What are they?"

"I think I know." Pidòhu smiled. "But I'm not worthy to name it."

Before Rutejìmo could ask more questions, Chimípu came up. Her left hand was still curled in a hook from carrying the frame. "The collector is set up. We should have clean water come morning. How are we on skins?"

Pidòhu lifted one up. "Last one."

Chimípu looked around. Then she focused on Rutejìmo. "Dòhu?" she asked without moving her gaze from Rutejìmo. "Do you mind if we hunt for food?"

Rutejìmo's stomach lurched. He was suddenly afraid of the hard gaze fixing him in place.

Pidòhu shook his head. "No, Mípu. I'll be fine for now."

"We'll stay close," she said. Taking a step back, she beckoned for Rutejìmo.

Nervous, he got to his feet.

Chimípu gathered up some strips of cloth from the frame and a few rocks, wrapped them together, and then hoisted the bundle over her shoulder. She gave Rutejìmo a look that commanded him to follow.

He gulped.

She jogged along the ridge, heading toward a field of rocks and gravel.

Exhausted, Rutejìmo almost sat back down.

"Go on, Jìmo. The Shimusògo run."

Rutejìmo gave Pidòhu a smile and then jogged after Chimípu. She was ahead of him, and he pushed to catch up. At first, his body was tight and unresponsive, but as the heat of jogging worked at his joints, he relaxed into the comfort of running.

Chimípu ran down the side of a ridge and along the base of a shallow valley.

CHAPTER 17. AN EVENING RUN

Rutejìmo followed, pushing himself to run faster. Exhaustion tore at him, but anticipation grew as he raced. His body sung with joy as he felt the dépa arriving, a flicker of feather and a trail of prints.

And then it was ahead of him, a tiny bird speeding along the rocks with a streamer of dust behind it.

Grinning, Rutejìmo focused on catching up with the dépa. As he concentrated on running, the aches and pain melted away. The sun no longer burned his skin and his breath came easier. He accelerated, pulling closer to Chimípu.

The dépa sprinted forward until it was running in front of both of them. Chimípu didn't appear to respond to it, and he wondered if he was the only one who could see it. Pidòhu said that Chimípu had already felt Shimusògo, but he couldn't tell if that was true.

They came up to where the valley split in two. The dépa swerved to the side, but Chimípu was heading down the other fork.

Rutejìmo was torn over which one to follow, but then Chimípu veered after the dépa.

Her feet traced the dépa's path too accurately not to see it.

Rutejìmo felt jealous but elated. He wasn't hallucinating. Biting his lip, he pushed his body to its limit. The ground blurred underneath him as his world became only three things: Rutejìmo, Chimípu, and the dépa.

With feet pounding on the rocks, he realized he was running side by side with Chimípu. There was no pain, no exhaustion. Just a liquid pleasure slipping through his veins. He was keeping up with her. Years of being in her shadow and somehow he was even with her.

He almost cried out in joy.

She shot him a glare, but there was the same excitement in her eyes. Their bodies were moving in sync, feet hitting the ground at the same time and the world blurring around them. Wind, hot and cool at the same time, whipped across his face.

The dépa came up on the end of a valley and then disappeared a few feet shy of a ridge top.

Rutejìmo and Chimípu ran past the spot it faded and to the top. When Rutejìmo started to crest over the top, he saw movement in the valley beyond. With a yelp, he tried to stop, but his body kept on moving. He lurched to the side and dug his feet in. The ground tore up around him, sand and rocks bursting in all directions as he carved a deep gouge into the gravel.

When he came to a stop, he was shaking. He stared back behind him, and there was a trench in the rock and sand a chain in length, sixty feet of his body tearing into the ground. He looked at his hand, expecting to see it bloody but it was unharmed. His feet were also unharmed, despite leaving a deep gouge in rock and gravel.

Next to him, Chimípu let out a yelp of joy as she stumbled out of a cloud of dust and sand. She also smiled broadly, her first real smile Rutejìmo had ever seen up close. Her eyes twinkled as she looked him over. Breathing softly, as if she hadn't just spent ten minutes sprinting, she looked him over. "You really can see Shimusògo, can't you? The dépa?"

Surprised, Rutejìmo let out a croaking noise.

She smiled and looked up to the sun, a quiet prayer to Tachìra moving her lips. When she spoke, it was a whisper. "It's a rush, isn't it?"

Rutejìmo gulped and glanced back at the ground. There were two long gouges in the earth from their stopping. He felt voiceless as he moved his mouth, but he couldn't form the words.

Chimípu glanced at him and then back at the gouges. "I haven't figured out how to stop either." She gave him another smile and he felt dizzy. "The others make it look so easy."

"I-I... how? How did you know?"

She gestured back the way they came. "I heard you last night."

He tensed up, a whimper rising in his throat. He hadn't thought she'd heard him being honest with Pidòhu.

Chimípu took a step to him. He cringed but she hugged him tightly, their bodies hot against each other. She stepped back after a heartbeat, her cheeks dark. She looked away, toward the horizon. "When my mother died... I was so upset. She spent a week dying in front of me, and there was nothing I could do in the end. I just"—tears welled up in her eyes—"started screaming."

She stared at the ground. "Hyonèku heard me and chased me out of my mother's cave and the valley. Made me run, but he wouldn't stop following me." She toed the ground, kicking rocks into the trench she had made with stopping. "I kept running and running. I thought I was going to pass out, but the pain wouldn't go away. Just when I was about to drop to my knees, I saw him. Shimusògo."

Rutejìmo thought about the dépa and how it drove him forward. He hadn't wanted to give up then and it came to him. He said, "I know, right when you are about to break."

When she looked up, there was a smile on her lips and tears in her eyes. "We are Shimusògo, aren't we?"

Rutejìmo gulped at the dryness in his throat. "I... I think so."

Chimípu nodded, then gestured to the valley they had almost entered.

Rutejìmo blushed when he realized why they stopped. In the valley below, there were thousands of nests. It was the nesting ground for rock fishers, a large bird that fed on cactuses and small insects. Feathers fluttered as the birds regarded them; a few took off when Rutejìmo stepped back.

"Dinner," Chimípu said.

"You going to catch them?"

She shook her head. "No, I need practice throwing."

"Throwing?" Rutejìmo frowned.

He watched as Chimípu took the rock and cloth she had taken with her. She formed a makeshift sling and held both ends of the fabric. "Great Shimusogo Desòchu showed this to me once as a girl. After seeing Shimusògo, I finally figured out how to do it." She gave him a sheepish smile. "Though I'm not very good yet. Step back."

Rutejìmo obeyed and leaned against a rock.

Chimípu planted her feet and held the fabric with both hands. Taking a deep breath, she spun around in full circle around, then another. Her feet stomped on the ground as she spun in the same spot. The sling swung out from her, and Rutejìmo cringed in fear that she would drop it.

But she kept spinning. He was expecting her to fall down with dizziness, but she pushed harder.

And then the dépa was there, sprinting in a circle around Chimípu. Her movements accelerated, and a vortex of dust rose up around her, blurring her form. The sling formed a disk as it spun with her.

She stopped suddenly and released one end of the cloth. The rock shot out and crossed the valley in an instant. It left ripples in the air as raw power rolled off the stone. A crack of air shook Rutejìmo from its passing. The stone shattered at the base one of the nests, and there was a shower of blood and feathers.

Rutejìmo gasped and stared in shock. "Drown me in sands! My brother can do that?"

Panting, Chimípu grinned at him and nodded. "The hunting bolas are a lot more accurate, and deadlier. Your brother says that a warrior can break a neck a mile away with one of them."

"I... he never showed me that."

She hefted a rock. "Want to try?"

Chapter 18

Quiet-Voiced Threat

The Moon Clans, also known the clans of night, gain power from the icy darkness.

— Kakasaba Mioshigàma

Rutejìmo sat on the ridge of the rock. He stared out into the darkness, seeing nothing but not daring to close his eyes. The last time he did, he woke up minutes later in a surge of guilt and fear. He didn't dare do it again, not with the two sleeping below counting on his vigilance.

The only illumination came from the few flickering stars above him. He spent the first hour amusing himself by counting them and trying to remember their names; there were only a hundred or so visible, but his exhaustion made it difficult for him to remember more than thirty.

He wanted to light up the glow egg, but it would only highlight his location and do nothing to push back the void. Rutejìmo was stuck listening to the wind around them and his own thoughts.

Something had changed that day. Chimípu had smiled at him, an honest smile that wasn't mocking or insulting. And then she taught him how to fire the rocks at high speed. He was horrible at it and nearly took out her foot with one shot, but the rush of using clan magic burned bright in his veins. He had somehow earned Shimusògo's respect, but he didn't deserve it.

In the distance and to his right, something moved, and he heard the crunch of a weight on rocks.

Rutejìmo gripped his knife, wary of accidentally stabbing Chimípu or Pidòhu. He had heard enough horror stories of accidents while guarding to be careful. His breath came faster, and he strained to listen.

When no other sounds rose up, he relaxed but didn't release the knife. He hated the darkness that smothered him. On the moonless nights, such as that current one, there was nothing to see or focus on.

It wasn't something he had ever experienced before. The valley was always lit. And when the clan traveled, they had a fire or glow lamps pushing back the night, not to mention someone standing on guard.

A warm breeze tickled the back of his neck. He spun around, fighting a scream. He flailed his hands out, but he only felt empty air. Realizing his blade was out, he set it carefully down in his lap with a flash of embarrassment. He didn't know how or when Chimípu would take her turn.

Rutejìmo also didn't know if he would detect danger before it attacked them. But the clan always had guards at night, and it felt right to sit there, even blind.

A shiver ran down his spine.

He inhaled a shuddering breath. Straining, he tried to listen but all he could hear was his own pounding heart.

There was sharp prick at his neck. He waved at it, to chase away the insect biting him.

But his hand struck something hard and smooth. With a gasp, he gingerly touched it until he identified it: a tazágu, a fighting spike. A whimper rising his throat, he felt down the weapon. It was about two feet in length with a leather-and-hemp braided handle.

A strong hand covered his mouth, pressing down against his jaw. The gloved fingers dug into the side of his cheek as he was pulled into someone's chest and against small breasts underneath thin, layered fabric. The ridge of the woman's hand pressed against his nostrils, cutting off his breath.

To his embarrassment, Rutejìmo lost control of his bladder. He felt the hot urine pouring down his leg, and the stench of it added to his humiliation.

"Damn the darkness," the woman whispered in his ear, "you're nothing but a kid." She had a light accent from the southern reaches.

He couldn't breathe, not because of her hand, but lungs that refused to move. He tried to shift, but a sharp stab stopped him. She didn't break skin, but his entire world was focused on the point poised to drive into his throat.

"Who are you?" she whispered. Her grip loosened over his mouth. "And if you call the others, you'll be dead before they wake."

Rutejìmo sobbed, trying to calm himself and failing. His shoulders shook, and tears ran down his cheeks. He was a failure and he was going to die in the dark.

Suddenly, the woman shoved herself back, the point of her weapon leaving a burning line across his throat.

Rutejìmo clapped his hand against it, terrified she had cut his throat, but only a trickle of blood damped his fingers.

A thud vibrated through the rock as someone landed on it. There was a blast of air as the second person accelerated away, leaving only the scent of her passing—Chimípu. Wind howled around him, and he lost his balance. With a scream, he hit the ground, and the impact drove the air from his lungs.

As Rutejìmo struggled to breathe, he could hear metal crashing into metal. It came fast, rapid parries and attacks, but there was no noise from the fighters themselves. The fight circled around the rock but he could only hear it from grunts from Chimípu and the other woman, the crunch of sand and rock as they spun around, and the occasional hiss of pain.

Rutejìmo didn't know how Chimípu was fighting in the pitch-darkness, but it sounded as though she was holding her own. More importantly, after a few seconds, he could still hear the sound of fighting.

Light burst from an impact, and he saw the runes of Chimípu's blade flare with the impact of the other woman's spike. Each letter was bright as sunlight but faded instantly. With the next attack, the runes flashed again. As Chimípu rained down blows, their attacks became a lighting storm of attack and parry.

Rutejìmo's lungs started to work. He inhaled sharply and struggled to his feet, but Pidòhu held him down.

"No, Jìmo."

"But—"

"You will only get in the way."

"How is she fighting?"

"Shimusògo," Pidòhu said as if it explained everything.

"Dòhu, I don't—"

Metal snapped loudly, halting Rutejìmo's words. Something whizzed past him and hit the rock wall near his head. It rang out loudly, almost deafening him, and then landed in his lap. Reflexively, he reached down, but when he encountered searing metal, he snatched his hand back. Scrambling to his feet, he slammed

CHAPTER 18. QUIET-VOICED THREAT

his head into the rock, and bright sparks exploded across his vision.

Silence crushed them, an overpowering tension as Rutejìmo strained to identify the winner.

"Darkness," came the woman's voice, annoyed and frustrated, "you're all children. This is a damn rite, isn't it?"

Pidòhu called out, his voice a broken whisper. "Is... Is Chimípu... alive?"

The woman scoffed. "Pathetic."

Icy blue light began to glow in the darkness. It was the color of moonlight and came from the runes along the woman's tazágu and quickly formed a pool of light around her and Chimípu.

She was kneeling on Chimípu's stomach, her tazágu against Chimípu's left breast and aimed straight for her heart. The woman held the weapon in place with one hand and had her other palm pressed against the base of the weapon. Her body was a coiled spring, and there was no question that she was ready to kill Chimípu.

Chimípu's head was off the ground as she glared at her opponent. Her hands were balled into fists as she trembled. A tear in the corner of her eye sparkled in the light, but it refused to surrender to gravity.

The woman never took her eyes off Chimípu. "Who are you, girl?"

Chimípu's jaw tightened, but then she answered. "Shimusogo Chimípu."

"And your boys?"

Chimípu glanced over at Rutejìmo, and he shivered at her look. He could see the frustration, helplessness, and rage boiling in her gaze. She tightened her lips into a thin line for a moment and glared up at the woman pinning her. "The injured one is Pidòhu and the other is Rutejìmo, both of Shimusògo."

"I am Mikáryo and I speak for Pabinkúe. I'm looking for my sister's horse."

"We don't have a horse," said Chimípu.

"I know that, but one of your clan stole her. And I can smell that one." She pulled the spike away and used the point to aim directly at Rutejìmo.

Rutejìmo froze, his entire body clenching tightly with fear.

"Which means that he was there. And that is guilt, if only by association."

Mikáryo still wore the dark outfit Rutejìmo saw at the campsite. It consisted of long lengths of a thin, black fabric wrapped around her body, granting her protection from the sun while sacrificing mobility. He had seen a similar outfit before, from a traveling smith, and knew there would be wires in the fabric. When she stood up from Chimípu, there wasn't even a whisper of sound.

The woman tossed her tazágu into the ground, stepped back, and then put her arms behind her back. She turned back to Chimípu, who was scrambling to her feet. "Girl, this is your rite of passage?"

Chimípu flushed. "Yes," she said. She dropped the shattered hilt of her knife to the ground.

Behind Mikáryo, a horse stepped out of the darkness. He was as black as the cloth around her. Dark eyes glittered as he took in the people, then snorted. His tail snapped back and forth but made no noise.

Mikáryo stepped to the side of the horse as she addressed Chimípu. "Then tell the adults following you that Pabinkúe demands a life for a life. If you don't bring me the horse thief and my sister's murderer, I will take one of yours."

Both Rutejìmo and Chimípu gasped.

Rutejìmo stared at Mikáryo in shock. "Tsubàyo...?"

Everyone turned toward him.

The woman had a look of distaste. She had dark tattoos covering her face and arms. They were elegant dark prints of horses and runes, and he could barely see her brown skin underneath the black ink. "Shimusogo Tsubàyo? Is he one of yours? Another child?"

Chimípu glared at Rutejìmo, but nodded. "Yes, Great Pabinkue Mikáryo. He is also on his rite of passage." The muscles in her jaw jumped at using the honorific version of Mikáryo's name.

"Then, if he is the one, I will take his name." Mikáryo pulled a second tazágu from behind her back. It was different than the first one, wrapped in a dark blue leather with black rope, but Rutejìmo saw that it was also unnamed. No runes identified the length of the spike. According to tradition, a blade was named for the first thing it killed. It would also keep a portion of the victim's soul.

Rutejìmo shivered, then he remembered something Mikáryo said. "There are no adults. They abandoned us."

Mikáryo scoffed and sheathed her weapon. She kept her other hand behind her back. "It would be best, boy, if you just kept your mouth shut and let the big girls speak."

Rutejìmo closed his mouth with a snap, his cheeks burning with humiliation.

"Your elders are close enough, near enough to watch the stupid things you've done but far enough you can't hear their laughter. And, between a boy who can't control his dick—"

Rutejìmo blushed even hotter and clamped his jaw tight to avoid yelling at her.

"—and one who managed to break his leg probably in the first hour, I'm guessing they are laughing so hard they are bent over in pain." She turned her attention back to Chimípu, looking her over with a sneer. "Of course, they say the more suffering during your rite, the closer you'll reach your spirit. I bet babysitting these two screwups"—she gestured to Rutejìmo and Pidòhu—"is getting you real close to your Shimusògo, isn't it?"

Chimípu stood there, back straight and hands balled into fists.

"Don't worry, girl, I'm not going to kill any of you tonight."

In the uncomfortable silence, Mikáryo picked up the glowing tazágu and caressed its length. Darkness plunged across their shelter as the runes snuffed out.

"Remember," her voice drifted from the darkness, "you may be nothing but children, but that won't stop me from killing one of you. You have three nights to find my sister's murderer. Until then, you have no reason to fear me or my clan. But, if you don't... I don't care which one of you dies."

And then nothing. No scrunch of sands or the nicker of a horse. Just the faint breeze.

Rutejìmo held himself still for a long moment, heart pounding.

When a flickering glow filled the site, he jumped back and slammed his head against the rock. Clutching his head, he sank to the ground.

Chimípu held up a glow egg. "No reason to hide if she found us so easily. We'll use light for the rest of the night. Jìmo?"

"Yes, Great Shimusogo Chimípu."

"Clean yourself up," she sniffed, "and then help me move Pidòhu. No reason we have to smell you all night, either."

Humiliated, Rutejìmo activated his own glow egg and sulked into the darkness. He waited until he was out of sight and hearing before he began to cry.

Chapter 19

Humiliated

The worse critic is the voice inside your head.

— Kormar Proverb

Rutejìmo woke up thinking about his actions the night before. The humiliation still burned bright, and he kept replaying the encounter in his head, pretending he wasn't as pathetic as Mikáryo said he was. But, no matter how dramatic his fantasies, there was no way to take back what he had done. He had failed them. Any hopes of being as good as Chimípu were blown away in a single night; he could never fight in the darkness that way, blind but somehow defending the clan against a superior opponent.

He sniffed and looked at the others. Pidòhu was sitting up, but his body shook with every movement. The injured teenager kept wiping his brow as he struggled to hold the water skin to his lips.

Chimípu knelt down next to him, her gaze fixed on him. She held her hand underneath the water skin, ready to catch it if it fell. She spoke to him quietly, a whisper too soft for Rutejìmo to hear.

Pidòhu said something and she smirked.

Rutejìmo felt ostracized by the only clan he had. He got up and trudged away, to answer the pressure in his bladder and to avoid the people who saw him at his weakest.

His feet scuffed on the sand and rocks. He headed back to the rock they spent the first part of the night under. He couldn't stain it any worse, and it gave him privacy.

Thoughts spiraling into depression, he finished what he needed to and circled around the rock. He had done everything wrong on the trip: didn't stop Karawàbi from knocking Pidòhu off of the Tooth, going with the wrong group, and then making a coward of himself when they needed him most. Rutejìmo wondered if he deserved to be a man or to see the dépa.

For the first time, he wanted to run simply for the need to run. It was a strange feeling, but he hoped that it would clear the shadows from his thoughts. He glanced back at their new camp; Pidòhu and Chimípu were still talking. He shook his head and picked a direction and ran. He would only go a few chains at most and then come back.

Shimusògo appeared as he got up to speed, the little dépa sprinting ahead of him. Rutejìmo smiled into the wind. It felt right when he was chasing the clan spirit. He bore down and accelerated, racing after the bird he would never catch.

When he ran, he couldn't think. His mind grew empty until there was nothing but the dépa and the blur of the world. He kept on running, keeping along the curves of the rocks as they turned into dunes. When he hit the soft sand, he expected to stumble, but the sand was as solid as a rock. He found purchase even running along the sandy ridges.

CHAPTER 19. HUMILIATED

Elation filled him and it spread out to suffuse his entire body. When he was running, he didn't feel like a fool and a coward. He felt like a runner, a courier of Shimusògo.

The dépa fluttered and it sprinted away from him. The feathered crest bounced with its movement as it left a trail of dust.

Rutejìmo stumbled, remembering how it had disappeared before the valley, but the bird was still visible. He regained his pace and pushed himself harder, struggling to catch up again. His legs and arms moved in an easy rhythm, but they burned with his efforts.

The world spun past him, a blur of rocks and sand. He chased the dépa, trusting the spirit to guide him to where he needed to go.

He didn't know how long he ran. He was lost in the movement, but catching up to the dépa. He focused on the bird, but the spirit was slowing him down. He thought he could catch up, but his own speed faltered with the bird's. Ahead of him, he saw a set of Wind's Teeth sticking out of the ground. There were five of them, like jagged fingers poking out of the desert.

Rutejìmo slid to his side and skidded to a halt. His hands and feet tore through the dunes, leaving a deep slash from his slowing. His momentum threw him into one of the towering rocks. He hit it with a thud and fell to the ground, stunned. He shook his head to clear the stars from his vision.

Images of Pidòhu's injuries flashed through his mind. Gasping, he sat up and felt his legs and hands, but he had not even a cut. The Tooth, on the other hand, had a large fragment broken off from the impact. Rutejìmo slumped back and chuckled. He wasn't even winded.

With a smile, he crawled to his feet. He spied a shard of rock that broke off upon his impact and picked it up. It was heavy. He hefted it before he felt the heat rolling off it. With a hiss, he tossed it aside before it burned him. It bounced off and came to a rest in a patch of disturbed sand.

Rutejìmo froze and looked around. He saw the remains of a camp. To his side, in a large circle, were impressions of tents and bags. Paths crossed over the sand, circling around the buried remains of a fire. He spotted some threads clinging to a sharp edge of a rock. They were the same reds and yellows he grew up with: Shimusògo's colors.

Mikáryo's words came to mind. The clan was watching him.

Rutejìmo looked up, but he didn't see anything. Only the wide expanses of the desert in all directions. He gulped and turned back the way he came. He could see his path across the sand, but the wind was already erasing parts of it.

He felt a prickle of fear and hope. With a start, he ran. When the dépa appeared, he chased it but kept an eye on his surroundings. He watched for landmarks and tried to memorize each one as he passed.

He came up to the outcropping he had turned around and saw three tents still fluttering in the wind. He stumbled, but then kept on running, mapping out the route. There were some things that shouldn't be explored alone.

It felt like only ten minutes before he came up to their camp again. He circled around the rock and skidded to a halt next to it. His stopping was more precise, if only from practice, and he managed to avoid hitting the stone or tripping. A smile stretched across his face, and he hopped in a circle as excitement pumped through his veins.

He trotted back to Pidòhu.

"Good run?"

Rutejìmo sat down heavily next to him. The joy faded slightly. "Yeah," he said, "it was. I'm sorry, I should have told you."

"Shimusògo run." He said it as if it explained everything. After the last few days, it did. He felt better after running.

"Look, about last night...," he started.

Pidòhu shook his head, then stopped abruptly as he paled. He braced himself against the ground and took a deep breath. "Last night was last night. No reason to bring it up."

"I... made a fool of myself."

"Yeah, you did," murmured Pidòhu as he drank from his cup.

Rutejìmo colored, but Pidòhu kept speaking.

"But you've always been a fool, so nothing really changed."

Rutejìmo stared in shock, wondering if the quiet words were insulting or playful.

Pidòhu answered with a wink and a weak smile. He wiped the sweat from his face and then on his leg. There were already wet streaks on the fabric.

Letting out his breath, Rutejìmo chuckled. "Yeah, I seem to keep making a fool of myself."

"Here, Jìmo, eat." Pidòhu handed him the last of the bird from last night. "Mípu is catching more for later... and," he said with a grin, "probably running out her own frustrations."

"How can she be frustrated? She defended us." He sighed. "And Mikáryo thinks I'm useless."

"There is a lot more to the path she's on. She is at the crux of giving up a lot more to Shimusògo than you ever will be."

Rutejìmo clamped his mouth shut, a surge of jealousy rising up. "What do you mean? She's going to be even better at magic?"

"Probably, but there is a cost."

"What?"

"Ever notice your brother never married?"

Rutejìmo shook his head. "What does that have to do with it?"

"Think, Jìmo. How many warriors have children?"

Rutejìmo frowned. He had never noticed it, but he realized there was only one. "Grandfather was a warrior."

"But he isn't your mother's father. Great Shimusogo Tejíko lost her first husband before you were born. The man you call grandfather was later, when her children had grown up and he was too injured to continue."

Curling his feet up, Rutejìmo stared at Pidòhu. "I know, but why...." Realization dawned. "He has no children, does he?"

Pidòhu shook his head. "Neither will your brother. And neither will Chimípu. A warrior's path is a very lonely, barren path."

"Why?"

"To defend us. They give everything to Shimusògo, and he gives them powers to protect our clan. Mípu knows that. Last night made it clear to her; she is going to lose everything for Shimusògo. And, I suspect, she already figured out the question but she needs to run around to come to the obvious answer. Like someone else I know."

"S-Should I do anything?"

Pidòhu pointed to him. "I'd say be yourself, but you can't help that. I'm going to say that our shared incompetence"—he paused for a deep breath—"is going to point out that she is herself, you are yourself, and I am me."

Rutejìmo blushed. "I'm a little slow, aren't I?"

Pidòhu sipped his cup again. "Yes."

Shooting a mock glare at Pidòhu, Rutejìmo said, "I could run you to the ground… if you could run."

"Yes," Pidòhu said over his cup, "but I'm not Shimusògo."

Icy cold ran down Rutejìmo's spine and his skin began to tingle. "W-What?"

"Shimusògo is never going to accept me."

"Nonsense, we'll just get you healed up—"

"Jìmo."

Frustrated, Rutejìmo continued, "—and then we'll run—"

"Jìmo!"

Rutejìmo clamped his mouth shut.

Pidòhu finished his cup and set it down. "I"—he pointed to himself—"am not Shimusògo."

CHAPTER 19. HUMILIATED

"You can't give up, Dòhu!"

"I'm not." Pidòhu was smiling. "But I... look, do you see that?" He pointed out on the sand.

Rutejìmo peered out across the dunes lit up by the morning light. He saw nothing. "No."

"I see it. A large shadow of a raptor flying above us. It has been circling all morning."

Staring, Rutejìmo saw nothing. "Pidòhu, I think you are...." His voice trailed off as a large shadow crossed the sands. Behind it, the sand kicked up in little eddies of wind, dying down a heartbeat later.

He turned back to Pidòhu just as the injured boy was finishing a sweep of his hand. "What was that?"

"Tateshyúso."

Rutejìmo had heard the name before. It was the clan spirit to Jyotekábi, the frail woman who lived in the valley with two others. "Tateshyúso? Why would you be seeing Tateshyúso?"

"I don't know, but I can feel those shadows. And I realized that I can do this." He swept his hand, and a breeze rose up around Rutejìmo.

Rutejìmo caught a hint of movement in the corner of his eyes, but when he turned there was nothing. Confused, he turned back. "Can that happen? Can you be called by another clan spirit?"

Pidòhu shrugged. "Seems like it."

"Did you tell Mípu?"

"Tell me what?" asked Chimípu as she sat down. She had a brace of birds on her waist, already stripped of feathers and gutted.

"About the shadows across the sand," replied Pidòhu.

She glared at him and then at Rutejìmo. "You are pushing yourself too much, Dòhu. You are hallucinating."

"No, I think it's real. It is real. It is Tat—"

She knelt down, slapped the birds against a rock, and then spread them out.

The impact quieted Pidòhu, and he closed his mouth.

She looked up at him. "Dòhu, you need rest." Her tone allowed for no disagreement.

In the silence, she pulled out a travel bag filled with salt and spices. It was used to preserve meat for a few days. After shoving the carcasses inside, she wrapped it tight before opening a small vial attached to the bag. She poured it inside. The liquid hissed loudly, and she tied the bag shut. When they stopped for the evening, time and movement would have cooked and seasoned the meat. She attached it to Pidòhu's stretcher.

When she finished, she stood up. "Ready to go?"

It was obvious Chimípu didn't want to talk about Tateshyúso.

Rutejìmo choked down his food even as he stood up. He swallowed hard before saying, "Yes, Great Shimusogo Chimípu."

Chimípu shielded her eyes and looked out across the desert. "Any idea which way to go?"

Rutejìmo smiled and pointed the direction he ran. "We camped about a day's drag away. Beyond that, there are some Wind's Teeth about a day past that. I saw signs of a camp there too so it's probably safe."

She shot him a look, surprised but otherwise unreadable.

Rutejìmo kept his smile inside. "I-I had to run."

For a moment, she said nothing. Then she lowered her hand to her belt, to the empty sheath. She sighed and stared out in the direction he pointed.

Rutejìmo got an idea. He pulled out his knife before handing it to her hilt first.

Chimípu looked at it before she regarded him.

"You"—he realized it was easier to admit it—"you are a better fighter than me."

She took it with a quick bow. "Thank you, Great Shimusogo Rutejìmo."

Chapter 20

Shimusogo Karawàbi

In the end, the cruel get their comeuppance, but rarely do victims cheer.

— Mistan Palarin, *The Iron King's Betrayal* (Act 3, Scene 2)

By midday, Rutejìmo was exhausted. He strained to pull Pidòhu. His back screamed out in agony, and his legs were on fire. But he couldn't stop pulling.

"Damn it, Jìmo, let me carry Pidòhu."

"No!" he gasped, and forced his feet forward.

"You've been dragging him all morning. You need to let me—" Chimípu reached out for the handles.

Rutejìmo lurched to the side to avoid her and almost fell over. Sweat ran down his face, and he regained his footing. Glaring at her, he forced himself to drag the frame farther along. They were almost up to the point where Tsubàyo, Karawàbi, and he stopped the first night. He knew there was shelter, and this time, when he arrived, it would be with pride instead of shame.

"Damn the sands, Jìmo. Let me!"

"No!" he said.

"Why not!?" Her voice was shrill and tense.

"Because you need your strength."

"For what?"

"Mikáryo."

Chimípu stopped and stared. "Is this what this is about? Look, Jìmo, everyone gets scared, and it isn't your fault that you—"

Rutejìmo closed his eyes tightly. "Please don't finish that sentence."

Chimípu sighed and paced him. "What is it then?"

"You...." He gasped and trudged forward. His foot slipped, and he dropped to one knee. With a sigh, he slumped. "I... can't do that." He looked up, his heart tearing as he spoke. "I can't fight for us. I can't do the same things as you. But I can do this. And if I'm going to be helpful, then let me do what I need to do."

She crouched down next to him. "Jìmo, you don't—"

"No. I do," he pleaded, "Please. Let me do this. You can't do everything."

Chimípu's gaze softened, then the corner of her lips quirked up. "Pidòhu's been gossiping, hasn't he?"

Pidòhu craned is neck to look at them. "Just making observations."

Chimípu leaned over and smacked him playfully on the shoulder.

With a chuckle, Pidòhu batted her back, but it was a weak, helpless strike.

"So," Chimípu asked both of them, "if I'm going to be the great defender of this pathetic group of clan members, what should I do?"

Rutejìmo shrugged and caught his breath. "I don't know. I'm still working on holding up my share."

She smiled at him and gave his shoulder a smack. "Not doing that bad at all, Jìmo."

Rutejìmo's heart skipped a beat with joy. He smiled and rubbed his shoulder where it stung.

"Well, if you are done beating on each other," Pidòhu said as he pointed past them, "maybe Great Shimusogo Chimípu could find out why there are vultures circling over the rocks we're heading for."

Rutejìmo and Chimípu looked in the direction he pointed. Six vultures sailed in a lazy spiral and a dozen more hopping on the rocks. They were staring down at the camp. Occasionally one would flap its wings and cry out.

Chimípu stood up. "You said the camp was there, right?" She asked as if she hoped Rutejìmo would say no. "Maybe it's just food rotting."

"M-Maybe." But Rutejìmo had a bad feeling in his gut.

"I"—Chimípu stroked the knife at her belt—"why don't I go check?"

She jogged forward about a rod, then accelerated in a blast of air. Her sprinting left a trail of dust behind her, and it bloomed into a cloud before the desert wind dispersed it.

Rutejìmo sighed and grabbed the handles. A blister on his hand broke, and he winced at the pain, but still wrapped his fingers around the wood and lifted it up. "Come on, Dòhu."

Pidòhu grunted. "Thank you, Rutejìmo."

Rutejìmo smiled and dragged the stretcher along, watching the rocks with fascination.

A few moments after Chimípu arrived, the vultures took off. They rose and joined the others, spiraling like a miniature tornado over the rocks. Their screeches were loud and piercing, and soon there were more circling around.

Chimípu came back at a high-speed sprint. She came to a long halt, exploding one dune before she stopped less than a few feet in front of Rutejìmo. She held out her hand and shook her head. Her face was pale, and she looked shaken. "No, circle around. We can't go there."

Rutejìmo stopped. "Why?"

"It was... it's...." Her face was pale and she gulped. "Karawàbi. He's dead."

Rutejìmo dropped to his knees in shock. He almost dropped Pidòhu, but clutched the handles tightly at the last minute. "D-Dead? How?" The world spun around him, and he almost threw up.

"S-Someone cut his throat." There was a terrified look on her face.

Rutejìmo gasped, and the blood drained from his face. "Who?"

Gulping, Chimípu shook her head and clutched her stomach. "H-How? Why?"

"I-I don't know. There is blood everywhere and... and...." She shook her head again. "No, I can't."

Rutejìmo knelt there, stunned for a long moment.

Pidòhu broke the silence. "Are the tents still there?"

Surprised, Rutejìmo stared at him.

Pidòhu, already pale, shrugged. "I've seen a lot of blood lately. Most of it mine. If it wasn't for you, I'd be dead, so.... I guess I'm being practical here. If there is something that can help us, one of us has to go and get it. I had medicine in my pack and I need it."

Chimípu whimpered. "I can't go back, not without...." The words failed her.

Rutejìmo took a deep breath. "What if we all go?"

She looked at him with hope.

Rutejìmo shrugged as casually as he could, but his stomach was twisting left and right with every passing second. "Come on," he grunted as he picked up the frame again, "before I lose my courage."

All three of them headed into the camp. There was a bittersweet smell in the air, a tickling sweetness of spoiled meat. It surrounded the rocks and fouled the air.

As he dragged Pidòhu in, Rutejìmo stopped by the three tents. One flap fluttered in the air and sand had piled inside it, but he could see rations and a blanket inside.

The smell was stronger around the corner, in the shadows under the rocks. Rutejìmo set down the stretcher and headed for the tents. He stopped at the first one and emptied it out, setting the supplies on the ground before working to take down the tent itself.

Chimípu joined him in silence. Neither said anything about the sickening smell or the insects that buzzed around them. Shadows circled around the corpse: the vultures waiting for their dinner, and they were impatient.

Rutejìmo found Pidòhu's pack. Inside, there was a number of medicine packets. He carried them over to Pidòhu and set them down. He didn't want to speak.

Pale and shaking, Pidòhu dumped them out and began to sort through them.

Once he was sure Pidòhu was set, Rutejìmo headed to his tent and tore it down. Chimípu finished and joined him.

The heat bore down on him, and he was sweating as he finished the third tent. He stood up to stretch and caught sight of Karawàbi's corpse.

The large boy was leaning against the shade of the rock as if he was taking a nap. His head lulled to the side but the angle was wrong. Someone had cut across his throat, slicing deep enough that Rutejìmo saw the flash of white bone. Karawàbi's shirt was soaked in dried blood, and it stained the sand in all directions. More splatters discolored the sand over a yard away.

Surprised by the sight, Rutejìmo spun around as bile rose up in his throat. He staggered to the side and vomited on the ground. A few yards away, he noticed that Chimípu had done the same thing. Sobbing, he closed his eyes as he emptied out his stomach. Soon nothing came but dry heaves.

Chimípu knelt next to him. "Calm down, Jìmo. Calm down." She was almost tender as she patted his back. "He's dead. Just look away. Don't think about it."

Gasping, Rutejìmo braced himself. "Who could have done that? Mikáryo?"

"No," said Chimípu, "I don't think so. When we were fighting, she used the tazágu and I didn't see any knives. Whoever killed Karawàbi used a straight blade; the wound is too clean and deep."

Rutejìmo looked at her, surprised and fearful of the haunted tone in her voice. "How close did you get?"

"Close enough," she said in a tone that didn't encourage questions.

Rutejìmo started to glance at the corpse again, but Chimípu grabbed his head and turned him away.

"No, Jìmo. Don't look."

"Who could have done it? Tsubàyo?"

Chimípu frowned. "He wouldn't kill clan."

"He isn't clan," Rutejìmo said, remembering Tsubàyo's bitter words outside the camp. "He was turning his back on Shimusògo."

Her lips tightened into a thin line. "I forgot you told me that. But he can't walk away. Even if he did, Karawàbi was his friend. He would have asked Wàbi to join him, not cut his throat."

"I don't know, Mípu. I don't know."

From the other side of the camp, Pidòhu called out, "Um, could we get out of here... now?"

No answer was needed.

Chapter 21

From the Shadows

We step through the shadows on silent hooves of steel.

— Pabinkue Zabīno, *Birth of the Pabinkúe*

They walked in silence, each one lost in thought. The only sounds were the scuff of sand, the whisper of the breeze, and Pidòhu's labored breathing. The heated wind burned Rutejìmo's skin, and he wished he could run, if just for the breeze, but also to escape his own thoughts.

Even through the pain and exhaustion, Rutejìmo couldn't stop thinking about Karawàbi's corpse. The look of Karawàbi's face and the sight of blood had burned itself into his memories. Even worse, he kept imagining himself in the murdered boy's place. He wondered if Karawàbi knew death was coming or if it was a surprise. If it was Tsubàyo, did he sneak up? Did they talk? Did they fight?

Each scenario made him sicker, but he couldn't stop his morbid imagination. Instead, he just walked in despair and silence.

They reached the Wind's Teeth in early evening. The campsite Rutejìmo had seen was completely obliterated by the wind, but the hunk of rock he had broken off marked their destination. Without a word, he set down Pidòhu and began to pitch the tents.

A moment later, Chimípu joined him.

He was startled by the quiet companionship she gave him. With Tsubàyo and Karawàbi, he had bristled under their constant commands and attitude. But Chimípu worked without question, and he felt the need to keep up. He was reminded of his brother's last advice to him, a suggestion to help Pidòhu make dinner. Now, days later, he could appreciate the advice of simply doing what needed to be done.

"Jìmo," Chimípu asked as they finished the tents, "after dinner, do you want to run? Just around the Teeth." She didn't need to mention Karawàbi or Mikáryo, but Rutejìmo could see the fear in her eyes.

With a grunt, he said, "I'd like that."

They shared a brief smile.

Chimípu looked around. "If you get Dòhu comfortable, I'll start dinner. That way, we'll have time before the sun goes down."

Rutejìmo finished the last tie and headed over to Pidòhu. At his side, he knelt down and loosened the ropes to give Pidòhu a chance to move around—as much as he could with a broken leg.

Pidòhu lifted his gaze to Rutejìmo, his eyes steadier than they had been in a while. He reached out with one hand and swatted a fly trying to burrow into his bloody bandages.

"Feeling better, Dòhu?"

"Yes, much better." Pidòhu stretched his arm out before resting it back on his lap. "The fever-block and the pain killers are helping. Everything hurts, but at least the throb is bearable."

"Do you need me to change the dressing?"

"Please?"

Rutejìmo peeled back the bloody bandage. Seeing it no longer brought the bile up, but the smell was overpowering. It was sweet and coppery; it reminded him too much of Karawàbi's blood. He stopped at the final wrapping, where the blood had turned the bandage crimson.

"I can do this," whispered Pidòhu. "You don't have to."

Rutejìmo gave him a thin smile. "Might as well, right? Just tell me if it hurts."

"Of course, Great Shimusogo Rutejìmo."

"I don't deserve that," snapped Rutejìmo as he focused on pulling back the bandage.

"Of course, Great Shimusogo Rutejìmo."

Rutejìmo gave Pidòhu a glare, but the thinner boy just smiled.

"It doesn't matter if you think you deserve it or not. I'm going to use it."

"Why? I'm a...." Rutejìmo couldn't find the words. He found a fresh bandage and began to wrap the wound back up, flicking off some flies that landed on the crusty edges.

"Hopeless? Irresponsible? Disrespectful?"

"Yeah," he replied, "all that." It hurt, but Pidòhu was right. He looped the bandage over and brought it back over the cloth pad, careful to avoid the exposed bone. "So why are you calling me great?"

"Because you came back."

Rutejìmo chuckled. "Just like that?"

Pidòhu didn't answer.

Rutejìmo finished wrapping the bandage. When he tied it off, he looked up to see Pidòhu staring at him. "What?"

"Why won't you let Chimípu pull me?"

Surprised by the question, Rutejìmo looked away.

"Because of Karawàbi? Or something before?"

Rutejìmo felt tears burning in his eyes. He sighed and stood up. "I'll set up the water collection."

Pidòhu stopped him by grabbing his trouser. "Rutejìmo?"

Fighting the tears, Rutejìmo wiped his face. He looked down at the sick, injured teenager. "B-Because I'm not strong."

"You're strong enough."

"No, I'm not. I was worse than useless against Mikáryo. I couldn't... didn't stop Tsubàyo and Karawàbi from knocking you off the rocks. I could have stopped Tsubàyo before he stole that horse and killed a woman. I knew it was wrong, but I just ran away. And, looking back, I realize my brother and Gemènyo and Hyonèku were all trying to help me and I just"—he waved his hands—"didn't see it."

Pidòhu said nothing, but he had a sympathetic look on his face.

"And Chimípu. She can do everything and she's amazing. When I think I finally start to get better than her, she's already blowing past me. Run across the desert, and she'd be at the far end, enjoying the sun. Everything, and I mean everything, she does is better than me. How can I compare to that?" He realized he was venting, but the words kept coming out. "She's going to be a warrior, like my brother. She'll no doubt have an honorable life and be revered. Everyone is going to love her and they'll sing song about her deeds. But... I'm going to be just a runner. They won't sing songs about me," he sniffed, "not like her."

The hairs on the back of his neck rose. Rutejìmo groaned. "Damn the sands, she's listening, isn't she?"

From behind him, Chimípu coughed into her hand.

Pidòhu shrugged and held out his hands. "You were talking rather loudly." He grinned. "I think they heard you in Wamifuko City with that last bit."

Rutejìmo turned around, blushing.

CHAPTER 21. FROM THE SHADOWS

About a rod away, Chimípu stood by the fire pit. The alchemical fire from Pidòhu's pack was hissing underneath the birds she stored in her travel pouch. Her green gaze was locked on him, but her face was unreadable.

"Um"—Rutejìmo struggled for a moment—"Great Shimusogo Chimípu, I didn't, I mean, I—" He stopped when she held up her hand.

Clearing her throat, she looked around at the Wind's Teeth, the tents, and Pidòhu. "Pidòhu...?" she left the question unfinished.

Rutejìmo turned back.

"Shimusògo run." Pidòhu grinned, then pointed to another set of Wind's Teeth a number of miles away. "Try there."

"No. That's too far." Chimípu shook her head. "What if Mikáryo comes back?"

"I'm not worried about her, actually. She could have killed Rutejìmo last night. I saw the blood on his neck; it would have taken just a second to kill him and you would have never known."

Rutejìmo tensed at the memory of his shameful behavior.

"But," Chimípu insisted, "what about her threat? She wants to kill one of us."

"Oh," Pidòhu said, "I think that's real. But she said three nights. And those rocks are only, what, two leagues at the most? You'll be back in twenty minutes. I think I can stall that long."

Rutejìmo spoke up. "What about Tsubàyo?"

Pidòhu gave a sudden grin. "I'll scream really loudly and crawl away. You won't get enough speed running in a small circle. You need distance to run, not to just jog around. Just" –he pointed to his leg—"come back?"

Chimípu stepped back. She looked around, then returned her attention to him. "Are you sure, Dòhu? We don't—"

"Shimusògo run," he answered.

Rutejìmo looked at Chimípu. Together, they jogged toward the other Wind's Teeth, quickly accelerating into a run. They followed the curve of the dunes without missing a beat. Everywhere Rutejìmo stepped, the ground was solid and gripped him. He had no fear or pain when he ran, as long as he didn't stop moving.

Ahead of them, the dépa appeared, and he felt joy at the sight of the small bird. The world was right when he ran with Shimusògo. With a grin, he chased after it, letting the world blur until the only thing left was Shimusògo, Chimípu, and himself.

The second group of Wind's Teeth were tall, narrow rocks. Each was only ten feet across, but there were over a dozen of them. They looked like weeds sticking out of a plain of rocks.

The dépa slowed a few chains shy of the rocks, and so did Chimípu and Rutejìmo. It disappeared as they shifted from a jog into a walk. But Rutejìmo still felt a connection to Shimusògo, a sense he was loved and cherished.

"Do you," Chimípu asked suddenly, "really think I'm that great?"

Her question wasn't a surprise, but Rutejìmo couldn't answer for a moment. "Yes, Great Shimusogo Chimípu."

She gave him a light punch on the shoulder. "Don't call me that."

He remembered Pidòhu's response and grinned. He bowed deeply. "Yes, Great Shimusogo Chimípu."

She punched him again but, when she looked away, she was smirking.

Rubbing his arm, he walked next to her. He didn't want to stop, but even a simple walk was relaxing. "Ever since we were kids, you were always better than me. A better fighter, a faster runner. You managed to steal the ancestors' ashes three times, and the closest I got earned me a beating by my own grandmother."

She grinned. "Great Shimusogo Tejíko pounds on everyone. You remember the time she caught me stealing food?"

Rutejìmo chuckled and grunted. "I never saw you run so fast. You almost made it to the mouth of the valley before she caught you. They heard your screams in the shrine house."

"She wasn't trying very hard. Only a few bruises and no broken bones."

"She was old."

Chimípu's smile dropped.

Wondering if he said something wrong, Rutejìmo snapped his mouth shut.

She didn't stop walking, so he continued to pace with her. It was a few minutes before she spoke again. "Jìmo?" she asked as they came around one of the stones. "You ever notice that there is only one warrior who made it to old age in the valley? Your grandfather."

Rutejìmo sighed. "I don't notice a lot. But Dòhu mentioned it to me. I never thought about it, really. Not a lot of people live past their forties, do they? But none of the warriors are over thirty."

Her footsteps crunched on the rocks. A few pebbles bounced away as they threaded their way through the Wind's Teeth.

Rutejìmo realized Chimípu doubted her own abilities as much as he doubted himself. It was strange to see her struggling with anything, but there was a storm of emotions behind her expressions, and sadness seemed to be the strongest.

"When I was younger," she started, "I told my mother that I wanted to marry Desòchu."

He stopped, staring at her in surprise. He never thought of Chimípu as desiring anything, much less his brother.

"He was always"—she held out her hands—"there, I guess. Strong, powerful, and handsome. Even at twenty-one, he wasn't married, and I hoped—begged Shimusògo, actually—that he was waiting for me."

Rutejìmo felt a prickle of discomfort at the idea of his brother and Chimípu. He wanted to say something, but didn't. Instead, he thought about his own words to Pidòhu. And he guessed that all three of them were struggling with fears and doubts in the last few days.

If Pidòhu could give Rutejìmo an ear to listen and a hand to hold, then so could he. Rutejìmo shoved aside his own fears and listened.

"My mother told me about the warriors that night. About how Desòchu will never grow old in the valley." A tear ran down her cheek. "Never have children. He will die out there"—she pointed to the desert—"far from home."

Rutejìmo toed the ground. He knew she didn't need him to speak, but remaining silent was uncomfortable.

"I cried when she told me that. I wanted to deny it. But, as the years passed, I saw it was true. Every time he went without the others, you could see it in his eyes. He may not come back. If he ever had to choose between himself and the rest of the clan, he would die with pride. It was terrifying that he could do it. One day… one day, I asked him how he could keep running. You know what he did?" She looked up and gave him a sad smile. "He smiled."

Rutejìmo pictured his brother, his easy attitude and the kind words. He was friendly to the entire clan. His brother had given his life to the clan. Not to one woman and not to his children, but to every one of them.

Chimípu started walking again. "A few years ago, I realized I wanted to be the same. I would give up on my legacy so I could be like him. Love and protect everyone, not just myself."

"I-Is it worth it?"

She smiled at him, her eyes shimmering. "Well, you're still an asshole, but you're getting tolerable."

"Oh," Rutejìmo responded with a mock glare, "glad to hear that. I'll try to keep my ass from speaking in the future."

She grinned, then burst into laughter.

Rutejìmo joined in with a snort.

Together, they kept walking around the Teeth.

When they regained their composure, Rutejìmo finally asked one of the questions that was haunting him. "Mípu? How did you fight Mikáryo? It was dark and you didn't have light."

"It was strange." She rubbed her arm. "I woke up when I felt Shimusògo's feathers against my cheek. I almost made a noise, but then the feathers were against my lips. So I held still and listened. As Mikáryo threatened you, I realized I could... feel her. Like a silhouette in the darkness."

"Why did you attack her?"

"When she threatened you, everything became clear as glass. Shimusògo moved and so did I. I did the same thing as we ran, chased after the dépa, but it was... it was...." She sighed. "I can't really explained. I chased Shimusògo and we fought her together."

Rutejìmo chuckled. "I'm glad one of us did."

Chimípu grinned and punched his arm.

He stumbled to the side and rubbed it. "Ow."

"Stop doubting yourself, Jìmo. You see Shimusògo. Even if you think it's a fluke, do you think Shimusògo would show himself to Karawàbi? Or Tsubàyo?"

Rutejìmo sighed. "I know, but—"

"No," said Tsubàyo. "I found something better."

Chimípu responded first. She used her right hand to push Rutejìmo behind her as she pulled out the knife. The blade shone in the sunlight as she aimed the point at the deepest shadow of the Teeth.

Rutejìmo couldn't see what she saw, but he remained behind her. His heart thumped louder as he peered around, just in case Chimípu was wrong. When he didn't see anything, he peered over her shoulder.

Blackness stirred within the shadows before it oozed out into the shape of a massive black horse. Rutejìmo couldn't tell how the horse managed to hide, but somehow it did. Fear clutched his heart as the creature continued to step out of the shadows. It was huge, six feet at the shoulder, and with pitch-black hair. The eyes were two black orbs, but, as the horse stepped into the sun, the pupils contracted into two tiny points of inky darkness.

Tsubàyo crouched over the back of the horse. He clutched to the mane tight enough that his knuckles were almost white. There were dark shadows around his eyes, giving them a sunken appearance. With his scar, he had the mask of a rikunámi—a nuisance, prairie creature known for stealing shiny trinkets. He still wore the same clothes Rutejìmo last saw him in, and he smelled as though he hadn't cleaned himself in days.

"Tsubàyo!?" Chimípu stepped forward. "Where have you been?"

"Riding," he said in a gravelly whisper, "and it feels good."

"You stole a horse."

"Yeah, I guess I did." A smile crossed his lips.

"And the Pabinkúe woman?"

Tsubàyo looked to the side, back in the shadows. His eyes scanned the darkness for a long moment, before he turned back. "I needed the horse." He patted the equine underneath him. "She was in my way. It was easy... easier than I thought it would be."

The horse lifted its head and exhaled hard. It lifted one foot and stamped. Tiny rocks vibrated from the impact.

Chimípu stepped back, pushing Rutejìmo's chest as she moved.

He followed her silent command, unable to take his eyes off the massive equine or the teenage boy on top. He had grown up with Tsubàyo, but there was no familiarity or compassion in Tsubàyo's eyes. There never was, but as he looked at the teenager, Rutejìmo felt as though he was staring at a stranger.

Tsubàyo looked back at the shadows again, a nervous look briefly crossing his face. "Where is Dòhu? Was he honorable and finally die?"

CHAPTER 21. FROM THE SHADOWS

Rutejìmo gasped.

Chimípu snapped at him. "No! He didn't. He's... he's close enough."

"Not that close. I saw you running up." Tsubàyo chuckled. "I'd say he's about two or three leagues that way, isn't he?" He pointed back the way Chimípu and Rutejìmo had come.

"You'll never get to him before we do."

Tsubàyo favored her with a smile, his lips pulled back to show the brightness of his teeth. "Ryachuikùo here is very fast in the night. I don't really have to outrun you, though, since you'd never see me coming."

Chimípu tensed, the hand against Rutejìmo's chest trembling with her emotions. "You will not touch my clan."

"Your clan!? We don't have a clan. That bird abandoned us. The adults left us. They left us to die in the desert!"

Rutejìmo snapped loudly, "No, they didn't!"

Tsubàyo lifted his gaze to stare directly at Rutejìmo. His eyes were angry and dark, hatred almost palpable in his eyes. "Any spirit which would take you, Jìmo, is a fool."

The horse stepped back, a slow and measured movement despite Tsubàyo not saying or commanding it. Its tail disappeared into the shadows, and Rutejìmo couldn't even see a hint of movement in the darkness.

Tsubàyo glared at both of them. "And I don't have time for fools."

The horse took another step back, and Tsubàyo leaned into the movement. As he crossed the threshold of light and shadow, his body disappeared.

"Tsubàyo!" called Chimípu.

Tsubàyo leaned back into the light. "Yes, girl?"

Chimípu didn't rise to the insult.

"You killed that woman, didn't you?" Both her voice and body were tense. Rutejìmo could see her muscles jumping as she crouched down. The knuckles on the knife were pale as she prepared to strike.

Tsubàyo looked into the shadows, his body disappearing into darkness as he did. When he looked back, his eyes were black orbs before they slowly adjusted to the light. "Why?"

Chimípu said, "Pabinkue Mikáryo is looking for a life in return for the one you stole."

"Really?" Tsubàyo smiled. "Then I guess one of you better sacrifice yourself, because I'm not getting off this horse."

Rutejìmo spoke up again. "How? How could you do that? Shimusògo run. We don't ride."

"Yes, I heard that pointless saying my entire life. Shimusògo run," he said sardonically, "but there is power up here. Power to hide in shadows and watch the fools run across the sands. I can feel it every time I ride."

Chimípu stepped forward, brandishing her knife. "You must give yourself up. We only have three nights."

"No, girl, I don't."

"We won't die for you, Tsubàyo."

"No," he said as the horse stepped back, "you're going to die because she's going to kill you." His voice faded along with his body. "Because she won't find me."

With a scream of rage, Chimípu exploded into movement. Dust and rock slammed into Rutejìmo, throwing him back as she charged. Her body glowed with liquid sunlight as she plunged into the shadows. The darkness peeled back as she slashed with the knife, trying to find him with the edge of her blade.

But, despite Tsubàyo and the massive horse stepping into the shadows just moments before, she hit nothing.

"Damn that bastard!" Chimípu threw back her head and screamed in rage. It was a high-pitched screech that sounded uncomfortably like that of a bird. Her body ignited with a golden flame that burned away the shadows around her. She became a blinding sun in an instant as a translucent dépa superimposed itself over her body. The image expanded to twice her height before it dissipated in swirls of golden sparks.

Rutejìmo whimpered at the noise, his hands halfway to his ears, but it was too late to block the sound.

Her scream echoed against the rocks, fading quickly. She took a step out of the shadows. Her body swayed once, and then all the tension left her limbs.

Rutejìmo saw her falling and he panicked. He froze, unable to act. But then all the frustration that he wasn't good enough shoved him into movement. He sprinted forward and covered the short distance between them. He caught her and held her tight to his body as he skidded to a halt.

As he stopped, the dépa faded away from where it appeared for his short sprint.

His momentum carried him a chain past the Wind's Teeth. He landed on his knees, cradling her. "Mípu? Mípu!"

Groaning, Chimípu opened her eyes. "What happened? Did Tsubàyo hurt me?"

"I-I don't know. You let out a scream, ignited in flames, and then passed out."

"I—" She groaned and pushed him away. Slumping to the ground, she gasped for breath. "I don't remember. I... I was angry, and then I felt Shimusògo inside me."

"I saw that..." his voice trailed off as his mind spun. He gasped. "I've seen that. Desòchu can do that!"

She pushed him away and staggered to her feet.

Rutejìmo stood up with her, holding out his hands in case she fell. "Mípu, we need to go back."

"I think," she groaned again, "that is a good idea."

Chapter 22

Shadows from Sunlight

Tateshyúso cannot be seen, only felt as she passes.

— Shimusogo Nedorómi, *Courtship of Shimusògo and Tateshyúso* (Verse 3)

"Rutejìmo? Jìmo?"

Rutejìmo opened his eyes to see Chimípu crouching at the entrance to his tent.

She was fretting with the handle of the knife. Her body shuddered as she tapped her foot. "Wake up, Jìmo."

He groaned. "I'm up, Mípu. What's wrong?"

"I... we need to get moving."

Rutejìmo yawned and looked past her. It was first light, a beautiful morning right before the spears of light crossed over the sands. It was still cool but the heat was already increasing. "Why?"

"Come on." Her expression faded into a pleading one. "Please?"

He searched her face. She was scared about something. He opened his mouth to speak but stopped at her look. He grunted. "Yes, Great Shimusogo Chimípu."

With relief naked on her face, she stepped back and moved to wake up Pidòhu.

Rutejìmo crawled out of bed and found a spot to relieve himself. He returned to find her digging out breakfast, the wooden boards placed around her. She moved with a frantic energy, practically throwing the plate of food in his lap before serving Pidòhu.

Feeling Chimípu's desperation, Rutejìmo ate quickly.

Pidòhu ate slower, but his movements were steadier, and he wasn't as pale as the day before. He didn't shake, but he still struggled to hold the board up. Rutejìmo reached over and steadied it for him. As he struggled with his food, Pidòhu watched Chimípu carefully. "Mípu? What's wrong?"

"Nothing."

Pidòhu continued to stare at her.

Chimípu glanced up, and then back down at her food. "I said nothing."

His eyebrow rose and his gaze never left her.

After a few seconds of her choking down her food, she slammed her plate down. "Okay, I ruined everything! Better?"

A smile ghosted across Pidòhu's face. "Oh, is that it?"

Chimípu glared at him.

Pidòhu stuck out his tongue at her and resumed eating. Between the bites, he said, "I mean, none of us have screwed up during these rites at all. Of course, forcing us to wake up early is far worse than me falling off a rock and breaking my leg. Or Rutejìmo marking the rocks."

Rutejìmo shot Pidòhu a glare but then focused on eating.

"It isn't that," snapped Chimípu. "It's Tsubàyo."

"What about him?"

"I told him about Mikáryo. I shouldn't have."

"So?"

"He knows that she wants one of us."

Pidòhu nodded and sighed. "And you are worried that he's going to do something stupid like kill one of us to save his own balls?"

Chimípu froze, her fingers inches from her mouth. She sighed and gave a rueful smile. "Damn, yes."

"Well," Pidòhu said with a dramatic shrug of modesty, "I'm pretty observant." He grinned. "Or, I don't have anything better to think about."

Rolling her eyes, she finished her bite.

"Am I right, Great Shimusogo Chimípu?"

"Yes, yes, you are." She stared at her plate. "I shouldn't have told him. And then, when I realized that he had gotten away, I got so angry, I had to scream."

"I know. Rutejìmo told me while you were sleeping."

She looked away, her lips pressed into a thin line. "I'm supposed to be the warrior. I don't know if I can protect you against him."

"We grew up with Tsubàyo. He is a bully and a bastard. I have no doubt you will succeed."

"But he did that... thing with the horse. He could be anywhere." She pointed to a large shadow on the side of the rock. "I-I don't know how to defend against that."

"You will."

She sighed and looked out over the rocky plain surrounding them. It was flat in all directions for at least a mile.

Rutejìmo swallowed his food and pointed out to the south. "Why don't you run? It will help."

"No," she said, shaking her head. "We can't leave Pidòhu alone now."

Rutejìmo gestured at her and then to the desert.

"Me?" Chimípu looked surprised. "By myself?"

Rutejìmo grunted. "Yes. Just run. It will clear your head. If Tsubàyo shows up, we'll just... stall."

She stood up, but didn't move. "Are you sure?" There was hope in her voice. "Just a few miles?"

Rutejìmo nodded.

Pidòhu gestured in the same direction. "Go on, but more than a few miles. Just run—"

She disappeared in a rush of air. The wind sucked along her path as she left a trail of blossoming rocks and dust in her path.

"—until you feel better," finished Pidòhu with a grin.

Rutejìmo followed Chimípu's movement with his eyes. She was moving faster than he ever could, ripping along the distance with startling speed. She raced in a straight line for a few minutes, then began to circle around them.

"Jìmo?"

Rutejìmo glanced down at his plate. It was empty. He stood up as he regarded Pidòhu. "Yeah?"

"What does it feel like?"

"Running?" Rutejìmo gathered up the plates and found a spot to scrape them clean. "It is... hard to be angry or upset. When I start moving, I can't really think about anything besides Shimusògo."

"Do you feel anything? Exhaustion? A tickling sensation?"

Rutejìmo thought for a moment before he shook his head.

"I wish I could feel it. You've changed a lot since you started running. You enjoy it, don't you?"

"Yeah," Rutejìmo muttered, "never thought I'd say that."

"Not hard to see why they say that your true self comes out during the rite of passage."

In mid-step, Rutejìmo paused. He wondered who he was, now that he ran with Shimusògo. Shaking his head to clear it, he packed away breakfast, took down the tents, and changed Pidòhu's bandage.

"She's still running," said Pidòhu. He pointed to the cloud of dust circling around them.

"Shimusògo run."

"Should we wait for her?"

Rutejìmo shook his head. "She can catch up no matter how far I drag you. We should get started; it's going to be a hot day."

He made sure Pidòhu was settled into the stretcher. Grabbing the handle, he felt the ache coursing up his raw palms. He could have fashioned makeshift gloves for his hands, but the pain was a constant reminder of his duty. With a grunt, he leaned forward to start moving. After a bit of friction, the ends of the frame started to move and he dragged Pidòhu across the rocky field.

"C-Can I try something?" It was only a few minutes after they started. Pidòhu was stuck on some rocks that looked flat when Rutejìmo headed for them, but the sharp edges caught on the wooden frame, and he had to pull hard to keep moving.

"Of... course...." gasped Rutejìmo.

"Don't tell Chimípu, though, if I fail. I'm not exactly sure what I'm doing."

Rutejìmo chuckled as the sweat dripped down his brow. He freed Pidòhu and resumed dragging him. "None of us know what we're doing, Dòhu."

"True."

After a few minutes of silence, Rutejìmo broke it. "Dòhu?"

Pidòhu sighed. "Damn, I almost had it."

"What are you doing?"

"I was thinking about you and Chimípu. And doubting myself."

"Done that, doesn't help."

Pidòhu sighed. "I feel useless."

Rutejìmo chuckled. "Done that. Peed my trousers. Doesn't help, either."

"What if I felt like a burden?" There was an amused tone to Pidòhu's voice.

With a grin, Rutejìmo said, "Done that. Got beaten up. Still didn't help."

Rutejìmo found a smoother path and aimed for it. The stretcher vibrated in his grip over the rough rocks, but dragging grew easier once he reached the path. Mapping out his route, he pulled Pidòhu along.

"All right," Pidòhu said, "let me try again."

"What are you doing?"

Silence.

Rutejìmo shrugged and kept on dragging. Sweat trickled down his back and chest, adding to his discomfort. He couldn't stop, he refused to stop.

Chimípu was still running, circling around them. He wished he would have the chance to do the same. He could see why Pidòhu said he was changing. He had never found joy in moving or running, but he ached for it now. Everything was right when he was chasing the dépa.

"I'm," gasped Pidòhu, "trying to call Tateshyúso. I can see the shadows, but I can't bring them closer."

"How are you calling for her?"

"Calling out... with my mind, I guess. It isn't working."

Rutejìmo pondered it for a moment. "Well, Chimípu and I chase the dépa. I know you can't run with Tateshyúso, but what does she do? Just fly around?"

"Yeah, usually on the hot air up above where the wind is stronger."

He thought about the massive shadows he saw. "How big is Tateshyúso?"

"Bigger than I can describe. Too big to be a real raptor."

CHAPTER 22. SHADOWS FROM SUNLIGHT

"Can you... I don't know. When Chimípu got angry, she said she felt Shimusògo inside her. She was part of Shimusògo. Maybe—"

"Oh!" Pidòhu gasped. "That gave me an idea!"

Rutejìmo smiled and kept on dragging. When Pidòhu didn't say anything else, he let his mind drift off.

And then he saw a shadow in the corner of his eyes. Gasping, he followed it with his gaze as the massive silhouette raced along the ground, spiraling toward them. He looked up, but he couldn't see anything but clear, burning skies.

The shadow continued to circle for a moment, then it passed over him. There was a blessed kiss of shade.

"That felt good for a second."

"Yeah," Pidòhu sounded distracted.

A moment later, the shade of Tateshyúso came back. But, instead of flying past, it hovered over Rutejìmo and Pidòhu, bathing them in coolness despite the heat.

Rutejìmo stumbled and looked up. There was nothing, but the shade felt good against his skin. "I-Is that you, Pidòhu?"

"This... is hard to maintain, Jìmo. I'm going to need practice."

The shadow shot off, and the heat rushed back.

Rutejìmo chuckled. "Well, we have a long walk ahead of us."

"Are you saying I have plenty of time?"

"No, but a bit of shade felt good. And, if someone were to help a fellow clan drag an injured boy across the desert, I know I'd be appreciative."

"I'm not Shimusògo."

"If our clan spirits are bound together, then so are we. So you can help me deliver you back home."

Tateshyúso's shadow circled around them again, coming closer.

Rutejìmo kept dragging, patiently waiting for the shade he knew would come.

Chapter 23

One Mistake

> It only takes a second for everything to change.
>
> — Proverb

Rutejìmo struggled to set one foot in front of the other. After a day of dragging Pidòhu across the desert, each agony had become painfully familiar. The muscles in his back screamed and his legs shuddered with the effort to pull the wooden frame along the rolling rocks and sharp stones.

Every time the wooden frame slipped in his palms, the memory of Pidòhu's fall slammed into him. He clenched tightly to the handles, despite the blisters and the sharp pains. Memories drove him to keep pulling. If it wasn't the heart-stopping fall, it was Karawàbi's empty gaze or the smell of his corpse. He was haunted by the terrible things that had happened and the guilt that burned in his throat. He was responsible, and even if it took them a month to get home, he wouldn't stop dragging.

A shadow circled around them—Tateshyúso. Rutejìmo followed the spirit's passing with his eyes as he forced himself to step forward. His heart quickened with anticipation as the shadow spiraled closer.

Pidòhu groaned softly, and the frame shifted in Rutejìmo's grip. "Come on, please, come on," he whispered.

"Don't force it," Rutejìmo said. He gripped tighter.

Pidòhu chuckled. "You're an expert now?"

"After listening to you for eight hours?" Rutejìmo grinned. "Yes, I am. Every time you start struggling and talking, that shadow"—he gestured with his chin—"slides away. And when you relax and doze, it stays above us."

"It isn't dozing, it's...." Pidòhu sounded hurt and frustrated. "I can't describe it, how it feels."

Rutejìmo struggled to drag the frame over a larger ridge. "Give me a better word."

"Word for what?"

"When you find that all your fears fade away and you have this... this... presence inside you. When you feel Shimusògo running in your heart and there is no time or place to be upset, angry, or even hurt. I-I, I can't explain it, either."

"Rapture." Pidòhu chuckled dryly, then groaned in pain. "Though I'll take your word for Shimusògo. When I doze as you said, it is the same thing. My leg doesn't hurt, and I stop thinking about all the things I should have done instead of getting up on that rock."

Rutejìmo froze in mid-step. "You too?"

"Yes. But then I realize that if I never broke my leg, I may have never heard Tateshyúso. I was never for Shimusògo, no matter how much I hoped. The idea that Tateshyúso would be there for me, to hear her whisper in the back of my head and feel that shadow, was the furthest thing from my dreams. But, now that I feel her, I have a craving to feel her shadow on my skin."

CHAPTER 23. ONE MISTAKE

As he spoke, Tateshyúso's shadow spiraled out and then dove back in. It sailed past Rutejìmo and Pidòhu before coming up.

As the blanket of coolness draped over them, Rutejìmo let out a soft moan of relief. "That feels good."

"I know." Pidòhu's voice was strained. "But I don't think I can hold her much longer. I'm getting tired."

"As long as you can." Rutejìmo bore down on the pain, gripped the handles tightly, and pulled forward. He couldn't move fast enough for Shimusògo, but he needed to take advantage of the dark comfort of Tateshyúso as long as it would last.

He followed Chimípu's half-hidden footsteps as the wind erased her passing. Her path took him up to the crest of a dune. He knew she was on the other side, but it felt like miles when it was only a few chains. Gasping for breath, he drove his feet into the shifting sands and concentrated on each step.

He had almost made it to the ridge when the shadow disappeared.

"I'm sorry," gasped Pidòhu, "I can't hold her any longer."

The heat bore down on Rutejìmo, but he shook his head. "It's only another chain. I can make it."

"Damn the sands," Pidòhu said with a sniff. "I feel useless."

"I know the feeling."

Every step was agony, but Rutejìmo drove himself to keep pulling. He jammed his feet into the sand and balanced himself before dragging Pidòhu up the side of the dune. His back screamed in pain, and he felt the burn in his thighs and shoulders, but the memories shoved him farther. When he reached the top, he let out a cry of relief and stood there, fingers frozen around the wood, and his body shaking with the effort.

The valley was long and steep-edged, empty except for four boulders arranged in a crescent at one end. Sand had piled up along the rocks, but the crescent formed a shelter from the wind.

Inside the rocks, Chimípu had already pitched the tents and started dinner. She moved quickly, rushing from a tent to the fire to the rocks. Her body blurred with her speed, and Shimusògo flickered into existence and faded away.

Rutejìmo stopped in shock. After a second, he pulled Pidòhu around so he could also see. "What's she doing?"

Pidòhu lifted himself with a groan to look. "Running, or at least trying."

"But she keeps stopping. That isn't a good run. We need distance to feel Shimusògo." Rutejìmo frowned. "She seems…." He struggled for the word. "Anxious? Desperate?"

Pidòhu gestured with his fingers. "She's scared. Look at her. She keeps looking at the shadows and holding her knife when she stops. She's afraid to be alone."

"Tsubàyo?"

"Probably."

Rutejìmo watched Chimípu flit around the camp. The dust rose up in a spiral, and the dépa was always ahead of her: standing by the tent, near the fire, on the rock. Everywhere Shimusògo stopped, she raced toward him.

"Jìmo, Mípu needs to run. Run straight and long. I don't know what else to say."

"Shimusògo run." Rutejìmo chuckled, "But she won't. Not knowing Tsubàyo is near."

Chimípu stopped suddenly, and the dust settled around her. She jerked her head to the side and her fingers tightened around the hilt of the blade. Slowly, she circled in place and peered along the ridges of the valley until her gaze focused on Rutejìmo and Pidòhu. She disappeared in a blast of movement, a cloud of dust and rocks exploding in a plume.

Rutejìmo watched as she covered the distance between the camp and him in a heartbeat. He braced himself and turned to shield Pidòhu when she stopped.

CHAPTER 23. ONE MISTAKE

The searing-hot air struck his back, pummeling his skin with shards of rocks. "It there something wrong?" snapped Chimípu.

"No, just talking."

"Come down from the open, please?"

Pidòhu whispered from underneath Rutejìmo's arm. "It's okay, Mípu."

"Please?" she asked.

Getting a nod from Pidòhu, Rutejìmo gripped the frame and started down the curve of the valley.

Chimípu ran off, her form blurring with her speed until she stopped near the camp. She bounced back and forth, checking everything impatiently as Rutejìmo made his way down. When he dragged Pidòhu to her, she snatched the frame from Rutejìmo and eased it down.

Rutejìmo gasped to catch his breath, then said, "You need to run."

"Absolutely not," snapped Chimípu. "We can't leave Dòhu alone."

Pidòhu grabbed Chimípu's arm to stop her. His knuckles grew white when she tried to pull away. "Mípu, he said you," he forced out the word, "need to run. Not the both of you, just you."

Chimípu froze and shook her head. "No, I can't."

"You're being a bitch. And those little sprints aren't going to help you feel better."

Chimípu growled. "I'm not trying to feel better. I'm trying to protect you! I can't... I couldn't stop Tsubàyo. And he could be anywhere!"

"But he needs shadows, right? You said he disappeared in the darkness."

"There are shadows everywhere!" Her shrill voice echoed against the rocks.

"But," Pidòhu said as he continued to grip her arm, "there is still sunlight."

She spun on her heel, but Pidòhu wasn't done. "Besides," he said with a grin, "Great Shimusogo Chimípu is being rather difficult right now. And I'd like to enjoy dinner without her running around and kicking sand in my food."

"I...." She worried her lip. "I already ran. This morning. And I ran ahead to set up." She pointed back to the camp.

"No," Rutejìmo said with a grim smile, "you didn't. You had a little stroll. But you know that a few miles run isn't enough for you anymore. I can see that—"

"I—" She screwed her face, "I already ran."

"And yet," Pidòhu added, "you feel the longing to do it again."

Chimípu looked guilty.

Rutejìmo pointed out to the desert. "Go on."

"But Great Shimusogo Chimípu," Pidòhu added in mock begging, "please don't accelerate until your blast won't rip my bandages off."

Chimípu grinned. "All right, but promise me you'll be okay." She looked directly at Rutejìmo. "Promise me."

Rutejìmo felt a prickle of fear, but he bowed. "I promise, Great Shimusogo Chimípu. I will keep Tateshyuso Pidòhu safe."

From the corner of his eyes, he saw Pidòhu flinch.

She didn't say anything, her eyes flickering back and forth as she stared at him.

He gulped. "With my life, if needed."

Chimípu stepped back. "It won't come to that. I'll be back, I promise. Just a little run."

Pidòhu grinned. "And don't say twenty minutes like last time. You never come back that fast. Run until the sun turns red, then come back. We'll... well, Jìmo will have dinner ready. Right?"

Rutejìmo nodded.

"O-Okay. I feel like—"

Rutejìmo pointed again. "Run."

CHAPTER 23. ONE MISTAKE

Chimípu bowed to both of them, then stepped back farther. She turned on her heels and jogged out a few chains before accelerating in a cloud of sand and dust.

Pidòhu chuckled as they watched her disappear. "You know, Jìmo. It sounded right when you called me Tateshyuso Pidòhu. But it scared me a lot."

Rutejìmo patted Pidòhu on the shoulder before removing the ropes. "But it is who you are. Right? I won't call you that, if you don't want."

Pidòhu stretched and smiled. "No, I'm pretty sure that I can hear Tateshyúso now. It is fair enough... at least until the elders say otherwise. Now, drag some food over, and I'll start preparing."

Chimípu came back when the sun was kissing the horizon and the red streaks of light stretched across the sky. The valley was in shadows, and everything was cast in a dark-red glow. She was sweating lightly as she bounded into the campsite with a smile on her face. Panting, she sat gracefully down on a rock.

Pidòhu handed her a board with food. "Good run?"

She nodded. She turned to Rutejìmo. "You should run too."

A longing filled him. He looked at the red sunlight.

"Just don't go as far," Pidòhu said.

"Well, if Great Shimusogo Chimípu isn't allowed to resist, I won't, either." He stood up, his heart pounding faster with anticipation. "I'll be back soon." With a grin, he looked over Chimípu from head to toe. "I'm not fast enough to run back home and back."

She stood up. "I didn't...." The outrage turned to a smile. "Shimusògo run."

Rutejìmo bowed. "Shimusògo run."

He jogged to the ridge of the valley, then sprinted forward. The dépa appeared, and he threw himself into chasing it. Running came with a rush, a pleasure that coursed through every vein in his body. It felt right to run, to let his feet pound the sands and to feel the wind on his face. Even the relief of Tateshyúso's shadow was nothing compared to racing along the desert. Rapture was a good word for it.

With a grin, he threw himself into a slide. His feet dug into the ground, leaving a deep trench. As soon as he stopped, he kicked off and accelerated in the opposite direction.

The dépa remained with him, spinning around when he stopped and sprinting ahead as he turned.

Rutejìmo threw himself into running and sliding, just pushing himself to the limits of his flagging strength. He loved every moment of it: his feet striking the ground, the wind blowing on his face, and the rush of running faster than he had ever run before. He felt alive out in the desert, breathing in the wind that whipped at his face and feeling the thrill that coursed through his legs.

The sun was almost below the horizon when he stopped. Looking out over the trails he left in the desert, he smiled. There was nothing around him. Not a rock, not a valley. Just the fading light and fine sand between his toes.

The dépa raced past him, heading back to their campsite.

Rutejìmo dug his feet into the sand and raced after it. Moving in a straight line, he blew across the desert as fast as his feet could carry him. Magic flowed through him as the world blurred into a haze of speed and light.

He was gasping when he reached the valley, but there was a smile on his face. He came to a skidding halt, blasting through the top ridge before landing on the side. He used his momentum to slide down to the bottom and then a rod up the far slope.

And then he saw one of the tents burning.

All the joy and pleasure left him in a rush. He sprinted to the campsite, calling out to the others. "Mípu!? Dòhu!?"

His tent was on fire. The alchemical fire had rolled into it. The sand and rock on the ground were torn up. Pidòhu's tent had collapsed, and the fabric fluttered in the window.

"Pidòhu!?"

He spun around, looking for the others. His heart pounded, the steady thump sending waves of agony across his ribs.

"Chimípu!?"

The sun hadn't set, but there was barely enough light to see. He accelerated into a sprint and raced down the valley, looking for any sign of Chimípu or Pidòhu. Finding neither, he spun on his heel and raced down the other length. He called out for them as he ran the length of the valley.

He almost missed the body in the shadows. He dug his feet into the ground to stop, and then raced back. The wind howled around him as he came to a halt next to Chimípu's prone form.

"Mípu!?" He grabbed her and pulled her up to his chest. He was terrified that she would be dead, her throat cut just like Karawàbi. Without thinking, he reached for her neck, his stomach clenching in fear, but he only found soft skin underneath his fingers. "Oh, thank the sands."

Chimípu moaned, her eyelids fluttering. "J-Jìmo?"

"Mípu? Are you okay?"

"I was...." She held up her hand to a bruise forming on her forehead. Her eyes widened. Chimípu surged to her feet. "The bastard hit me with a horse! A sands-damned horse!" Her body began to glow with golden flames. She spun around. "Where is Pidòhu!?"

"I couldn't find him." Rutejìmo cringed anticipating the response he knew would come.

She stepped back from him. "No, he couldn't have. Bàyo, um, Tsubàyo would never take him." She spun on her heel and then disappeared in a streak of golden flames. The air exploded around him, sucking sand and wind after her as she reached the valley in a heartbeat.

She was already tearing apart the tents when he caught up to her. "Damn it, he took him! That bastard took my clan!" She grabbed her knife from near the fire and stopped in front of Rutejìmo. "We're going after him."

Rutejìmo held out his hand. "Mípu, I—"

"Hurry up, Jìmo." She turned on him. "We have to go."

"Mípu!"

She glared at him.

"Do you know where he is?"

She frowned and shook her head. She spun once and pointed down the valley. "That way. He's there, I know it." She stepped forward. "Come on, it shouldn't be more than an hour."

Rutejìmo froze with the memory of Tsubàyo telling him almost the same thing. He remembered the darkness that surrounded him as they walked across the sand. And the suffocating loneliness as he wandered back. He looked around at the shadows filling the valley. "Mípu, it's night."

"The dark doesn't scare me." Her voice was proud and furious. She tapped her foot and glanced in the direction she pointed.

"I—" He gulped. He wanted to help, but he knew he was useless in the night. "I-I can't go with you."

"Jìmo! It is Pidòhu! He needs us."

"No," he said, stepping back, "he needs you. Mípu. If anyone can save him, it will be you."

"No, I can't leave you behind."

"And I can't keep up, Mípu. Not in the dark. No matter how much you want, can you defend us both?"

She let out a groan. "Damn it."

"I'll build a fire and keep still. In the valley, no one will find me, and Tsubàyo wouldn't bother coming back for me. He has Great Tateshyuso Pidòhu and is probably going to give him to Mikáryo."

Chimípu held out her hand, gesturing him to stay. "J-Just be safe. I'll be back soon."

Rutejìmo bowed. "Yes, Great Shimusogo Chimípu."

And then she was gone in a rush of wind and sand.

Chapter 24

Alone in the Dark

The clans of day and the clans of night will only talk over naked blades.

— Chidomifu Kapōra

Rutejìmo sat alone in the dark.

Only an hour ago, the sun had dipped below the horizon, but it felt like years. He stared at the alchemical flame in the center of the ruined campsite. The normally pale light was painfully bright in the inky darkness of the desert.

Remembering how Tsubàyo stepped out of the night, Rutejìmo had spread out the glow eggs in a large circle. Each one was a tiny pool of flickering blue light, a weak illumination but he hoped enough to give him a second's warning if Tsubàyo came for him.

He couldn't sleep. He didn't realize how much he depended on having the other two near him. Knowing that Chimípu watched over him had given him a peace of mind, at least quelled the fears enough for him to sleep. Alone once again, he didn't dare crawl into either of the remaining tents in fear that he would never wake up. He kept seeing Karawàbi's corpse.

Sighing, he dug into the meat pouch and snapped off a wing. Fitting it on a stick, he set it over the fire and waited for it to warm up. The alchemical mixture inside the pouch had cooked the meat and killed any parasites, but gnawing on cold meat didn't appeal to his clenching stomach. Soon, the meat was warm enough to eat, and he plucked it from the fire.

He glanced up at the night sky, wondering if he should try to name the stars again. To the east, he could see the faintest sliver of the moon. He shivered in fear. Just as Tachìra was the sun, Chobìre was the spirit of the moon.

Legends said that both spirits used to be best friends, but then they both fell in love with Mifúno, the desert spirit and mother of the world. It quickly became a violent rivalry, and the two clans, clans of day and clans of night, were drawn into the conflict. He shuddered, remembering the horror stories his grandmother had told him about Chobìre and the clans who gained power from the dark spirit.

Tearing his thoughts away, he chewed on his dinner. The meat was heavily spiced, and the travel pouch gave it a metallic taste. He had to force it down his dry throat.

"Sands," he muttered, "I never thought I'd be wishing for salted meat." He chuckled again. "I'm pathetic."

His brother's stories about the horrid alchemical meals hit him, and he laughed. He could understand the longing Desòchu had when he relished the meals cooking in the valley. He missed the variety of flavors and the taste of woodsmoke in the food.

The alchemical flame sizzled as grease dripped into it. The smell of roasted meat drifted across his senses, and he breathed in the smoke. He smiled and leaned back, enjoying the memories.

CHAPTER 24. ALONE IN THE DARK

And then Rutejìmo realized the smoke came from burning wood.

"You aren't going to pee again, are you?" asked Mikáryo in a soft voice.

Rutejìmo lowered his head to look over the flames. She was on the far side of the fire, and he shook at the sight of her.

She smirked as she reached over and picked up her tazágu from where it was braced between her foot and a rock. The pointed weapon had a hunk of dripping meat jammed on the top of it. Juices ran down the short spike and gathered at a circular guard above the grip. The liquid dripped from a small hook on the edge of the guard and hit the ground with faint splats.

"P-Please don't kill me."

Mikáryo looked up with a humorless smile. "Shimusogo Rute... jìbo, right?" He could barely see the white of her eyes. Her pupils were unnaturally large.

"Rutejìmo."

"Well, Jìmo"—she leaned back and pulled off the meat with her teeth—"if I wanted to kill you, I probably would have stabbed you in the throat two nights ago. And, if for some reason, I thought you were suddenly a threat, I probably would have Bàpo crush your skull in while you were staring at me."

Rutejìmo felt something looming over him. Mikáryo's horse stepped over his head. Rutejìmo didn't even feel a whisper of hair or breeze of movement as the horse continued past him, around the fire, and then settled on the ground next to Mikáryo.

She didn't look up as she held out an unfamiliar, red fruit for him.

The horse took it and chewed noisily. Rutejìmo couldn't tell if it was staring at him or something else. Like his mistress, his eyes only had the faintest of white rings around the large, black pupils.

Mikáryo leaned over to an open bag and speared more meat on the end of her weapon. She set the weapon against the rock with her boot. She pulled out another fruit, sliced it in quarters, and shoed the four parts on the point.

Rutejìmo found the courage to speak, surprised how much his body shook in fear. "What do you want, Great Pabinkue Mikáryo?"

She smiled at him. "Your little warrior girl is an idiot, isn't she?"

"Chimípu?"

Mikáryo nodded and said, "I remembered her name, but she doesn't deserve it right now. No matter how fast she runs, she'll never catch a Pabinkúe at night. She was a fool to leave you alone."

"She was—"

The woman held up her hand. "Listen, Jìmo."

Rutejìmo was uncomfortable with her using the familiar form of his name, but he was too afraid to say anything.

"I don't know what they teach the clans up here, but the night is a very dangerous place to be alone. There are things out there that hunt lone fools."

"I-I wasn't sleeping."

"You were going to stay up all night, jumping at every noise?"

"Um...."

Mikáryo shook her head. "You are young"—she grinned suddenly—"and very stupid. But I expect that of you. You're pathetic. But your little warrior girl, I'd be tempted to teach her a lesson."

He inhaled sharply.

"Not you, Jìmo. I have something more important to do than following children barely out of their diapers around the desert."

"What?"

"Your friend, Tsubàyo. He's riding Pabinkue Ryachuikùo."

"The horse?"

"Were you dropped on your head? Of course the horse."

Rutejìmo flushed hotly. He wanted to stand up and fight, but he knew he would die.

Mikáryo watched him, a slight smile on her lips.

Finally, Rutejìmo regained control of his temper. "Yes, he is riding, Great Pabinkue Mikáryo."

"I thought so. I can smell him in the wind, and he is moving too fast to be on foot."

"The Shimusògo are—"

"He's not one of your clan, is he?"

Rutejìmo hesitated, but then shook his head.

"So, tell me, Jìmo. Can he disappear into shadows?"

He gasped, then nodded.

"Did you ever see him disappear in one shadow and then not be there when you," she snorted, "excuse me, your warrior girl went after him?"

Another nod.

"Only one horse though, right?"

"Yes, Great Pabinkue Mikáryo."

"Call me Káryo, Jìmo." It was her familiar name, only used with children and close friends.

He shook his head. "No, I-I couldn't."

"Suit yourself. I don't enjoy calling anyone great. Kissing ass is for the villages and cities, not for travelers in the dark. The fight between night and day doesn't mean anything out here, does it? Not when Mitúno can keep secrets...." Her eyes glittered as she favored him with a predatory smile.

Rutejìmo tensed up, feeling like prey. There was something in her green eyes that forced him to stare into them. It was a sultry, smoldering look that brought a heat through his body. It sank down into his groin, and sudden thoughts blossomed in his head. He blushed hotly and turned away to hide his expression.

Mikáryo chuckled and relaxed. "Don't worry, boy, you have a long way to go before I consider riding you."

Rutejìmo whimpered and clamped his jaw shut as he tried to tear his thoughts away from the sudden ideas she gave him.

She laughed, a booming noise out of place of her slender body. "You are too easy, Jìmo. You also need to relax a lot more when you grow up. Otherwise, you'll rot from the inside."

He stared at the ground, unable to answer or look back.

Mikáryo said nothing, and he listened to her eating. His stomach rumbled at the smells.

She broke the silence after a few minutes. "He's a Pabinkúe, you realize."

"Tsubàyo?" Rutejìmo turned back to her, but kept his gaze averted.

She grunted in agreement. "He rides one of the horses and he can step through shadows. There is no doubt he is riding the spirit of my clan."

He finally looked up at her. "Then why don't you just take him? Then he would leave us alone."

Another smile. "The same reason your clan is watching from a distance. I want to see his measure. I want to know what type of man he's becoming."

"And if he isn't the right"—he gulped—"type of man?"

She lifted up her weapon. "You are at that wonderful crux of being a man and a boy. No one ever says you have to live through your rites."

A strange thought drifted through Rutejìmo's mind. He imagined Karawàbi's death, but it was his brother cutting the teenager's throat. He shook his head to clear it. "No, he couldn't," he whispered before he raised his voice for her. "Mikáryo? Did you kill Karawàbi?"

"Karawàbi? I don't know him, but I haven't killed anyone in months."

CHAPTER 24. ALONE IN THE DARK

The image came up again, and Rutejìmo force it out of his mind. Desòchu would never kill another member of the clan.

Mikáryo added more meat to the end of her tazágu and set it over the fading flames.

Rutejìmo yawned, the exhaustion dragging him down. He blinked and tried to stay awake.

When the meat was done, she picked up her weapon and held it out to him, point first. "Here."

Rutejìmo stared at her in surprise.

"Take it. A boy like you needs food. Maybe when you grow up, you won't be so helpless."

"T-Thank you, Great...." he trailed off at her glare. "Thank you, Káryo." He slipped the meat off, the heat searing his fingers.

She gave an approving nod.

Rutejìmo nibbled on his meal. It was juicy and rich in flavor, but he couldn't place the type. It tasted like roasted snake. In a few seconds, he was licking his fingers clean. "Thank you," he said in a quiet voice.

Mikáryo chuckled, her gaze never leaving him. She had a strange smile on her lips.

"What?"

"Oh," she said, "when you aren't peeing yourself, you are almost adorably pathetic."

Rutejìmo blushed. "I don't mean to."

"I noticed. I watched you trying to be brave for a while now. The boy I thought I saw earlier would have been cowering in a tent or against the rocks. But you are pretending to be a warrior, standing guard over yourself."

"Um...."

"That's a compliment, Jìmo."

"Oh, thank you, Káryo."

"Good boy." She smiled again and speared a piece of fruit with her weapon. She lifted it to Rutejìmo, who took it. It had a sweet taste with a hint of spices.

The horse stood up, took a few steps, and sank back down behind Mikáryo. She leaned back against his side and crossed her arms. "Go to sleep, Jìmo. We'll watch over you."

"Why?"

"Because you can't guard yourself while you sleep."

"No, why… why didn't you kill me? Why are you helping?"

Mikáryo smiled and reached up to stroke her horse's mane. "Because, a long time ago, I was also young and stupid. I thought I could take on the sun and hold back the light. I couldn't and I failed." A sad smile crossed her face. "If it wasn't for a kind soul, I would be just bones on the rocks. I'm just returning the favor, Jìmo. Nothing more."

She pointed to the standing tents. "So sleep. You'll wake up safe in the morning. I promise."

Chapter 25

Lessons Taught

<blockquote>Children in the desert have a special place, beyond the wars of night and day.

— Kimichyufi Garèki</blockquote>

Rutejìmo woke to the smells of a wood fire and cooking meat.
 He snapped open his eyes and stared up at the unfamiliar tent above him. For a moment, he didn't know where he was, but as the events of the night drifted through his mind, he remembered crawling into Pidòhu's tent. He rolling on his stomach and peered out between the gap between the tent flaps.
 It was still night, but barely. There was a sharp edge where sunlight began to reach over the horizon, but the desert remained in shadows. The air was crisp, and he felt the bite of the night's coolness against his skin.
 He crawled out and stood up. He breathed in the exotic scent of wood and followed it to a campfire.

Mikáryo had her back to him as she crouched over the flames. She had stripped down to a loincloth and a black top that wrapped around her chest. She balanced on the balls of her feet, which she had dug into the sand. Black tattoos covered her entire body, except for a bare patch centered on her spine. The unmarked area of her skin was in the shape of a horse head. She had fresh wounds across her back and arms that he hadn't notice the night before. Dark-gray bandages wrapped over them, but there were bright-crimson stains in the center.

Even with her injuries, he remembered the look she gave him over the fire. She was exotic, and he had became painfully aware of her femininity and strength. A strange tingle ran along his skin, an unfamiliar sensation. And then it was gone, leaving behind only a pounding heartbeat.

She looked over her shoulder at him, her eyes dark and a smile across her brown lips. "You aren't ready for that, Jìmo."

"I-I—"

"You should just stop talking," she said wryly. "You'll just embarrass yourself."

Rutejìmo sighed. "Sorry, Great Pabinkue—" He hesitated at the glare ghosting across her face. "Káryo."

"Good. Now, come over here and eat. You need to eat. And Tachìra will be rising in a half hour"—she gestured to the brightening horizon—"and he and my clan don't always see eye-to-eye."

He inched forward as she spoke and looked at the hunks of meat sizzling on both of her tazágu. It was the same meal as the previous night, but far better than the rations or the meat from the alchemical bag.

"Eat so I can have my weapons back."

Grabbing a wooden board, he eased the meat from the spike and sat back. "Káryo?"

Mikáryo stood a rod away, wrapping the long black cloth around her body. She had one foot up on her horse as she covered her leg. "Yes?"

"Why are you doing this?"

She looked back at him, shook her head with a smile, and returned back to dressing. "You keep asking that. Do you not like the answer?"

"No, but you're a clan of the...."

"Oh," she said, "you want to know why the evil murdering, stealing, and no doubt raping, assassin of the night is helping the noble warrior of light and justice?"

Rutejìmo blushed hotly. "I'm not a noble warrior."

"And that," she said in a whisper as she strolled closer, "is why I'm helping you." She reached down and caught his chin with her fingers.

His heart thumped, and he felt the burn of embarrassment searing his cheeks.

"You are utterly helpless. Pathetically, in fact." She smiled, one corner of her lips curling with her amusement.

Rutejìmo's emotions turned to a sharp anger.

Mikáryo chuckled and released him. She bounded back to her horse, the long cloth trailing behind her. When she reached her mount, she braced her foot on his flanks and drew up the fabric. "Your little warrior girl should have never left you."

"She was going after Pidòhu."

"But you don't leave your clan alone. Especially not one as clueless and vulnerable as yourself." She gestured to the meat in front of him.

Getting used to her insults, Rutejìmo grabbed the food and began to eat.

"I almost didn't come down here," Mikáryo chuckled, "but let's say the decision was made for me."

"By who?"

She gestured toward the rocks. "Finish eating first. And then wake up your warrior girl."

"Chimípu? She's here?" He started to stand up.

"Eat, then wake her up," commanded Mikáryo.

He dropped back down. "Yes, Káryo."

Grinning, she moved to her other leg. Her hands were sure and graceful as she covered her body. By the time she finished dressing in the dark cloth, Rutejìmo was licking the last of the juices from his fingers.

Standing up, he hurried toward the tents just as Chimípu came around the boulder. He stopped. "Mípu?"

Chimípu glanced at him, then at the boulders. Her face was pale. "I'm sorry, Jìmo, I couldn't save Pidòhu."

He cocked his head, trying to figure out the proper response, but she wasn't done.

"And I failed you."

"What? No, you were defending your clan."

Chimípu glanced back around the boulders, in the direction Mikáryo had pointed earlier. She turned back. "I shouldn't have left." Without another word, she pushed past him and headed toward the fire.

Curious, Rutejìmo headed back around the rocks. His feet scuffed along the ground as he walked. He didn't see anything until he came around the far edge, but he smelled blood. A tremor ran down his spine as he inched forward, peeking around the last rock.

Behind the boulder was the largest snake he had ever seen. It was over a hundred feet, maybe even two chains. The creature's jaw was larger than his head. One of the fangs had been snapped off but the other was buried in the ground. The black, unseeing eyes seem to stare at him.

Along the side, in the fleshy underbelly, he could see where Mikáryo had been carving out hunks of the dead snake, his dinner and breakfast. Footsteps marked the sand and rock. He could see swaths carved out from the charge of Mikáryo's horse and even Chimípu's footprints as she went out to investigate it.

"Don't."

He jumped at Mikáryo's voice.

She continued, "Don't say anything to your warrior girl. No reason to beat a corpse I've already killed." She patted him on the shoulder. "I think she figured out the lesson."

Mikáryo walked past him. She made no noise in the sand as she passed, just the black shadow of a body flowing along the ground. She knelt down at the jaw of the snake and forced it open. She kept pulling until there was a muted crack.

Rutejìmo jumped at the noise. He cleared his throat to cover his embarrassment. "What did she learn?" He didn't want the answer, but had to hear it.

"If you leave the weak alone in the dark, there is a good chance you'll come back to a corpse." Mikáryo glanced at him, her eyes hard.

Rutejìmo shivered. "I should thank you, shouldn't I?"

She tore the snake's fang out of its mouth. Blood sluggishly ran from the gaping wound. Holding it with both hands, she slammed it down repeatedly on a rock until the tip of the fang snapped off. She snatched the tip from the ground and walked over to Rutejìmo holding it. She pressed the fang and a length of leather into his palm.

He stared down at it. His throat was dry.

"But you, Jìmo, are a bit too slow for lessons like these. So," she said as she folded his fingers over the fang, "wear this until you learn your place in your clan. You are like a wounded rabbit out here, and if you don't grow up, you'll be a vulture's dinner before long."

Rutejìmo stared into her eyes for a long moment. "Thank you, Great Pabinkue Mikáryo."

She left him to his thoughts.

He walked around the snake twice, trying to remember the fear from being so close to death, and then returned to the dying fire.

Chimípu had finished eating and left Mikáryo's two tazágu on the empty board. She was pulling down the tents and tearing apart Pidòhu's frame, moving with rapid speed, and keeping her back to Mikáryo. When she did look back, it was to glare at the Pabinkúe woman.

"So, little warrior girl—" drawled Mikáryo.

Chimípu stiffened.

"—do you remember which direction you were running blindly in the dark?"

With a nod, Chimípu finished packing Rutejìmo's pack. She tossed it aside and started on her own.

"Do you know where Pabinkue Bàyo will be tonight?"

"I can find him," snapped Chimípu.

"I have no doubt about that. But, for Jìmo's sake, I recommend that you head to a set of Wind's Teeth about thirty leagues in that direction." She pointed to the south. "There is a large arch a number of chains in length and maybe a chain or so in height. He'll be there."

Chimípu glared at her. "How do you know?"

"Some generations back, the Pabinkúe lost a battle there, and a lot of our blood was shed on those sands. He doesn't know it, but he'll be drawn there. The spirits always return to their blood."

"Why should I trust you?"

Rutejìmo opened his mouth, but Chimípu silenced him with a glare.

"You don't or you do"—Mikáryo shrugged—"I don't care either way. But, if you leave Jìmo alone in the dark again, who is going to save him?"

He flushed, but forced himself to remain silent.

Chimípu stalked toward Mikáryo. "Are you threatening him?"

CHAPTER 25. LESSONS TAUGHT

Mikáryo seemed unperturbed. "No, little warrior girl, I'm not. I have no interest in you, Jìmo, or Pidòhu."

"Then why do you still want a sacrifice?" Chimípu dropped her hand down to her knife.

"Pabinkúe doesn't want you anymore, girl. I want Tsubàyo. He has ridden my spirit, and I cannot accept anything else."

"That isn't what you said!" The knife drew out an inch from the sheath.

"Things change like the winds of the desert. I wanted blood for my sister's death, but now Pabinkúe demands what is hers. When it comes down to it, my clan's needs will always be more important than my own."

"You can have him," Chimípu said.

Mikáryo smiled broadly. "I will, but I'd like to know if I'm cutting his throat before he reaches home or not. So, go get your little Pidòhu back and show me the man Tsubàyo will become."

"And you'll just follow to kill us?"

"No," came the reply, "I won't. This is something between the children of the clans, not from the elders. I'll watch like the ones watching you, laughing at Jìmo and wondering who will come out on top."

Rutejìmo stared down at the fang in his hand. He closed his fingers over it and felt the sharp edges cutting into his palm.

Chimípu sighed and grabbed her pack. Slinging it over her shoulder, she said, "Rutejìmo, it is time to go."

He grunted and walked around Mikáryo. At her amused snort, he gave her a guilty look but then knelt down to gather up his belongings. When he got to his pack, he discreetly looked inside for his stones. He found them wrapped in some cloth at the bottom. He also took half of Pidòhu's but left the remaining with Chimípu's rocks. He added the tooth to the cloth and shoved everything into his pocket.

Rutejìmo looked over the empty campsite and then to the woman who saved him. He peeked at the furious Chimípu and then gave Mikáryo a deep bow.

Mikáryo smiled and bowed back. "Safe journeys, Jìmo."

He turned back and caught a glare from Chimípu. Blushing, he stepped back.

Still glaring, Chimípu turned and inspected her route.

"Warrior girl." Mikáryo walked over to her, her tazágu in her hands.

Chimípu stepped back, her hand on her knife.

Moving faster than Rutejìmo could see, Mikáryo swung the tazágu.

Chimípu parried with a ring of metal.

"Your weapon is a boy's toy."

Rutejìmo flushed. Mikáryo glance at him, then grinned. "An immature boy's toy at that." She flipped the tazágu over and handed it to Chimípu hilt-first. "Warriors need real weapons, not toys."

Chimípu stared at the unmarked blade. "This is nameless."

"Yes, but my other has personal significance. And you need a weapon for the coming days."

The teenage girl's jaw tightened. "I'm about to fight someone claimed by your clan."

"So?"

"Are you telling me to kill him?"

"No," Mikáryo said, "I'm giving a little girl a real weapon because she is about to be fighting not only her life, but for two others. How she uses it is entirely on her soul, not mine."

Chimípu paled, still staring at the weapon.

"Take it as a gift. No obligations, no promises. And, if you kill someone, name it Shimusògo, not Pabinkúe."

CHAPTER 25. LESSONS TAUGHT

Sheathing the knife, Chimípu took the weapon. "Thank you, Great Pabinkue Mikáryo." The muscles in her neck tightened as she spoke.

As the sharp point slipped from Mikáryo's fingers, her body dissolved into shadows. Darkness flooded across the campsite and poured into the dark spots formed by the rocks and boulders. It passed over Rutejìmo with a wave of coolness, and then Mikáryo was gone.

Chimípu stared down at the weapon, her fingers tight around the hilt.

"Mípu?"

She looked up. Then up in the direction of Tsubàyo. "Come on, Jìmo. We have to save Pidòhu."

He was afraid she was going to say "kill Tsubàyo" but he knew it was on her thoughts.

Chapter 26

Preparing for Battle

Death should never be planned lightly.

— Kormar Proverb

Without having to drag Pidòhu, Rutejìmo ran as fast as he could. He stopped feeling the blisters on his hands or the ache in his back. His fears and self-doubts disappeared under the comforting speed and closeness to the clan spirit. There was nothing but him, Chimípu, and Shimusògo.

Even though he didn't have Tateshyúso's shadow over him, he felt neither the oppressive heat nor the sand against his feet. The heat was there, he knew it, but it didn't sap his strength or steal his breath. His feet never slipped on sand or rocks.

Ahead of him, Chimípu ran in silence. He knew she could go faster, but she was pacing him as she ran along Shimusògo. No doubt, Mikáryo's lessons were burning on her mind. He felt relieved that she wouldn't leave him, but also felt guilty that she couldn't run as fast as her powers would take her.

Before he knew it, they were slowing. He saw no sign or signal, but the wind no longer ripped along his skin, and the dépa grew hazy with every step. As he shifted from a run into a jog, the spirit disappeared from sight.

Chimípu jogged for a few chains before coming to a stop. She was breathing lightly, and her limbs glistened with a thin sheen of sweat. A triangle of sweat also soaked the collar of her shirt. As she strode up the slope of a dune, she had a set to her jaw that frightened Rutejìmo.

She reached the top and crouched down. Her knee scrunched on the sand. Rutejìmo joined her, kneeling as they peered over the dune.

A quarter mile away was the stone arch Mikáryo had described. It was on the threshold of a mountainous region, with sharp-edged cliffs and ragged rocks. The arch was on a rocky hill. The nearest side of the hill was sandy but behind it was a gentle slope leading up to the cliffs. As the wind blew, it kicked sand into eddies that disappeared beneath the shadows of the outcropping.

The arch was larger than he imagined, stretching a few hundred feet across the sands and reaching about a hundred feet at its peak. Both ends were steeply sloped to the ground; he would have been hard-pressed to climb either end. In the shadow of the arch, he saw the silhouettes of more rocks. He had no doubt they would be sharp and jagged.

Rutejìmo whispered to Chimípu, "Do you know where Dòhu is?"

She nodded silently. Her finger was rock-steady as she pointed to one end of the arch.

He followed her gesture, frowning as he focused into the shadows. He spotted Pidòhu after a few seconds. The injured boy was curled up in the shadows, clutching his leg and rocking back and

CHAPTER 26. PREPARING FOR BATTLE

forth. Rutejìmo thought he saw a puddle underneath Pidòhu and he felt sick to his stomach.

"He's hurt," Chimípu whispered back, "and bleeding."

"Where is Bàyo?"

She gestured to the rocks underneath the arch. "Hiding and waiting. It's a trap. He knows we're coming."

"What do we do?"

"He hurt Dòhu. I'll kill him." She lifted her attention to the sky. "But I need to get started. There is only about thirty minutes of sunlight left, then he gains power as I lose it." She stood up.

Rutejìmo grabbed her arm to stop her. At her glare, he shook his head. "No, not you, we. We need to stop him."

She grunted and knelt back down. "Jìmo, I have to do this. It's my"—she gulped—"duty."

"Your duty to kill… stop Tsubàyo. But that doesn't mean I can't help."

She glanced at the stone arch, then back at Rutejìmo.

"Come on, Mípu. Dòhu is our friend, and after everything, I can't give up on him now."

A smile quirked her lips. "Grew some balls last night, didn't you?"

Rutejìmo blushed.

"With the night bitch? Did you do anything else?" Her voice was sharp and probing.

He thought of Mikáryo crouching over the flames, nearly naked. He shook his head sharply even as the blush grew hotter. "No."

She stared at him for a long moment, then sighed. "Good. Stay away from her. She's evil."

Desperate to change the conversation, Rutejìmo pointed to the rocks. "So let me help."

"Okay, but promise me something. If you have a chance, you grab Pidòhu and run. Just run. Don't turn around, don't try to look for me." She leaned next to him, her breath warm on his face. "All that matters is saving Pidòhu and you."

His heart thumped loudly. Gulping, he nodded.

"I'll"—she glanced toward the arch—"catch up as soon as I can."

He said nothing as he watched the storm of expression across her face. There was doubt and anger, but also fear. He could tell she was still struggling with her duties as the clan warrior, a fighter to protect him. But the fear was something else. Guardians died protecting the couriers. She was already his guardian, and there was a very real possibility she would die that day.

There was nothing he could say. She was on her own path, and he was on his own. He rested his hand on his pocket, feeling the fang sticking through the fabric.

She would always be better than he. The realization hurt, but he finally needed to acknowledge it. He closed his eyes and sighed. "Tell me what to do, Great Shimusogo Chimípu."

It was easier to bare his throat to her knife.

Chimípu's eyes widened with surprise. Then she gave a single nod without looking at him. She hesitated for a moment, then pointed to the arch. She spoke in a tense voice, her body trembling with her emotions. "When we were practicing firing rocks at bird's nests, you weren't very accurate beyond two chains. You can run a chain in about two seconds from a dead sprint. That means you need to stay about a chain or so away and fire rocks at Tsubàyo. When you have a chance, grab Dòhu and run. You'll only have thirty, maybe forty seconds."

"That isn't a lot of time."

"He won't give you much. He can come out of the shadows in a charge. He doesn't need to accelerate, which is why he put Pidòhu there."

"You want me to wait here?"

CHAPTER 26. PREPARING FOR BATTLE

"No, he'll figure it out if you just stand there waiting." She turned and dumped her pack on the ground. "We'll start by using the packs for slingshots. Pull everything apart and make as many shots as you can."

Rutejìmo nodded and dropped next to her. He emptied his bag out on the sands before sorting everything into four piles of equal weight and size. Once finished, he turned his attention to his bag. Using his cooking knife, he tore out long strips of canvas and wrapped the fabric around each pile to create four impromptu projectiles.

Chimípu added six shots from her own bag to the pile. She raised on her knees and shrugged out of her shirt. Underneath, the white band around her chest was stained with dried blood and grime. She tore her shirt in half and braided it together into a sling that could take the strain of firing their impromptu shots.

Her muscular body was slick with sweat, and her skin was dark. Rutejìmo peeked at her, but he didn't feel the same attraction that he had for Mikáryo. Tearing his attention away, he pulled off his own shirt and formed a second sling.

When they finished, he leaned back on his heels. Ten shots from the packs and two slings didn't look like a lot. He wasn't sure if he could use them, but he felt determination rising inside him. He had to help. Even if he missed, he would be a distraction.

"Mípu?"

"Yes?" she asked as she looked back over the dune.

"Are you going to kill him?"

Her jaw tightened. "Yes." She toyed with the tazágu, tracing along the spike where a name would be. She glanced at him. "Do you...?"

He shook his head. "No. That's your choice, Great Shimusogo Chimípu."

A muscle twitched in her cheek. She finally looked at him, tears shimmering in her eyes. "But I don't know if I can. I keep thinking about it. He kidnapped Dòhu and he tried to kill me. But, when I imagine stabbing him"—her hand tightened on the hilt of her weapon—"I feel sick."

He reached out and rested his hand on her shoulder. The muscles underneath bunched up for a moment, then she rested her palm over his wrist.

Neither said anything for a long moment.

She broke the silence as she stood up, letting his hand slip from between her palm and shoulder.

He pulled back and stared up at her, frightened but determined to do his part.

"Come on, Jìmo. It is time to fight."

"Yes, Great Shimusogo Chimípu."

She gestured to the ten shots they made at their feet. "And don't miss."

Chapter 27

Pabinkue Tsubàyo

It takes only a single word to ruin a surprise.

— Ralador Markin, *A Girl's Secret*

Rutejìmo came sliding to a halt along the flat patch of sand Chimípu had pointed out. It had a thin crust over the top and, when he stopped, it cracked underneath his weight. He stumbled as he sank down an inch into the softer layer. Some of the projectiles spilled out of his arms and hit the ground in a series of thumps.

He glanced over his shoulder and watched Chimípu circle around to the far end of the arch. A plume of sand and dust rose behind her, billowing out and adding to the haze from a light breeze rippling across the desert. She straightened into a line and sprinted for the arch, her body blurring as she accelerated for an attack.

Bile rose in his throat, and he turned away sharply. As much as he hated Tsubàyo for what he did, kidnapping Pidòhu and killing Mikáryo's sister, he couldn't bear the thought of seeing the teenager's death. Karawàbi's corpse still haunted him. In the last few days, he realized he didn't have the taste to even imagine killing someone.

He looked back just as Chimípu reached the arch. From their plan, she would draw Tsubàyo out of the darkness and into the sands where he didn't have shadows to hide in. Rutejìmo imagined Chimípu watching the shadows warily as she approached. Her tazágu glinted in the sunlight as she held it ready to strike.

As she came in, the shadows bulged out and Tsubàyo came barreling out of the darkness on the back of his horse. He crouched low to the black creature with a spear in his hand. They moved as a single creature. Rutejìmo didn't know where Tsubàyo had gotten a spear until he realized it was Tsubàyo's knife tied to the end of a tent pole, crude but no doubt effective.

Tsubàyo's horse lashed out at Chimípu, teeth snapping in air.

She dodged to the side. Her momentum blasted through the sand as she planted her foot on one of the fallen rocks. The impact stopped her instantly, and the rock cracked in half from her speed. Before the sand settled down, she kicked off, rolled backward into a jump, and landed on her feet. Sand rose in the air as she dove underneath the horse and accelerated away from the arch, but at a far slower rate than her top speed.

Tsubàyo charged after her. As he and his horse ran along the dunes, he readied his spear to attack.

Feeling guilty for not responding faster, Rutejìmo grabbed the sling and a shot. He set the bundle in the center of the sling, made sure it was secure, and then spun on his heels. He could feel the shot tugging away from him, but he wasn't moving fast enough. Trying to remember the sensation when he practiced earlier, he threw himself into each rotation.

CHAPTER 27. PABINKUE TSUBÀYO

When Shimusògo appeared at his feet, his spin accelerated, and the sand rose up in a vortex around him.

Between the rotations, he saw Tsubàyo reach Chimípu and attack. His spear slashed out in a wide swath. It left a faint blue haze as it cut through the air.

Chimípu ducked at the last minute, and the blade narrowly avoided her. She spun on her heels and grabbed at the shaft. She missed but yanked her tazágu up before Tsubàyo's backswing struck her.

Rutejìmo felt himself getting up to speed. With a grunt, he released the end of the sling, and the shot rocketed across the sands. The speed tore up the ground, sucking sand and dust behind it in a long trail as it cracked through the air.

He stumbled as he watched it. It flew straight, but it would miss. Swearing, he fumbled as he grabbed another shot. He jammed it into the sling and violently spun up to speed.

The first shot slammed into the ground a rod behind Tsubàyo. Neither Tsubàyo nor Chimípu would have noticed the miss, but the impact launched shrapnel and sand everywhere. A cloud of rocks and camping supplies blossomed out.

In the rain of sand, Tsubàyo ducked against the horse, and the equine spun on his forelegs. The creature's back legs snapped out and caught Chimípu in the chest. The impact hit with an explosion of air.

Chimípu rocketed out of the cloud, flying backward. She hit the ground on her feet. Her hands dug into the sand, gouging out a long line. As soon as she came to a stop, she shot forward again, holding her spiked weapon with both hands.

Tsubàyo sprinted back for the shadows. He reached them and disappeared just as Chimípu caught up to him.

Chimípu raced into the darkness of the arch, her body igniting in golden flames. But, as the light peeled back the darkness, Tsubàyo was gone. She continued under the arch and came out the other side, the wind howling around her as she circled around it in a wide loop.

Tsubàyo stepped back out of the shadows a few feet away from Pidòhu. A cruel smile was on his face as he looked around. He stopped when he met Rutejìmo's gaze and then gave a little wave as if they were friends.

With a snarl, Rutejìmo fired the shot in his sling.

Tsubàyo shook his head. Just before the shot hit him, the horse stepped back, and Rutejìmo missed. It hit the rock near Pidòhu and exploded, showering him in rock dust.

Pidòhu cowered against the rock, and his wail rose up over the thuds of falling stones.

Rutejìmo gasped and cringed. "Sorry," he said, even though Pidòhu couldn't hear him.

The shadows swelled before peeling away from Tsubàyo. From the back of the horse, Tsubàyo yelled out cheerfully, "Don't hit Dòhu, Jìmo!"

Pidòhu continued to cry out in pain. Even in the shadows, Rutejìmo could see him clutching his broken leg as he tried to cower against the rocks.

Guilt slammed into Rutejìmo, and he wiped the tears from his eyes. He wasn't a warrior, he couldn't fight.

Chimípu jumped through the darkness as a translucent dépa appeared over her body. The flames around her became blindingly bright as she landed on the back of the horse. She slashed with her weapon, a blow aimed for Tsubàyo's throat.

Tsubàyo's spear flashed. He parried Chimípu's attack but slid back from the horse. Only a frantic grab of the mane kept him seated.

Chimípu screamed in rage as she swung at his face, punching him across the jaw.

The horse reared up. Tsubàyo flowed with the movement, but Chimípu tumbled off. With a jump forward, the creature lurched

CHAPTER 27. PABINKUE TSUBÀYO

forward, landed on its front legs, and kicked hard.

The world exploded around the two fighters, a large cloud of sand bursting out with blinding speed. Chimípu's glowing body was flung back across the stone arch and slammed into the far end. Even with the thunder rolling across the sands, he heard the dull crack of the impact.

Her flame died out as she fell to the ground in the darkness, disappearing as the sand rained down around her.

Rutejìmo gasped. He fumbled with the shots at his feet. One slipped through his fingers and he swore violently. He glanced up to the battle.

Tsubàyo stalked Chimípu, and his horse stepped easily around the rocks.

Whimpering with frustration, Rutejìmo grabbed a shot and set it in the sling. He threw himself into a spin as he stood up. He put everything he could into moving and he felt the power ripping through his limbs.

He released the sling and grabbed a second shot without slowing. Wrapping it into the sling, he spun violently and fired before the first attack hit.

Both projectiles tore across the ground. To his surprise, both of them were burning with light as they shone like two stars racing across the desert. He could feel the crack of air as they streaked at Tsubàyo's back.

He held his breath while he watched the shot. It left his lungs in a moan of despair when the first only clipped Tsubàyo's ear before rocketing past the arch and into the rocks beyond.

Startled, Tsubàyo jerked in the opposite direction and stumbled into the path of the second. The world seemed to slow down as the second projectile punched into the side of the black horse and exploded.

The horse stumbled as it staggered back.

Tsubàyo grabbed the creature's mane to keep his balance.

Chimípu burst into flames as she launched herself out of the darkness. Her scream of rage echoed as she grabbed Tsubàyo with both hands. She tore him off the horse and threw him out into the sunlight.

Tsubàyo scrambled to his feet, but Chimípu raced past him. For a moment, Rutejìmo thought she had passed him, but then he saw that she dragged Tsubàyo by his arms. Tsubàyo's head bounced on the sand as she crested a dune.

Shimusògo appeared in front of Chimípu, already spinning in a circle. Chimípu grabbed Tsubàyo's arm with both hands and wrenched him into a spin of her own.

Tsubàyo's scream rose in waves as he was pulled out from her arm, his legs flailing around helplessly. Rutejìmo found it hard to focus as Chimípu continued to accelerate, spinning Tsubàyo like a slingshot. Their bodies blurred as a vortex of dust around her.

She released him.

Tsubàyo cried out he sailed across the sands. The air howled around him, rippling as he hit the dune. He struck the first dune on his shoulders, and the impact flipped him over. He bounced off and hit the second, and then the third. The fourth dune exploded as Tsubàyo crashed into it and rolled over the far side.

"Jìmo! Get Pidòhu!" Chimípu spun on her heels and raced back to the far end of the arch. She blurred as she rushed through. On the other side, she was holding the tazágu. She came into a wide circle as she charged after Tsubàyo.

Gasping, Rutejìmo scrambled back to his feet and sprinted for Pidòhu. The air rushed around him as he covered the distance in a few seconds and came to a sliding halt in front of Pidòhu. "Dòhu!"

Pidòhu looked up with tears in his eyes. His hands were bloody as he clutched his leg. The sharp ends of his bones stuck through his fingers. The coppery stench surrounded him as he shook. "J-Jìmo." He gave a pained smile. "I can't say how happy I am to see you."

Panting, Rutejìmo knelt down next to him. "Yeah, me too." He looked over Pidòhu. "Um, I don't know if I can safely carry you."

"I'll take all the pain if it gets me away from Bàyo."

"You should call him Tsubàyo; he isn't a friend anymore."

"Yeah," Pidòhu groaned, "but I'm having trouble remembering through the agony."

With a grim smile, Rutejìmo inched closer and slid his hands underneath Pidòhu.

Hot air struck the back of Rutejìmo's neck. He froze as a horse exhaled again. He could feel the threat, and his body began to shake. Looking up, he saw Pidòhu staring over his shoulder.

"J-Jìmo?" whispered Pidòhu.

Rutejìmo gulped, his body tensing painfully. "I'm about to get hurt, aren't I?"

A soft whimper escaped Pidòhu's throat. He gave a little nod.

"Sands," muttered Rutejìmo. He yanked his hands from Pidòhu and lurched to his feet. He felt the horse launching forward and dodged to the side.

The horse's teeth snapped on empty air.

Rutejìmo saw a flash of movement in the darkness. Dread filled him as he picked out the shadowed image of a second horse just as it kicked out with its back legs. He had a chance to inhale as the hooves hit his chest.

The world exploded into agony as his ribs cracked and his vision blurred into white. He clutched as his chest, trying to think through the pain. Rutejìmo could feel the wind whistling around him but it took him a heartbeat to realize he wasn't touching the ground.

He tried to inhale to yell out, but his lungs wouldn't work. The world flew past and the desert became a blur of sand and rock. He tried to move, but every twitch ended in agony.

Rutejìmo hit the sand hard, and the impact felt like rock against his skin. It tore the flesh along his back and arms before he bounced off and flew in a low arc to slam hard into the ground. The impact ground his cracked ribs into each other, and he sobbed at the agony. He tore at his chest, trying to force his lungs to work.

Sand crunched as someone walked up to him. "Did you know," asked Tsubàyo with a dry chuckle, "that I found more horses? Very useful, being able to command them without words. They'll do anything for me, including wait in the shadows for an idiot going for a cripple. Though, I was hoping that Mípu would get to Dòhu first. The look on her face would have made this all worth it."

Rutejìmo looked up with surprise. He gaped but he couldn't draw in a breath. He clawed at his throat as he crawled back.

Tsubàyo stepped down on Rutejìmo's foot and pinned him. "But I don't have time to chat."

He lifted the spear and held it with both hands.

Air rushed into Rutejìmo's lungs, and he could breathe again. He gasped for breath but couldn't look away from the spear poised to strike.

The flaming shot hit Tsubàyo square in the back, throwing him over Rutejìmo. It exploded in shreds of canvas and bedding. The spikes for the tents clipped Rutejìmo as they slammed into the ground.

A second, third, and fourth shot hit Tsubàyo in rapid succession, each one exploding as they picked Tsubàyo off the ground and tossed him like a pebble.

Stunned, Rutejìmo scrambled to his feet and stared as Tsubàyo hit the sands one last time. Every time Rutejìmo inhaled, he could feel sharp pains in his chest, but seeing Tsubàyo laid out gave him a fierce joy.

CHAPTER 27. PABINKUE TSUBÀYO

Behind him, Rutejìmo heard the rush of both Chimípu and a horse charging toward them.

Tsubàyo picked himself up, stumbling back as he clutched his head. "I'm ending this." His eyes flickered to the side.

Feeling a prickle of fear, Rutejìmo followed the gaze. Tsubàyo had focused on Pidòhu. In the darkness above the injured teenager, the shadows bulged out as the second horse stepped from the darkness.

Rutejìmo jerked. "Mípu! Save Dòhu now!" Even as he yelled, he knew she couldn't turn around fast enough.

In the shadows, the horse stepped over Pidòhu and lifted a hoof. It was poised to crush his head.

Pidòhu looked up, his eyes white in the shadows.

Moving instinctively, Rutejìmo reached out for Chimípu. "Spin!"

She grabbed his wrists, and he spun with all his might. Her momentum tore through him, and he felt muscles ripping and his ribs grinding into each other as he brought her around in a tight circle.

Working by instinct, he released her and she shot out in a flash of light for the horse and Pidòhu, moving faster than he had ever seen her move. It was like firing a slingshot, but using her as the ammunition.

The first horse, the one charging Rutejìmo, slammed into his side. The impact blasted him across the sand.

Rutejìmo screamed out in pain as he flew through the air, but then he hit the sand hard, and the impact drove the air out of him again. He flailed on the sand, trying to get purchase.

A hoof slammed down on his left forearm, and he heard bones crack. A heartbeat later, the pain tore through his senses, and he couldn't help but scream in agony. His entire body spasmed as he curled around the hoof, trying to move the massive weight off the grinding bones.

A high-pitched squeal cut through his panic. Rutejìmo jerked and looked over his shoulder as the second horse dropped to the ground. A blood spray arched high into the air before splattering down. It flailed its legs as it struggled to get back up.

Chimípu stood over Pidòhu, guarding him. Her tazágu dripped with blood as she snarled. Her body flickered with flames as she kept the point of her weapon aimed toward the creature's throat.

Tsubàyo let out a growl and swung himself on the horse pinning Rutejìmo. "Come on, let's save Ryachuikùo before she kills him." He chuckled as he looked down at Rutejìmo. He spoke in a low voice. "But your precious Mípu won't be able to save him from Ganifúma."

Rutejìmo froze when a memory slammed into him. Mikáryo had named Tsubàyo's horse Pabinkue Ryachuikùo. He glanced down at the horse underneath Tsubàyo. It was male and couldn't be Ganifúma, a female's name. With a start, he realized that Tsubàyo said horses, and Rutejìmo knew there were more.

He gasped and snapped his head around. The shadow next to Chimípu became suddenly threatening, and he imagined seeing something moving in the darkness. Panic tore through him. He inhaled before yelling as loud as he could. "Run!"

Chimípu's head jerked as she looked him.

"Run, damn it, run!"

Tsubàyo sighed and shook his head. His horse kicked out, catching Rutejìmo under the chin and slamming him back into the ground.

There was an explosion of movement and a howl of wind from near the arch.

Rutejìmo lifted his head, but his eyes weren't focusing. He saw a light burning across the desert, moving away from him faster than he could ever run. He knew that she carried Pidòhu.

His thoughts ended when Tsubàyo's horse kicked again.

Chapter 28

The Offer

> Over the centuries, the clans have specialized not only in their powers but what services they offer the world.
>
> — Jastor, *A Tactical Analysis of Kyōti Politics*

Rutejimo woke up crying. He could feel the tears running down his cheeks and his chest shuddering with every gasping sob, but he couldn't figure out how to stop. It felt as though his body was disconnected from his mind and he could only listen to himself as he pitifully cried.

He tried to lift his hand to wipe the tears from his face, but nothing happened. He slumped forward and winced as he felt bones grinding. Gasping for breath, he continued to sob as he tried to focus on his chest. It rose and felt with his ragged breathing, but someone had bound his arms to his sides with rope.

There was only one person who would have tied him up: Tsubàyo.

With a struggle, he lifted his head and looked around him. His eyes were blurred from the tears, and a fire in front of him blinded him. He slumped back, hitting his head against rock, and looked up. It took a moment for him to focus on the stars and not the pain of hitting his head.

Moving helped with his crying, and he managed to calm his ragged breaths. He gulped to ease his dry throat and looked back down at his bindings.

Tsubàyo had tied ropes around him: one around the pectorals and below his shoulders, another at his waist, and two on his legs. They dug into his sides, and the pressure ground his ribs together. Morbidly, he focused on his arm. A bruise had already formed on the skin and it was swollen. He concentrated on moving his fingers, but stopped when pain shot up into his shoulder.

Memories of Pidòhu's broken leg flashed through his mind, of the ragged wound and blood pooling underneath. His breath quickened, and he leaned to the side, looking for signs of an open wound. When he saw no puddles of blood or stains on the sand, he let out a sob of relief.

"Please tell me you are done babbling," grumbled Tsubàyo.

Rutejìmo peered across a fire at the teenager on the other side. The shadows cast Tsubàyo in relief, highlighting the scar tissue on the side of his head. He had bruises and cuts on his face. Only a tiny arc of Tsubàyo's glare was visible through Tsubàyo's swollen right eye.

"W-What?" Rutejìmo's voice was broken and raspy.

Tsubàyo shook his head. "You've been moaning and babbling for the last six hours. I thought if I hit you in the head again, you'd shut up, but I was afraid of killing you."

Rutejìmo groaned through a piercing headache and the agony of his broken bones. "Did Mípu get away?"

"Yes, and she took my sacrifice with her."

"Sacrifice?" He let out a sigh. "Pidòhu got away?"

CHAPTER 28. THE OFFER

"Yeah, which means you'll be Pabinkúe's sacrifice. You aren't really worth more than that."

He tensed. "Mikáryo?"

Tsubàyo let out a groan as he stood up. "You said three nights, but she hasn't shown up. I've been awake all night waiting for her." He sighed and stretched. "The strange part is that I'm not tired at night. It feels"—he smiled—"good. And I see things I never saw before. The desert is alive, Jìmo, but you'll never find out."

"She won't...." His voice trailed off with the feeling that he shouldn't say anything.

"Won't what?"

"I hope she kills you," he finished uncomfortably.

"Well, if she doesn't come before the sun rises"—Tsubàyo pulled out his knife—"then I'll make sure it will be your last."

Rutejìmo stared at the blade through the flames. It was named, but Tsubàyo had scraped off the runes for Shimusògo. It was one more sign that Tsubàyo had turned away from the clan. In the blade, he saw the light of the rising sun reflected in the metal. It was less than an hour before morning.

"Have no fear, Jìmo. I'll cut your throat nice and clean. I'll even give you a chance to see Tachìra one last time."

Memories slammed into Rutejìmo, and he choked back a fresh sob. "Did you kill Karawàbi?"

"Wàbi?" Tsubàyo frowned. "What are you talking about? I don't care what that slow-witted rock was doing. He would have just slowed me down."

"He's dead."

Tsubàyo hesitated, and then he shrugged. "The world is better without him."

"Why? We were all clan."

"You are an idiot, Jìmo, but you didn't listen. Instead of going with me, you ran back to Mípu like a little baby boy. Maybe Mikáryo's sister would be alive if you hadn't abandoned me."

"I didn't abandon you, Bàyo." Rutejìmo shifted and cringed at the pain. "Shimusògo didn't abandon us. I can run. Have you seen—?"

"Yes, you can run. But I found something better." He gestured to the three horses standing just outside of the circle of flames. One of them had fabric wrapped around its chest; it was stained crimson from Chimípu's attack. Each time it inhaled, it struggled to breathe. Another, the mare, leaned against the injured horse while the third rested on the ground.

"There is power in the herd. I can feel them in my head. It's a song," Tsubàyo's voice grew dazed, "and it's beautiful. Better than running in the sun or that pitiful life we had in the valley. No, as soon as I'm done with her, I'm going to take my little herd and I'm going to run. I don't care about Shimusògo or Pabinkúe."

"And," said Mikáryo as she stepped out of the darkness, "what if Pabinkúe won't let you run?" Her voice was tense and threatening, but didn't rise above a low tone.

Behind her, her horse circled around the light, moving with the same shadowy silence it always did. The other three horses lifted their heads as Mikáryo's mount approached them.

Tsubàyo hissed and brandished his knife at her. His foot scraped sand as he prepared for an attack.

Mikáryo circled the flames after him with a grim smile on her face. The dark fabric wrapping her body shifted with her movements, but didn't even make a rustle of noise. She held her left hand against her side, and Rutejìmo noticed she had the tazágu half-hidden in the folds of cloth.

Tsubàyo continued to back away from her. "What do you want?" Sweat glistened on his brow as he stared at her.

"Oh," Mikáryo said, "I've been listening to you screaming into the dark for a few hours now. Well, you have my attention, boy. What do you want?"

Tsubàyo stepped over Rutejìmo's legs. He waved the knife at him in a dismissive gesture. "You demanded a life. There he is."

Mikáryo didn't even look at Rutejìmo. "That boy? He's pathetic. He peed his own pants when I first met him."

Tsubàyo chuckled. "Sounds like Jìmo. He was always the weakest next to Dòhu... Pidòhu."

Rutejìmo flushed in humiliation.

"Yes. But," Mikáryo said as she stepped over to Rutejìmo, "that would make him a pathetic sacrifice, wouldn't it?"

Tsubàyo clenched the hilt of his knife tighter. "A life is a life."

"There are many different types of lives in the world, boy." Mikáryo strolled after Tsubàyo. She moved with an unhurried grace, her body swaying as she stalked after him. "And I'm thinking that Pabinkúe would be greatly interested in the"—she smiled—"richness of your life."

Tsubàyo stepped back and shook his head. "No, not me. Take him."

Mikáryo stopped. She finally looked at Rutejìmo. But he didn't see compassion in her eyes, only a cold, calculating look.

His stomach clenched at her dark eyes, the pupils hiding the whites completely. There was death in Mikáryo's gaze, and he wondered if the compassion she showed earlier was just a lie. Stories of the clan of night rushed through his mind, and a soft whimper rose in his throat.

She glided across the sands and knelt, one knee on either side of his. Her eyes looked over him and he wanted to crawl away from her cruel eyes.

"You," she said in a whisper, "are adorably pathetic, Jìmo."

He gasped and his eyes widened as he stared at her.

"But keep looking frightened. Otherwise, I'll have to gut you."

He whimpered.

"Just like that," she said with the barest hint of a smile.

Rutejìmo gulped, trying to ease the tightness in his throat. He trembled as she reached out and touched his leg. Her skin was cool and dry against his heated flesh.

"You have a fever." She trailed two fingernails up his leg.

He squirmed and she chuckled. He stared in shock as she pressed against his stomach, then up to his ribs. At the pressure, he hissed before she could reach his broken rib.

"That hurts?"

He whimpered and whispered, his voice cracking. "A-And my arm."

"Pathetic." She leaned into him as she stood up.

Rutejìmo froze when he felt the brush of her lips against his, but then she was turning away from him. He blushed hotly as he stared at her, unsure of what to say or what to do.

"He's too weak for Pabinkúe. My sister was worth twice him."

Tsubàyo snarled. "Then kill the bastard." He hefted his knife.

Rutejìmo tried to push away, but his feet just dragged through the sand and rocks. Every movement sent agony coursing up his arms and along his ribs. He ached from the inside, but the murderous look in Tsubàyo's eyes allowed no compassion.

Tsubàyo circled around the fire.

Mikáryo looked up sharply. A frown ghosted across her face, and then she smiled broadly. "Tsubàyo," she said. She lowered her head, and the smile dropped from her face. "You have other concerns to worry about."

"Like what?"

"As much as you pretend that Pabinkúe doesn't talk to you, I know you can hear her. That song? That's her. Your lovely horses that are coming to you? Those were my sister's."

Tsubàyo froze, his blade only a few feet away from Rutejìmo. He looked over his shoulder.

"Yes, the woman you killed. Someone has to lead her herd, and we have a job to do. The Kidokūku clan should have that scorpion of theirs ready to move tomorrow, and we must be ready."

Tsubàyo turned back to Rutejìmo. He gripped the knife tighter, staring at Rutejìmo.

"We have a job, Pabinkue Tsubàyo," Mikáryo said as she stepped closer, "and your little pissing match with Jìmo isn't going to help anyone."

Tsubàyo spun on his heels, brandishing his knife. "I won't go with you! I am not Pabinkúe!"

Mikáryo chuckled. "We'll find out in about an hour." She turned and headed toward the edge of light.

He shook his head. "An hour!? What's in an hour?"

She only smiled as she disappeared into the darkness.

Tsubàyo's feet thudded the ground as he stalked toward where she had stood. "What's in an hour!? Damn it! What's in an hour?"

"Kill Jìmo," her voice drifted from the dark, "and you'll find out sooner. Otherwise, in an hour, you'll be Pabinkue Tsubàyo or dead."

"Come out!" Tsubàyo yelled, "And tell me what is going on!"

There was only silence, except for the hiss and pop of the flames.

Tsubàyo spun back to Rutejìmo. He stormed over, his knife flashing.

Rutejìmo cringed away, but he couldn't move fast enough to avoid Tsubàyo as he crouched in front of him. He felt the cool blade on his neck, the sharp edge pressing against his delicate skin.

"I should kill you right here." He pushed harder, and Rutejìmo felt the flesh parting. A trickle of blood ran down his neck.

Terror pounded in Rutejìmo's ears. His heart slammed against his chest, every beat agony from his cracked ribs and broken arm.

He gulped and tried to put on a brave face, but he wanted to beg for mercy.

There was no compassion in Tsubàyo's gaze. There was never love, but now Rutejìmo only saw hatred in the dark eyes. The knife pressed harder against his neck, and more blood dribbled down.

"Damn it!" Tsubàyo yanked away the blade. "What did she mean!?"

Rutejìmo gasped for breath, fighting back the sobs that threatened to rise up.

Tsubàyo turned back to Rutejìmo. "You're lucky. You're going to live long enough to see the sun."

Chapter 29

Rescue

In the end, only the blood on the ground measures a woman.

— Chirodimu Funìgi, *Queen of the Chirodímu* (Act 3, Scene 12)

The wait for sunrise was excruciating. The false dawn refused to become anything more than a razor-thin line of light along the horizon. The dunes remained black waves in the ocean of sand. It was as if time had fixed itself still and he was frozen between the grains falling through an hourglass.

His body, on the other hand, refused to stop shaking. The cracked ribs and broken arm throbbed painfully. If he remained still, the bones didn't grind together, but then sooner or later, a muscle would twitch and fresh waves of pain ripped through him. He suffered; it was the only thing he could do.

Rutejìmo wanted to run. He wanted to scramble to his feet and just shoot out in any direction. Even if he could somehow loosen the ropes, the horses would catch up with him. If he had sun, he could outrace them, but Shimusògo's power came from Tachìra and, without the sun, there would be no magic.

He whispered a prayer to Tachìra and Shimusògo to pass the time. It wasn't empty words anymore, but honest hope that he would see the sun against his face and feel the dépa racing at his feet.

"Oh, just stop muttering, Jìmo."

Rutejìmo glanced over to Tsubàyo. The rites of passage had bored down on all of them and left their mark, but Tsubàyo showed the burden more than even Pidòhu. He was thin and drawn. Rutejìmo hadn't seen him eat or even try to drink. Tsubàyo's eyes were dark and inset, hidden in shadows, as he glared around. Even in the alchemical flames, they were only a thin circle of white in the pitch-black gaze.

The only two things that reflected light were his blades. He had his spear and Rutejìmo's blade. He toyed with both as he watched his prisoner carefully.

"Mikáryo," he said with a hiss, "seemed rather kind to you."

Rutejìmo glanced away and shrugged his one good shoulder. "I guess."

"I hoped she would gut you right there."

He had to fight the urge to deny Tsubàyo's words. Thinking furiously, he lied as smoothly as he could. "She is a clan of night; who knows what they do." He squirmed as a muscle twinged in his arm. "For all I know, she was probably seeing if I was edible."

Tsubàyo chuckled. "Probably not. Maybe I just need to give you and Dòhu to her? Chimípu, I'm going to kill."

"You can't win against her."

Tsubàyo smiled, his face tilting into darkness. "Maybe, maybe not. There are a lot of secrets in these shadows." He gestured to the rocks underneath the arch. The outcroppings were barely visible in the pale light of the alchemical fire and the light along the horizon that refused to brighten.

"More horses?"

He smiled broadly. "I can feel them. There are a lot more coming."

"Why not use all of them earlier? You just had the—"

Tsubàyo's smile dropped sharply "Shut up!" His voice rang out from the rocks.

Rutejìmo said, "You can't, can you? It takes skill to keep the herd."

"What would you know?"

"We live less than a league from the Ryozapòti for decades. I've seen them care for their horses."

"Ryozapòti is a riding spirit, not a herd spirit."

"What's the difference?"

"It is...." Tsubàyo's voice trailed off as his lips parted for a moment. He shook his head. "It is like being surrounded by friends, but they are close. Like lovers, maybe?"

Rutejìmo thought of Mikáryo and blushed at the uncomfortable feeling that rose up inside him.

Tsubàyo shook his head again. "It feels good. When I'm riding, I don't worry about things."

"All the world just seems to melt away, and you are just moving. The pain, hunger, and doubt cease to exist. You are just moving and it feels like you are chasing something that loves you with all his heart."

Tsubàyo looked at him with surprise. "Yeah, but how... how did you know?" He frowned. "You are talking about Shimusògo?"

Rutejìmo nodded. "Pidòhu calls it rapture. Chimípu and I feel it for Shimusògo. Pidòhu feels it for Tateshyúso."

"And you think I can feel it for Pabinkúe?"

Rutejìmo shrugged with his good shoulder.

Tsubàyo stood up. He sheathed Rutejìmo's knife in his belt. "Maybe, but I'm not going to tell that Mikáryo bitch that. She thinks she knows everything, but I'll be damned if I'm just going to roll over to her."

A warmth spread out across Rutejìmo's body. He looked around in surprise, trying to find the source. His eyes scanned along the horizon as the first curve of the sun rose up over the horizon. Sunlight lit up the tips of the dunes. He gasped as he stared at the sun, not sure if he would see another sunrise.

Tsubàyo spoke without looking at Rutejìmo. "I hate that feeling. Every time Tachìra rises, I get this sick feeling in my gut."

"You can feel it too?"

Tsubàyo nodded.

Rutejìmo glanced up at the arch above him. Thin fingers of light caressed the rock. He thought he saw some movement, but it was too hard to make out anything in the darkness. Sighing, he looked around. They were near the center of the arch. In front of him were the endless waves of sand, behind him the shallow slope of broken rocks leading up to the cliffs.

"Well, Jìmo, enjoy the sun. It will be your last."

Rutejìmo shuddered at Tsubàyo's hard words. He focused on the horizon and watched the sun. It was bright as it welled up, stretching into the pale sky. He could imagine the sun spirit, Tachìra, was looking at him and seeing him for who he was.

He felt ashamed in the growing light. As much as he tried to do the right thing, he couldn't see how Tachìra would ever forgive him for hurting Pidòhu. He was nothing but a small sand tick in the desert, a tiny little thing, and he wondered if Tachìra even knew he existed. It was a humbling and depressing thought.

Shimusògo forgave him. The dépa had run with him, and he had felt the rapture of running. He smiled and relaxed. If he was going to die, at least he was going to die as a clan member, not someone who abandoned them.

More sun stretched across the sand, pooling on the tops of the dunes and sinking into the valleys. As if to make up for freezing

CHAPTER 29. RESCUE

time, the sun rose quickly and soon it was a quarter above the horizon.

Movement caught his attention. It was a plume of dust coming toward him. At the head, he could see a single runner. He couldn't focus on her from that distance, but his heart swelled knowing she was coming.

And then, shadows spread out from the dust behind her and stretched out. Massive wings sailed along the waves of sand, giving the impression of a bird larger than the mountain but invisible to sight.

Rutejìmo's breath caught in his throat.

A flash of power rose from the plume, and a large dépa appeared and faded. The movement accelerated, the plume turning into a spiraling spear of sand as Chimípu pulled away and charged.

Tateshyúso's shadow rushed forward and overtook her. Behind the shadow, wind yanked sand and dust from the desert and pulled it into the air. In a matter of seconds, it was boiling in a massive cloud rushing toward them.

The air grew tense, and a breeze pushed against Rutejìmo's face. He stared as the rolling cloud of sand charged the arch, kicking up stones and more sand until it was nothing but a wall of an incoming storm.

His stomach clenched but he was smiling. Rutejìmo braced his feet on the ground and shoved himself up the rock. The movement sent fresh pains through his arm, but he wanted to be standing when the storm hit them.

Tsubàyo gasped. "What is that? Damn it, it's Mípu! To the shadows!"

The horses scrambled to their feet, but then the storm was on them.

Rutejìmo braced himself, cringing as he waited for the blast of air. The air howled around him, ripping at the ground. The sands below his feed rumbled from the ferocity of the winds that tore at the rocks and Tsubàyo. But, not a single grain hit his face. Surprised, Rutejìmo looked up to see the storm parting less than a foot from him. Turning, he saw he was in a bubble of calm air. The storm raged at the rock behind him and all around and left him untouched.

To the side, he could see Tsubàyo fighting against the wind. It tore at his face and arms, pushing him back with force that ripped the cloth from his chest.

Someone grabbed Rutejìmo's broken arm. He jerked it back with a scream, almost losing his balance. He backed into the wind and felt it tearing at his back. The air shifted and he was once again the center of the calm area.

Burning with glowing flames, Chimípu stepped into the bubble of calm. "Jìmo?"

"Mípu!"

She pulled out a knife and grabbed his ropes. She slicing them away before pulling him into a tight hug. "You're injured?"

Rutejìmo whimpered. "H-He broke my arm." He groaned at the pain. "And ribs."

She yanked away. "Sorry. I didn't see any blood."

"No, but it hurts to move, and I can't really feel my fingers."

Chimípu nodded and sheathed the dagger. Pulling out her tazágu, she toyed with the weapon. "Pidòhu won't be able to keep the storm up for long, so we need to hurry."

"What do I—"

"Run. Dòhu is safe from Tsubàyo, but you need to run away from here. I'll deal with Tsubàyo." She turned away from him as she tightened her grip on her weapon.

Rutejìmo stared at her back for a long moment, then he nodded. "Be safe, Mípu."

"Jìmo?" She looked over her shoulder. "That was very brave of you. Thank you."

CHAPTER 29. RESCUE

He chuckled. "I can't tell you how scared I was."

"Tonight, you'll be the one telling stories."

Rutejìmo bowed. "Be safe, Great Shimusogo Chimípu." He turned toward the storm and stepped into it. He expected it to rip at his face, but the bubble of calm spread out. He gripped his broken arm to reduce the grinding and ran. He didn't need to see where he was going, he just ran.

A moment later, he was racing fast enough to feel Shimusògo, and the pain faded away. A heartbeat later, he was out of the storm and into the sunlight. The light never felt as good as it did in that moment.

He ran just to enjoy the moment of peace, but he couldn't leave Chimípu. Slowing down, he jogged in a wide circle before stopping a few chains from the outer edge of the sandstorm. The pains in his body came back, throbbing and agonizing, but he couldn't stay moving forever.

The cloud was dark, but he saw flashes of sunlight in the depths. He knew it was Chimípu fighting with Tsubàyo. He hoped she was safe against Tsubàyo and his herd.

And then he noticed there was someone else. They were perched on top of the stone arch, hands held above them. At first, he thought it was Mikáryo, but there was energy rising up from the figure. It looked as though waves of heat clung to their form, curling up like smoke before they hit some invisible force. His eyes watched the mirage-like wavers roll along the shadow of a massive bird hovering above the arch. He had seen it before, but only in shadows.

"Tateshyúso."

Identifying the spirit, he knew there was only one person who could be on top of the arch. Pidòhu was balanced on the narrow rock, his legs stretched along the line of stone. He was chanting with his hands in the air, and the power rose through his fingers as the storm raged below him.

"H-How did he get there?" Rutejìmo was surprised. Then he remembered when Mikáryo looked up in the darkness and made the cryptic comment. He smiled. It was a clue, one that both he and Tsubàyo had missed.

Rutejìmo looked around for something to use as a sling. He didn't know anything else to do. But he couldn't find anything to use as a shot. Frustrated, he expanded his search and jogged around.

He ran completely around the stone arch, over the rocks and back down into the sand, when the howling wind stopped. He skidded to a halt and looked down at the battle. The sand from the storm was raining down, and Tateshyúso's shadow was gone. He glanced up for Pidòhu.

The boy was still on the arch, but he was slumped forward. The last of the haze had faded from around him, and he looked thin. For a heartbeat, he was worried that Pidòhu had somehow passed out, but then the frail teenager lifted his head.

Blades crashing into each other dragged Rutejìmo's attention down. Chimípu was in the center of a fight, her body surrounded by golden flames as her tazágu flashed with every strike. She was fighting Tsubàyo and two of the horses. The three figures had her surrounded and were lashing out with spear, hooves, and teeth.

Chimípu danced in the attacks. Her body moved gracefully as it blurred around weapons, teeth, and hooves. She missed more than she hit, but there was already blood staining the sand around them. Rutejìmo couldn't tell if it was hers or the others'.

Rutejìmo whimpered and looked around. He was near the spot Chimípu assigned him the day before. He spotted a dark shadow and rushed over to it. It was one of the shots they made from their pack. He dropped to his knees and dug into the sand. He found two other bullets and one of the slings.

With a surge of elation, he used his one good hand to load a shot. He struggled to push both ends into his palm before stand-

CHAPTER 29. RESCUE

ing up. Taking a deep breath, he gave a quick prayer to Shimusògo and began to spin. It was clumsy, working with one hand, but soon he was spinning fast enough for the dépa to circle him and sand to rise up. He felt the power coursing through his body.

He released the shot. It cracked the air as it rocketed toward the fight. The canvas ignited in the same golden flames that surrounded Chimípu. But, as it reached the midpoint, he realized it was going to miss.

"No!"

Chimípu stepped into the path of the shot.

He screamed at the top of his lungs. "Watch out!"

She didn't looked up. Instead, she slammed her foot on the ground and spun around. It looked as though she was about to throw one of her own shots, but she didn't have a sling.

He flinched as the shot reached her, but Chimípu plucked it out of the air and rotated even faster. Her body turned into a column of light and wind. It was just a blinding light with a streak for the glowing shot and another for the dépa sprinting around her feet.

Chimípu released the shot, and it shone brilliantly as it rocketed from her hand. It was aimed for Tsubàyo, but both of the pitch-black horses threw themselves in front of him. The shot caught the first horse in the chest, and there was an explosion of sand and flames.

The shot burst out the far end of the sudden cloud and kept going. It shot out of sight in a blink. A moment later, a crack slammed into Rutejìmo, a deafening roar of something moving too fast.

The sand from the explosion hit the ground, but the fight had been interrupted. In the middle was Chimípu, crouched down as she glowed with power. It rolled off her body, rising up in waves of heat and flickering flames.

Tsubàyo was almost a chain away, at the end of a large gouge. The other horse was scrambling to its feet from where it shielded

Tsubàyo with its body.

There was no sign of the other horse, not even blood or bone.

Tsubàyo swung himself up on the horse. Blood dripped down his face as he gripped his spear tightly.

Chimípu stood up with a glare on her face. She stepped forward, but Tsubàyo stopped her by pointing toward the arch. She peeked over her shoulder just as two horses charged out of the shadows.

Rutejìmo let out a groan. He thought she would have killed one of the horses, but it somehow escaped. He started for another of the shots, but then he saw more movement.

More horses were boiling out of the shadows, two, then four, and then six. They came out as a herd, spreading out as they charged toward Chimípu. Rutejìmo stopped counting at a dozen.

Chimípu burst into movement, sprinting away in a cloud of dust.

The herd followed after her, flowing along the sand like black water.

Wind howled around Rutejìmo as Chimípu stopped next to him. She was panting as she gave him a smile. "Thank you."

"H-How did you do that?"

Chimípu shrugged and held up her hands. "I'm making this up as I go. I have no clue, but it seems to work. But I saw it missing and thought I would try. Never thought it would do that much damage." She stepped to the side and turned to watch the horses racing toward them both. "The horses are slow, though, and they can't get behind me if they don't have a shadow to enter."

Rutejìmo looked for Tsubàyo among the herd. When he didn't see the teenager, he looked back to the arch until he saw him. Tsubàyo was racing for the far end. "What is Bàyo doing?"

"I don't know." Chimípu sounded worried.

Tsubàyo rode past the end, but he came to a halt a few rods away. Rearing up, he turned his mount around.

CHAPTER 29. RESCUE

"Mípu? I have a bad feeling."

Chimípu clenched her tazágu. "So do I."

With a yell, Tsubàyo spurred his horse into movement. The black mount charged toward the end of the stone arch.

Rutejìmo pointed. "Is Dòhu okay?"

"Of course. There is no way...." her voice trailed off as the horse reached the end of the arch.

Tsubàyo kicked hard, and the horse jumped up the arch. Its hooves struck the side of the stone in a shower of sparks. Instead of sliding back, the horse held its position. It made a small leap and jumped higher up on the steep rock, climbing.

"Sands!" Chimípu exploded into movement. She raced down toward the nearest end of the stone arch. It was a steeper climb, but Rutejìmo thought she was going to try the same thing.

She passed around the black herd. The horses split in half, spreading out as they circled around. Instead of chasing after Chimípu, they charged into each other. Rutejìmo held his breath as he watched with fascination. He couldn't imagine what they were doing.

The horses ran past each other. But, as they passed, the ones that were shadowed from the sun disappeared.

Rutejìmo gasped and looked up as the horses burst out of the darkness to block Chimípu.

She raced past them to head to the far end of the arch.

The horses raced in a sharp circle and dove back into the darkness. They came out in time to block Chimípu as she approached it.

Chimípu let out a scream of frustration and raced back to the first side, but the rest of the herd had covered the distance and blocked it. There was no way she could get on the arch without going through a gauntlet of horses.

Rutejìmo whimpered as he watched her run back and forth, trying to get past the horses. There was no other way up the arch.

Above, Tsubàyo was working his way up. His mount was struggling, climbing the stone in shorter jumps as it tried to climb the rock. Despite being a large creature with tiny hooves, it was making steady progress toward the peak. It would be only a few moments before Tsubàyo had Pidòhu.

Pidòhu noticed Tsubàyo and crawled back. His broken leg dragged behind him as he limped away, trying to keep his balance on the rock while avoiding the charging horse.

"Jìmo!" screamed Chimípu. "Throw me up!"

He stared at her in shock, but Chimípu sprinted in the opposite direction as she sheathed her tazágu. He didn't understand what she said, but then he saw Shimusògo race past him. Despite his confusion, he knew how to follow his clan spirit. He sprinted after it, accelerating until the world blurred.

Chimípu had turned around and was rushing toward him. Her own dépa was just as fast as she glowed with brilliant flames. She was faster than he, but they would still meet in the middle of the arch.

And then he figured it out. Bearing down, he pushed himself to his limits. His body ached as he charged forward. As he ran past the horses guarding the end, he threw himself into a slide. The ground tore into his back as he dug through the sand and rock. He skipped across the sand and each impact drove the air from his lungs. He struggled to pull up his arm and leg to give her a platform to jump from.

Chimípu reached him and took a small hop. She landed on his arm and leg, the impact crushing him into the ground. She was searing-hot as their momentum froze a moment.

And with a liquid surge that brought golden flames coursing along his body, he shoved up with both arms and legs. The magic of the clan flowed through him, and he tasted feathers and blood in his mouth. His world turned into a single flash of agony as the bones ground into each other.

CHAPTER 29. RESCUE

Energy flared between them as Chimípu flew straight up in an explosion of air and flames. The sand howled after her, sucked up by her passing as she rocketed above Tsubàyo.

Rutejìmo screamed in agony as he was crushed into the desert. The impact had dug him into a crater. Every pulse of his heart sent throbbing pain coursing through his body. He sobbed at the agony, trying to breathe.

Chimípu hit the apex of her flight and came down. She landed hard on back of Tsubàyo's horse. She grabbed the back of his head and slammed her fist into his back. The impact sounded like she struck solid bone. She punched Tsubàyo hard and fast, and the dull thuds drowned out the pounding of Rutejìmo's heart.

Tsubàyo slumped forward, but then the horse reared back.

She lost her grip but grabbed his torn shirt. Bouncing off the rump of the horse, she scissored her legs and kicked up. Releasing Tsubàyo, she flung herself up and around him to land on his chest. She kicked him hard in the face before grabbing the mane to hit him again.

The horse clamped its teeth down on her arm.

Chimípu yanked her hand from the equine's mouth, and her blood arced into the air. She punched the horse and then kicked Tsubàyo again. Grabbing tighter to the creature's ear, she repeatedly slammed her heel into Tsubàyo's face.

Rutejìmo jerked with every wet, meaty thud of her foot.

Tsubàyo tried to parry with his spear, but Chimípu brought her knee down on it and cracked it in half.

The horse surged forward, jumping to its front feet and kicking out.

She made no noise as she lost her grip and tumbled off. For a moment, she slid off the side of the rock and her feet were dangling over open air. She managed to grab the sharp rocks to stop her fall.

It was a hundred feet to the ground, and below her was nothing but sharp rocks.

Rutejìmo struggled to his feet, but he couldn't move fast enough. He kept struggling, unable to use his broken arm. The agony was intense, and the edges of his vision were red with pain.

Chimípu lost her grip with one hand. Her arm flung back, but instead of trying to get a new grip, she yanked the tazágu from her belt.

Tsubàyo's horse stepped up to her and lifted its hoof to crush her hand.

She surged up and punched the point of her weapon into the equine's leg. It pierced through the black flesh and came out the other side.

The horse's scream would haunt Rutejìmo's nightmares for the rest of his life. It jerked away from the pain and lost its balance. With sickening slowness, it tumbled off the rock and plummeted to the ground.

With her weapon still in the creature's leg, Chimípu was ripped off the stone. She made no noise as she fell after the horse.

Rutejìmo scrambled out of the crater. Everything hurt, but he couldn't let someone fall again. He raced as fast as he could. His broken arm flopped against his hip, and the agony tore through him, but he covered the distance in a heartbeat. Sliding to a halt, he held out his hand to catch Chimípu.

There was only a flash of darkness.

The horse slammed into the rocks next to him, a sickening crunch that shook the ground. He didn't dare look at the corpse as he stood up, trying to find her. He had missed her and failed her. His mind kept reliving her fall and he almost threw up.

A massive shadow flashed over him. The air rippled, and he saw translucent claws release Chimípu only a foot above the ground. She hit it hard, landing on her hands and knees. Panting, she froze as she tried to get her breath. Bright blood dripped

CHAPTER 29. RESCUE

from her face and it splattered on the sand. She was shaking as she tried to push herself up, but she stumbled and slumped back down.

She looked around, groaning as she tried to get up. "Where's Tsubàyo?"

Rutejìmo glanced around and then, with a sickening feeling, looked up.

Tsubàyo stood on top of the arch, his face lost in shadows. He had the broken end of his spear in one hand. "Looking for me, Mípu?" His voice was cracked and gasping.

Pidòhu was only a few feet away, still trying to crawl. A fresh bandage on his leg was stained crimson with fresh blood.

Chimípu looked up, a glare on her face.

"I'll be right down." The teenager turned and stalked toward Pidòhu.

"No," whimpered Rutejìmo.

But Pidòhu wasn't crawling back. He was on one knee and his hands.

There was a painful stillness in the air. Rutejìmo could hear every footstep as Tsubàyo walked over to Pidòhu.

"Time to die, Dòhu."

Pidòhu shook his head, but there was no tears or fear on his face. Instead, there was only determination. Ripples of power rose off him.

Rutejìmo gasped and looked around. He stood up and he looked for Tateshyúso's shadow.

The massive bird was coming in from the south, the darkness flowing across the sands. And, barely visible in the darkness, was the wind. It wasn't a howling wall but a single line of power forming a spear of swirling sand and rock.

Chimípu groaned and tried to push herself up. "J-Jìmo, I need to get up there."

Rutejìmo shook his head. "No."

"Jìmo! You can't—"

"Mípu"—he gulped—"this is Pidòhu's fight."

"He can't—"

"Tateshyúso's shadow."

On top of the arch, Tsubàyo didn't respond to the shadow as it rushed toward him. Instead, he lifted up his spear and stepped over Pidòhu.

The shadow washed over Rutejìmo and Chimípu. It blotted out the arch as the bird spirit raced past.

And then the wind hit. It was a stream of force that slammed into only Tsubàyo. The sand tore at his side and ripped his spear from his hand. He gasped and turned into it, bracing himself, but it continued to rip at him. Power rippled along the stream and it grew stronger, blasting sand against Tsubàyo's face and body. It tore at his clothes. Rocks slashed past him, and streaks of blood poured into the streaming sand.

"Goodbye, Tsubàyo," Pidòhu said, his voice as clear over the wind.

The impact of the wind sounded like a punch, and Tsubàyo was thrown off the rock. He screamed as he plummeted to the ground on the far side of the arch. The impact was the same sound Pidòhu had made when he hit the ground, a thud that shook Rutejìmo to the core.

On top of the rock, Pidòhu swayed as the wind cut off.

Chimípu groaned. "Jìmo?"

Rutejìmo surged to his feet. "I'll get him."

He was running even as Pidòhu tumbled off the edge. It was a short fall, no more than a rod or two, but Rutejìmo was there to catch him. The impact crushed them both into the sands. One of Rutejìmo's knees cracked against some rocks. Pidòhu slipped from his arms and hit the ground, but it was a hard blow instead of a fatal one on the rocks below them.

CHAPTER 29. RESCUE

Rutejìmo slammed face-first into the rocks. He sobbed at the pain, flailing with his one good arm as he flipped himself over. "Dòhu? Dòhu!?"

"Yeah," groaned Pidòhu next to him. "You caught me that time. You caught me."

"Y-Yeah?"

"Did that hurt you as much as me?"

Rutejìmo gasped at the sharp burning coursing up his legs. His arm refused to move and his vision was blurred with tears. "Yes. Let's not do that again."

"Deal. Where is Mípu?"

Struggling, Rutejìmo pushed himself into a sitting position. Every part of his body hurt. He wanted to crawl into a hole and never get out again.

Chimípu was twenty feet away, crouching over Tsubàyo's form. She had her tazágu out and held ready to strike. The point was bright on the nameless blade.

"Sands, she's going to kill him." He felt the bile rising up. He couldn't watch.

Rutejìmo, thankful to look away and praying she would kill Tsubàyo before he looked back, reached out to help Pidòhu into a sitting position. He let his hand linger, delaying the inevitable look back.

But he had no luck. When he turned back, she was still poised to strike. Her arm shook with exhaustion. Blood soaked her shoulder. She was covered in cuts and bruises.

Tsubàyo grabbed for her tazágu.

She snatched his wrist and slammed it down on the ground. Their bodies shuddered as they stared at each other, panting for breath and hatred in their eyes.

The silence stretched between them, interrupted only by their rapid breathing. Both of them were glowing, but it was the banked fires of the power inside them. It shimmered the air around them, rippling like a mirage.

Rutejìmo was afraid to make a noise. He didn't want to set off more fighting. He just wanted it to end. He couldn't handle death in front of him, not after everything else.

Chimípu jerked her hand up. "Damn you!" she screamed and slammed her weapon down.

Rutejìmo jerked and clamped his eyes shut. He waited for the scream or yell, but there was nothing. Tentatively, he opened his eye, fearing the worst.

Chimípu was crouched over Tsubàyo, panting heavily. Her shoulders rose and fell as sobs tore through her.

"You," Tsubàyo laughed from underneath her, "are just as bad as—"

She sat up and slammed him across the jaw with her fist.

Tsubàyo's hand reached up to block her.

Chimípu knocked his arm aside and punched him again. Tears ran down her cheeks as she struck again and again. The dull impacts of her hammering fists shot straight through Rutejìmo. He was horrified, but he couldn't stop her.

The wind rose up around them, kicking up streamers of sand that curled between the two.

A hand pried Rutejìmo's hand away from Pidòhu. "Let me have Tateshyuso Pidòhu, Shimusogo Rutejìmo." The speaker was an old woman with a cracked voice.

Rutejìmo gasped and spun around. He stared in shock until recognition dawned. Tateshyuso Jyotekábi crouched next to him, the old woman's thin robe did nothing to shield her old body from his sight. Despite her thin body, she was strong enough to scoop her hands underneath Pidòhu and lift him.

Pidòhu looked at him, his face showing his pain. "Tateshyúso?"

CHAPTER 29. RESCUE

Rutejìmo glanced around and saw the rest of the clan coming from all directions. Plumes of sand and dust billowed as they raced across the sands, their bodies blurred with their speed and the heat. He could see Shimusògo leading all of them, the delicate-looking dépas sailing across the ground.

He turned as a sob rose in his throat. It was over. The first of the runners reached the two fighters.

The wind crashed into all of them, and the dust swallowed up Chimípu and Tsubàyo. It sank to the ground almost instantly, and Desòchu stood there, holding Chimípu's arm as he looked down at her. "Enough, Chimípu."

Chimípu looked up, tears in her eyes and a torn look on her face. "D-Desòchu?"

He nodded and held out his hand. "Yes."

"H-He tried to kill Dòhu and Jìmo. I-I had...." She rose up. "I had to save them."

"I know," Rutejìmo's brother said, his voice filled with warmth.

Rutejìmo felt a surge of jealousy. He looked down as the rest of the clan arrived. The air crackled with their power, the clan's magic.

Gemènyo knelt down next to Rutejìmo. "You okay?"

Rutejìmo looked up, feeling tears in his own eyes. He shook his head.

With a sympathetic look, Gemènyo patted him lightly on the shoulder.

Rutejìmo winced at the pain.

"Broken arm?"

Rutejìmo nodded and let out a whimper. He felt broken and exhausted. It didn't seem real that the clan was there. "And my ribs."

"And," said Hyonèku as he knelt down on the other side, "you tore up your back. But, that was a nice maneuver to get Mípu up on the stone. You did good, Jìmo."

Startled, Rutejìmo stared in shock. He wasn't expecting a compliment.

Hyonèku grinned and pulled out a healer's kit. Tossing a few rolls of bandages over to Gemènyo, he gestured for Rutejìmo to raise his arm. "Don't look surprised, boy. Now, don't look at Mènyo, either; this is going to hurt."

Rutejìmo felt Gemènyo easing his arm up as he wrapped the bandage around his arm. As the runner did, he was testing the wound. Rutejìmo winced at the pain, but kept his mouth shut. He watched as two of the clan runners pulled Tsubàyo to his feet.

Tsubàyo's face was swollen and bruised. Blood trickled down from his nose and one eye. He glared at Chimípu and Desòchu. "Now what?"

Hyonèku spoke up sharply without looking away from Rutejìmo. "Kill him. End it here."

Assent rippled through the gathered clan.

Desòchu held up his hand. "Anyone disagree?"

Silence.

Tsubàyo looked back and forth. There was fear in his eyes.

"Actually," Mikáryo said as she stepped out of the shadows, "I might want a say in this." She was wrapped in darkness, but the cloth was pulled back from her head. Her dark tattoos seemed to suck in the sunlight as she strolled to the gathered clan.

Growls and hisses filled the air, followed by the rasp of weapons being drawn.

Mikáryo looked around, unperturbed by the drawn weapons. "So many threats against one person. Typical for the clans of day when they stand in Tachìra's light. I am Mikáryo and I speak for Pabinkúe."

Desòchu stepped forward. "I am Desòchu and I speak for Shimusògo."

From behind Rutejìmo, Jyotekábi announced, "I am Jyotekábi and I speak for Tateshyúso."

Mikáryo bowed once to Desòchu and then to Jyotekábi. She pointed to Tsubàyo, who stared at her with a strange combination of anger and hope. "That one is Pabinkúe's, and I'm here to collect him."

One of the other clan adults stepped forward. "I say kill both of them. Rid the sands of the night."

More agreed as they brandished their weapons.

Rutejìmo stared at them and cringed under the hatred rolling off them. He looked at Chimípu, who looked torn, and then at Pidòhu.

Pidòhu clutched to Jyotekábi's body, his face pale and fresh blood dripping from his leg to the sand beneath him.

Jyotekábi pulled him tight to her body as energy rippled around her. Behind the two, the broad shadow of Tateshyúso sailed across the sand toward the two. "Great Shimusogo Desòchu, Tateshyúso has no interest in this and Pidòhu needs help. We will meet you at the valley."

Desòchu nodded but didn't take his eyes off Mikáryo. There was a frown on his face, but unlike the others, he had no drawn weapon.

The shadow of Tateshyúso sailed over the clan, leaving behind a ripple of coolness. When it passed, Pidòhu and Tateshyúso were gone.

Mikáryo smiled, her lips curling back until her teeth were visible. "Do you really want to spill more blood, Great Shimusogo Desòchu?"

Another person said, "There are only two of them."

"Yes," Mikáryo purred, "only two of us."

From behind her, the shadows of the arch deepened and turned into pitch-black voids. A coolness rippled from the darkness as a horse stepped out in perfect silence. Behind it, more horses stepped out.

Rutejìmo inhaled as he watched the herd walk out of the darkness. He caught movement to the side and looked. The shadows cast by the surrounding clan were also pitch-black. A horse pulled itself out of the narrow strip as if it was crawling out of a hole. It moved in perfect silence as it turned around.

Gemènyo inhaled sharply. "Behind you!"

The clan spun around. As one, they took a double take at the twenty horses surrounding them. The black bodies were silent but there was no doubt of the threat.

Rutejìmo pushed away from Gemènyo and Hyonèku and scrambled to his feet. "Stop!"

Everyone froze. Mikáryo smiled and cocked her head as the others turned to look at Rutejìmo. There were bared weapons, but Rutejìmo couldn't stomach the idea of watching blood on the sand, not Tsubàyo's or anyone's.

He was the center of attention and he felt ashamed.

And then he saw the corner of Desòchu's lip curled into a smile.

Rutejìmo gulped and held up his good hand. "P-Please? No more fighting. No more blood. Let both of them go."

Hyonèku stood up. "No, kill her!" He stepped away from Rutejìmo with a glare.

Desòchu looked back and forth.

Rutejìmo whimpered and then fumbled with his pocket. He dug in until he found his voting stone; in front of others, he knew he only deserved to use one. He shook as he pulled it out and held in his palm. "Please?"

Turning on Rutejìmo, Hyonèku hissed, "What are you doing? This isn't a vote—"

A stone hit the ground at Rutejìmo's feet. It was Chimípu's. Rutejìmo stared down at it, a shiver coursing through his body. He was dizzy and sick to his stomach.

Chapter 29. Rescue

Someone tossed a handful of stones at Hyonèku. More landed in front of Rutejìmo, thrown by someone he didn't see. More stones smacked the ground at Hyonèku's feet. They littered the sands front of him.

Rutejìmo stared down the two piles. There were far more in front of Hyonèku than him.

Gemènyo poured over twenty rocks at Rutejìmo's feet. He straightened up and patted Rutejìmo on the shoulder. "You have balls, at least." He was smiling as he stepped back. "Stupid, but you have balls." He kicked one of his rocks in front of Hyonèku before stepping back.

Silence crushed against Rutejìmo. He wanted to crawl away but couldn't. Fighting back his fear, he stood up straight and turned to his brother.

Desòchu stood next to Chimípu, hefting a handful of his own voting stones in his hand. The rocks clinked as he rolled them in his palm. With a sigh, he tossed them in the air.

Rutejìmo flinched as they landed in the sand at his feet.

"She lives just as Tsubàyo will," announced his brother.

Tsubàyo let out his breath in a low gasp. His chest rose and fell as he stared at the rocks.

Hyonèku hissed and gathered up his stones. He turned his back on Rutejìmo and walked away. The other clan members came up to gather their rocks. Some of them patted Rutejìmo on the shoulder as they passed, but most moved in silence as they followed after Hyonèku.

Gemènyo gathered up his voting stones and stood. He handed Rutejìmo his single voting stone.

Rutejìmo took it, unsure of what to do.

Gemènyo leaned into him. "Stay as long as you want, but then join us."

He turned and jogged away. A moment later, the wind rushed as the clan sprinted off toward home.

Rutejìmo turned back. There were only five of them left. Even the horses had disappeared back into the shadows.

Desòchu looked around, his face grim. He bowed to Mikáryo. "I request a favor, Great," he choked on the word, "Pabinkue Mikáryo. He attacked my clan as one of yours. May Shimusògo get closure on the one who abandoned us?"

He spoke not as Rutejìmo's brother but as a warrior of the clan. Rutejìmo felt as if he had just lost his sibling.

Mikáryo chuckled. She rested her hand on the tazágu. She said nothing for a moment.

Tsubàyo looked at her, confusion on his face.

She gave a short nod. "Don't break any bones. We have a long ride."

Tsubàyo turned back to Desòchu, confusion naked in his expression. "What is she—?"

Chimípu's fist caught him across the face. The smack cracked the air.

Tsubàyo staggered to the side, but Desòchu was there. Growling, Desòchu backhanded Tsubàyo and threw him back into Chimípu's other fist.

Rutejìmo jerked as the punch caught Tsubàyo.

Tsubàyo flailed around in an attempt to block, but Desòchu's next strike hit him in the stomach, folding him over.

Chimípu grabbed Tsubàyo's head and slammed her knee into his face. He staggered back to Desòchu, who grabbed Tsubàyo with his right hand and punched him hard across the chin. A tooth flew out across the sand.

Tsubàyo slammed back on the ground. Fresh blood was pouring down his face. He looked up at Mikáryo. He reached out with a shaking hand. "Save me!"

Mikáryo shook her head. "This is a lesson, Bàyo," she spoke in a hard voice. "This time, try to learn it."

CHAPTER 29. RESCUE

Chimípu grabbed Tsubàyo and yanked him to his feet. He tried to pull back, but Desòchu slammed into his back. They alternated punching and kicking him. As they moved, the impacts grew louder. Golden flames grew around Desòchu and Chimípu as they attacked in perfect synchronization.

Rutejìmo was crying. He felt no joy as they brutalized Tsubàyo. For all the pain and bullying he went through, he couldn't take it. Sniffing and wiping at the tears on his cheeks, he stepped back away from the fight.

Mikáryo caught his eye. She gave him a small nod of approval, then blew him a kiss.

The beating continued with brutal efficiency. The strikes rocked the air as Tsubàyo cried out, interrupted only by the sound of fist on flesh or the sound of a kick slamming into him. He was helpless against the Shimusògo warriors as they took their revenge for Rutejìmo and Pidòhu.

Bile rising in his throat, Rutejìmo turned and fled.

Chapter 30

A Year Later

> During clan celebrations, nudity is neither a taboo nor sexual. It is freedom of constraints when viewed in public.
>
> — *Cultural Differences in Practice*

The valley celebrated the birth of Shimusògo, a tradition that had been carried for twenty-seven generations. A bonfire burned brightly, kicking up stars of embers high into the air.

Around the flames, half the valley danced with wild abandon. Dark flesh glistened with sweat from the heat. No one raced or sprinted, but everyone enjoyed moving with nothing but their own feet. Shimusògo wasn't needed that night; he was the one being celebrated.

Rutejìmo smiled sadly as he sat on the roof of the shrine house. He had a bottle of spirits in one hand and he had stripped down to a pair of shorts. The snake tooth hung around his neck. He wore it always even though Desòchu and Chimípu forbade it. Neither could accept what Mikáryo had done, but Rutejìmo refused to forget the woman who saved his life. Chimípu even abandoned the tazágu, and it was Rutejìmo who named it.

Down by the fire, Chimípu spun from partner to partner, moving with a warrior's grace. She caught Pidòhu and flung him around, laughing loudly as her dark red hair swirled in a crescent.

Pidòhu laughed just as loudly. He was stripped down to a loincloth, his skin shimmering in the light of the bonfire. He grabbed her and spun her around twice before bringing her close. Rutejìmo could only see him limping if he was looking for it.

They weren't lovers, but Rutejìmo knew they had shared a bed at least twice. Chimípu was a warrior; she would never mate. Just like Desòchu.

On the other side of the flames, Desòchu pounded on the drums. He was naked from a dare and laughing as one of the women tried to get a bottle of spirits to his mouth. He snaked one arm around her and kissed her before releasing her. He returned to the drums, smacking the top with a wild beat that shook the air.

Rutejìmo couldn't call him brother anymore. He was Desòchu just as Chimípu was herself. They were things he would never have again, but he had finally accepted it. He was Shimusògo now.

"You," Gemènyo said as he sat down next to Rutejìmo, "are supposed to be naked and dancing around like an idiot."

"Why aren't you?" Rutejìmo shot back.

"Eh, can't taste my pipe with all that laughter." He drew on the pipe and let out a long cloud of smoke. "Besides, that's the last bottle of the good stuff."

Rutejìmo handed it over with a smile. "Enjoy."

Gemènyo drained a quarter of the bottle before holding it up over his head.

Hyonèku took it and drained it before he sat down on the far side of Gemènyo. He let out a sigh and handed the bottle back to Rutejìmo.

Rutejìmo took it, toying with the expensive glass. It was from Wamifuko City and a gift from a thankful clan. It was Rutejìmo's fourth courier delivery, and Chimípu had given him the honor of handing the sealed message over to the grateful man.

"So," asked Hyonèku, "why are you sulking, Jìmo?"

"I'm not sulking."

"Sitting in the dark on the shrine? Sounds like sulking."

"No." Rutejìmo watched the dancing. There was so much joy in the clan and he felt it, but there was something still hanging in his thoughts. "I'm just...."

He felt them looking at him. He turned, then rolled his eyes before smiling. "What?"

"You tell us," said Gemènyo.

"Just... thinking."

Hyonèku said, "About what? Sour thoughts are for old men like us, not a boy like you."

Gemènyo smacked his friend. "I'm not that old."

"You're thirty-seven," snapped Hyonèku, "and if you keep sucking on that pipe, you'll be dead before me, old man."

Rutejìmo chuckled as he listened. He knew the smile dropped from his face, but he couldn't tear his thoughts away from the dark spiral.

Gemènyo tapped him on the thigh. "Even the darkest thought can't survive open air."

Rutejìmo looked at him. "Can I ask you... both of you something?"

"Of course."

"Who killed Karawàbi?" He knew the answer, but he wished it wasn't true. Rutejìmo didn't dare ask Desòchu, for fear of knowing.

Hyonèku inhaled sharply.

Gemènyo drew on his pipe and let the smoke out in a long streamer. "Damn, boy, I hoped you would never ask us that."

"It was Desòchu, wasn't it?"

The guilty looks told him the answer.

Leaning forward, Hyonèku peered at him. "Listen, Jìmo, there is—"

Rutejìmo held up his hand. "Desòchu protects the clan, even from itself, right? And if Karawàbi had stayed, he would have been poison to that." He gestured to the celebration below.

Neither said anything, so Rutejìmo continued. "He was a bully and cruel, just like Tsubàyo. I remember when Gemènyo tried to tell me to be a better man and Chimípu told me that he helped her too. All of you were trying to guide us, weren't you? Some of us just weren't listening very well."

Gemènyo nodded slowly.

"And"—Rutejìmo sighed for a moment as he remembered Karawàbi's corpse—"if Tsubàyo hadn't been claimed, his bones would have been bleaching in the sand somewhere."

Another nod.

Rutejìmo tilted back and looked up at the dark sky. He remembered Mikáryo on the opposite side of the flames. She had started a doubt that continued to grow inside him. For a year it had been festering, and he couldn't hold it in anymore.

"How close was I?"

He tensed as he waited for the answer, unable to look at the others.

"Damn, boy," whispered Hyonèku.

Rutejìmo felt the tears in his eyes. "It had to be Desòchu, wouldn't it?"

Gemènyo rested his hand on Rutejìmo's shoulder. "I'm sorry."

A tear ran down Rutejìmo's cheek. "How close?"

"We had already decided."

CHAPTER 30. A YEAR LATER

Rutejìmo's stomach lurched. He tightened his grip on the bottle until his knuckles ached.

"But then you and Tsubàyo headed toward that horse clan. He couldn't get close enough without starting a fight with them. We were going to end it the next day, but then you headed back."

Hyonèku said, "None of us believed it. You did the right thing. And when we saw you baring your throat to her, we decided that you deserved a second chance."

"I'm glad we gave you one. You finally grew up and became a good man."

Rutejìmo smiled grimly. He looked back down to the celebration. His brother was dancing with his grandmother, pulling her into circles as they bounded around the fire. There was no anger in Desòchu's face. He was just having fun and raising everyone's spirits. He would protect the clan with his life.

Gemènyo leaned into him. "What are you going to do? Knowing that?"

Rutejìmo drained the bottle and set it down. "Nothing. They"—he gestured to Chimípu and Desòchu—"protect the clan and will do for the rest of their lives. The only thing I can do is honor that is... by running."

"Shimusògo run," said Gemènyo and Hyonèku.

Rutejìmo smiled. "Shimusògo run."

They sat in silence, watching the celebrations and lost in their own thoughts.

Gemènyo broke the silence. "Nèku, your daughter is trying to sneak into the shrine."

Rutejìmo looked around to see Mapábyo creeping along the shadows toward the front door. Her bare feet rose and fell in quiet movements as she kept to the shadows from the light spilling out the door. She had a bag in one hand and clutched her dress with the other. She was trembling like a leaf as she headed for the unguarded door.

Hyonèku sighed. "Damn. I'll get her." He started to get to his feet.

Rutejìmo held out his hand to stop Hyonèku and stood up. "No, let me."

About D. Moonfire

D. Moonfire is the remarkable result from the intersection of a computer nerd, a scientist, and polymath. Instead of focusing on a single genre, he writes stories and novels in many different settings ranging from fantasy to science fiction. He also throws in the occasional romance or forensics murder mystery to mix things up.

In addition to having a borderline unhealthy obsession with the written word, he is also a developer who loves to code as much as he loves writing.

He lives near Cedar Rapids, Iowa with his wife, numerous pet computers, and a pair of highly mobile things of the male variety.

You can see more work by D. Moonfire at his website at http://d.moonfire.us/.

Colophon

This book was written in Markdown using Emacs and then transformed into DocBook 5 XML using the Python-based MfGames Writing tools. From there, the print version was generated using XeLaTeX and custom-written stylesheets. The ebook versions were generated using the same tools but different stylesheets along with a Makefile and a bit of Perl magic.

The font used on the front and spine is Vinque, while the body and back cover font is Corda in various weights.

The front cover was created with Photoshop and Gimp.